God's Dogs

Also by Mitch Wieland
Willy Slater's Lane

"Wieland's lovely first novel is likely to entrance readers with the sheer quixotic wonder of his telling of quenched lives. Through the brevity born of perfectly chosen words, and through the pervasive intimations of hope, Wieland transforms this story of lives on the edge into a psalm."
—*Publishers Weekly* (starred review)

"This small gem of a book offers a transcendent portrait of two eccentric, middle-aged brothers who could have come straight from the pages of a Sherwood Anderson novel. First-novelist Wieland is a meticulous craftsman using spare, quiet sentences to compose this spellbinding character study."
—*Booklist* (starred review)

"*Willy Slater's Lane*, with its simple plot and simple language, is immensely moving, reminding us that the story that seems the tritest can still turn out to be the truest."
—*The New York Times Book Review*

God's Dogs

A Novel in Stories

MITCH WIELAND

Southern Methodist University Press / Dallas

Requests for permission to reproduce material
from this work should be sent to:
Rights and Permissions
Southern Methodist University Press
PO Box 750415
Dallas, Texas 75275-0415

The following stories were previously published elsewhere:
"Beware the Pale Horse Comes Riding," The King of Infinite Space," and
"God's Dogs" in *The Sewanee Review*; "The Mistress of the Horse God"
in *The Southern Review*; "Swan's Song" in *The Kenyon Review*; "The Bones
of Hagerman" in *TriQuarterly*; "The Prodigal Son" in *Shenandoah*;
"Swan in Retreat" in *StoryQuarterly*; "Solstice" in *The Yale Review*;
and "Swan's Home" *in Prairie Schooner.*
"The Bones of Hagerman" was reprinted in *Best of the West.*

Cover art: "Coyote is Intrigued," Daniel Stolpe, color woodcut, 24" x 20",
edition 30, 1982, used by permission of NativeImagesGallery.com.

Jacket and text design: Kellye Sanford

Library of Congress Cataloging-in-Publication Data

Wieland, Mitch, 1961–
    God's dogs : a novel in stories / Mitch Wieland. — 1st ed.
        p. cm.
    ISBN 978-0-87074-553-9 (alk. paper)
    I. Title.
    PS3573.I345G63 2009
    813'.54—dc22
                                                            2008051374

Printed in the United States of America on acid-free paper

10   9   8   7   6   5   4   3   2   1

For my son, Benjamin.
The beat goes on . . .

Acknowledgments

Heartfelt thanks to the editors of the literary journals that first published these stories, most notably the inestimable George Core, whose encouragement led directly to the writing of this book. Equal gratitude to Kathryn Lang for her unflagging diligence in making these stories better than they deserved. Thanks to Wendy Weil for her steadfast support. A tip of the weathered Stetson to Dennis Covington, whose love of the Owyhee rangelands inspired the stories of Ferrell Swan.

I would like to thank the Idaho Commission on the Arts for its generous financial assistance during the writing of these stories.

Love to Cynthia and Ben. Norry, too, on the other side of the world.

Contents

Beware the Pale Horse Comes Riding

The day after Ferrell Swan turns sixty, entering what he views as the steep downhill slide of his life, his stepson appears at the door. The two haven't spoken three years running, not since the divorce from the boy's mother, and Ferrell suspects Levon's broke or bored or both to be showing up at his door.

When the boy arrives, Ferrell is sitting on the porch in the cool silk of the evening. The sunset light slants on the high desert, turns the emptiness into something special for a brief burning moment. He watches the dust sift above the lane, then drift eastward in spooky slow-mo. The car stops in the drive, its engine ticking against its own heat. Levon gets out and moves all wrong, like something's just whacked the breath from his lungs.

"What'd you do?" Ferrell asks, though he's not sure he cares to know.

"Busted my ribs."

Ferrell knows he'll learn how soon enough. "Are you here for a while?"

"Day or two at most."

Levon pulls a bulging duffel from the trunk of his car. He sees Ferrell eyeing him, and Ferrell marvels how quick they've slipped into their old roles: Ferrell casting a suspicious eye at all the boy does, Levon trying hard to outfox him.

"It's mostly dirty laundry," Levon says.

Ferrell nods, though he's not convinced.

Above the distant Owyhees, the sky has faded from high color into nothing at all. He'd hoped to sit on the porch until good dark, when the desert chilldown left him shivering in his skin. But the kid's standing in the drive, and next will be the required catching up, including how they *feel* about the things that happened—the kind of sharing the boy's mother used to want with compulsive, heartbreaking need. Back then he talked until his head hurt, until he said so many words he was sure to run dry, and then she'd want even more.

"Hungry?" Ferrell asks and rises from his chair. He doesn't wait for the boy to answer.

The next morning Ferrell's out in the barn, shoveling sheep shit and straw into the wheelbarrow. He bought the stock the end of his first year in Idaho, two years past. After a while it had seemed silly to have land as far as sight could reach, and nothing to raise. He'd wanted cows but didn't want the trouble, and decided on sheep by default, though he knew nothing about them other than the kinky farmer jokes. In fact, he almost didn't buy them *because* of the jokes, but then understood he didn't give a rat's ass what people thought or said. There was no one around to tease him anyway.

Ferrell pitchforks out the stall, then pushes the wheelbarrow into the pasture. He dumps the load along the fence line, a mulch heap for next year's garden. Somewhere along the way he's become a back-to-nature guy or a passive survival-ist—he's not sure which. All he knows is he wanted to be left be after the divorce, and if being left alone meant doing for yourself, then so be it. He grew up working his grandfather's farm in northeast Ohio—it wasn't like he was some fed-up lawyer or business suit quitting his hundred thousand per to move to Idaho or Montana and talk to God. In his eyes he was simply returning to his roots for lack of any other damn thing to do.

He looks to where Levon stands at the gate.

"You're the sorriest shepherd I've ever seen," the boy says.

Ferrell studies the flock grazing across the pasture. He's not thought of the word *shepherd* since he was a kid. It conjures his old children's Bible, colorful paintings of men in sandals and sackcloth, clutching lambs to their chests against God's potent ire. The kid's remark isn't altogether unpleasant.

"Did you eat breakfast?" Ferrell asks.

"I had some of that sawdust bread you made in there. You ever buy store-bought?"

"The nearest store's a fifty-mile round trip."

Levon leans against the top rail of the fence. "I never thought you'd end up hiding out in the middle of nowhere."

Ferrell guesses the boy's in the mood to stir things up. If nothing else, he inherited his mother's take-no-prisoners sar-casm, her ability to turn running out of coffee into a prime example of the weakness of Ferrell's character, of proof he was lacking some fundamental thing most breathing people shared tenfold.

"If you want to sound like your mother, you can leave."

Down the road sunlight flashes off chrome, and in the dust Ferrell sees the coal black of his neighbor's Dodge Ram, a massive diesel rig that cost as much as Ferrell's annual retirement. Cole is a retired forest ranger who spends his days raising conifers on an irrigated twenty acres, a miniforest where nothing should grow. When Ferrell passes Cole's spread, he always sees the man out amid the trunks, drifting like a ghost through the incongruous trees.

The truck rumbles even with the gate and shuts down. To Ferrell's disappointment, Cole's wife, not Cole, sits at the wheel, looking like a little girl in the oversized cab. The woman climbs down into the dust and hikes the scrub to the fence. Her name is Melody or Melanie—he can't remember which. In his head he calls her Moonbeam, since she seems to be into each New Age cure and preventative that comes down the pike. When he first met her, she said she had magnets in her undies, something about reverse polarity and the cycle of her womanhood. Ferrell finds her too easy a target for his generalized wrath, and promises himself to be nice.

"Coming back from town already?" he says when she makes earshot.

Moonbeam leans on the fence, dazzling him with cleavage before he averts his eyes. She's wearing tight western jeans and a man's work shirt knotted below her generous breasts. Her belly is tanned and muscle-flat. The woman's thirty at most, and Ferrell suspects she spends her days begging Cole to take a siesta from the trees.

She pulls something from her rear pocket. "I had new business cards printed in Boise."

Ferrell comes to the fence line. He wipes his hands across his backside and takes the card like it's something special. On the card is a watercolor of galloping bays and paints, a wild-eyed Appaloosa. Atop a chestnut mare rides a man who looks like Father Time: long hair and flowing beard, white robes trailing down. *Beware the pale horse,* the caption reads, *when he rides with the black and the red. Dreamworlds, Inc. Melody Cole, President. Free Consultations.*

"Nice, Melody," Ferrell says. He tries to give the card back, but she raises her hand.

"Oh, you keep it. You need my services, you just let me know."

Ferrell's not sure what she means, but doesn't want to ask. Moonbeam looks over his shoulder and smiles broadly. Her teeth are whiter than anything Ferrell has ever seen.

"Who's this young man?"

Ferrell's forgotten all about the boy. He steps to the side and waves him over.

"This is Levon, my son." Rilla used to ride Ferrell for introducing him as stepson, like he somehow wanted to disown him.

"You two look so different," Moonbeam says, referring, he supposes, to Ferrell's bald head and the boy's gushing black hair. Levon hit twenty-one this summer—youth and hormones beside Ferrell and his worn-out parts. "And what an interesting name."

"My mom was an Elton John fan," Levon says, his favorite line when people ask. "It's from one of his songs. You know, the oldies tune where this Levon dude names his son Jesus."

Ferrell rocks on his heels. The boy, he realizes with a shock, has been running from that song his entire life.

"That's one beautiful piece of music," Moonbeam says. "Like poetry."

"In their day, the Taupin-John team could not be beat," Levon says.

"Are you visiting your dad for long?"

Ferrell perks up at this one. He's been wanting the answer himself.

"I'm not sure," Levon says. "I've been hoping to find myself out here in all this space, but I keep getting more lost."

Moonbeam's eyes take a charge like she's been hit with high voltage. Ferrell isn't sure the boy means what he's saying, or if he has figured her number fast, and is playing her for all she's worth. Levon's been drop-dead handsome his whole life, with a face that puts women's hearts down low in their bellies. If nothing else, he knows which end is up.

"I used to live in northern California," Moonbeam says. "Outside Sebastopol, near where Brautigan took his head off with that gun. I couldn't think for all the trees. I moved out here for the open space. Nothing to get in the way of my thoughts."

Moonbeam lifts her gold-hued hair off her shoulders, but there's no breeze to cool her. "The heat hits so early now. I bet it'll be a hundred by noon. Makes me just want to melt down."

"I like the heat," Levon says. "The sweat makes you feel alive."

"But you lose too many aminos. Without the aminos

your thoughts literally run dry. Your brain's like a sponge left out in the sun."

Ferrell's heard enough for the day. He excuses himself and returns to the reassurance of his work. As he hefts the wheelbarrow handles, he sees the woman give Levon one of her cards.

The first week passes without much grief, and Ferrell thanks the North Star for that. The boy stays up late doing God knows what in the spare bedroom, then sleeps till noon and the full heat. As long as Ferrell can rise before the sun and take his coffee to the porch, he's happy enough to let things go. Summers he's learned to crave the morning chill, before the sun turns the land into an overexposed photograph. The brutal heat is a desert he must cross, and the morning is his sweet drink of water.

Ferrell lives on one hundred acres of sagebrush and chaparral, bought for next to nothing when he was teaching high school history in his quaint Ohio hometown. Rilla thought he was crazy at the time and, in point of fact, still does. His land lies eighty miles south-southeast of Boise, in the middle of not much else but the wide curving sky. On the phone Rilla wonders aloud if he's doing the crazed hermit thing, but he tells her he's not seen trip-wire vets or hatemongers within a stone's throw. He doesn't mention his other neighbor Din Winters, who lives underground.

When Ferrell first arrived, he camped in a tent on his property, up on the blustery ridge. The next morning, with dawn seeping like blood into the sky, he heated instant coffee on his Coleman. He'd just taken his first bitter sip when he spotted the coyote thirty yards out, a flash of tan and gray floating through the tufts of bunchgrass, moving fast, its paws as if not touching the ground. The thing was gone so fast he doubted he'd seen it at all. While still in sight the animal had seemed more ghost than real, and now that it was gone he wondered if the beast had sprung intact from his fertile mind. But that night he heard them across the darkness, below the bright cluster of the stars. The yipping rose to weave around itself, faded off, then gathered together again, climbing the scales in the pitch dark of the air. Though he couldn't explain to anyone why he'd come, he knew he did the right thing somehow, someway, at long stinking last.

The next noon, Ferrell eats lunch on the porch. In the sky a redtail rides the heat, wing feathers fanned like the air feels too damn good. Ferrell's drained from working the posthole digger until both arms went numb with blood. The sun scorch has taken his appetite, and he nibbles his ham sandwich without much interest.

The screen door creaks and slaps against the frame. Levon stands at the rail in his striped boxers, before the vast nothingness of the land.

"You couldn't do this down in L.A.," he says.

"I wouldn't want to."

"L.A.'s too wild, too nuts."

Ferrell takes his cue, too tired to do otherwise. "Is that where you were?"

"For the last year or so."

"Doing?"

"Fitness trainer."

"Like pushups and stuff?"

"It's called spinning. You get on an exercycle, then you lead people on a fitness journey."

"They follow you around?"

"You just pretend you're moving. You just tell them where they are, and they imagine it in their heads."

Ferrell decides to let that one go. He's long sensed he is lost behind something huge, but he doesn't want to know what it is. Inside he still has all the saltpeter he ever did, still feels his heart thrash and yearn in the night, crying out for something wonderful to wing down from heaven and eat him alive. Yet when people rattle off those unfamiliar phrases—*search engines, Internet provider, dial-up*—he feels left behind, feels like some old geezer driving his restored Model T down the freeway, a line of modern curvy cars pissed off behind him.

Levon goes back inside and comes out with a bowl of granola and a spoon. He sits beside Ferrell and starts crunching.

"Is that how you hurt yourself?" Ferrell asks.

"Eating granola?"

"The weird-assed fitness stuff."

Levon shakes his head. A dribble of milk hangs onto his chin, then falls to the bowl. The boy waits for Ferrell to ask again, but he won't play.

"I got mugged," Levon says.

"What?"

"I was leaving the club one night and some guy came up to ask the time. He wore chinos and one of them fancy pullover shirts. The sucker looked like he had more going

for him than I sure did. When I glanced at my watch, he
jammed the end of a lead pipe into my ribs and laid me out.
I couldn't breathe for just about forever. I stayed down with
my face on the sidewalk, thinking how the cement was still
warm, how pleasant the *warmth* really was. I could feel the
guy pulling out my wallet, taking the watch off my wrist, but
all I wanted to do was lie there and wait for the air to find a
way back into my body."

"Did they ever catch the guy?"

"Over a wallet and a watch? It wasn't exactly a drive-
by." Levon raises the bowl to his mouth and drains the milk.
"Sometimes I doubt it happened, but I got the three busted
ribs to help me remember."

Three weeks after Levon pulled his dirty laundry from
the car, he and Ferrell are out tagging his mix-and-match
flock.

"Have you heard from your mother?" Ferrell says, wondering why Rilla's name won't roll off his tongue when he
wants it to. He takes the sheep's ear and pulls it taut, then
grips the ear-tagger in his right hand. Levon rests on his
knees, bear-hugging the ewe's chest, looking the other way.
He doesn't want to see the hole punched like some giant ear-
ring stud, and Ferrell doesn't blame him.

"Not since Christmas."

Ferrell lines up the tagger on the ear and squeezes hard.
The animal shudders at the instant of bright pain, then looks
on like nothing's happened. Levon still holds the ewe, cheek
to the oily wool, eyes shut tight.

"You can let her go," Ferrell says.

Levon stands and wipes his hands on his jeans. He looks tired from being roused at sunbreak to help. When there was work to be done, Ferrell couldn't see the boy riding dreamland into noon. Ferrell's father worked forty-five years as a machinist, never late or absent one lousy day. When Ferrell was born, Maynard was out planting trees to make a little side money, and he stayed till he was done, missing Ferrell's arrival in the world by half a day. In his youth Ferrell was a slacker just to spite the old man, used to sit reading his books while his father worked in the yard, or hovered above some grease-black engine. But in recent years Ferrell feels himself slipping into his father's skin, feels goddamn *inhabited* by the old fart, driven from the house each day to accomplish something, to get work done before the sky goes dark and nothing wholesome can happen, only the nighttime things that leave you dead with shame come morning. Now Ferrell sets off into the dawn with something to do or else he's doomed. He likes to lean his old bones into some effort, something that will tap him out and make his porch time feel earned and good. Weariness, he's learned, keeps the hounds of sorrow at bay.

"Let's get another one," he tells the boy.

They wade into the gathered ewes, searching for one without the neon-yellow ear tag. Ferrell corners a California Red, and Levon works her other side. When she spooks, Levon jumps and lands butt down in the corral, sheep pellets like soft marbles under his hands. The look on the boy's face is too good to let pass.

Ferrell studies Levon on his duff in the sheep shit and laughs before he can stop himself. He bends over double with his hands on his knees, not knowing what's struck him so keen. He laughs until tears burn his cheeks and his bones tingle. Levon sits looking at his black-smeared hands, his fingers opening and closing like he's just discovered how to use them, then he's on his feet faster than Ferrell thought possible.

Ferrell sees the look in the boy's eyes and goes cold inside. There's a wildness loose in Levon's head, Ferrell can tell, something back a ways on the evolutionary tree, rooted deep in our animal past. Before Ferrell can think to duck, white light sparks in his head, and he is looking at nothing but clear blue sky. At first he's thankful he doesn't feel anything, but then the hurt slams home, and he believes he may be sick.

"You dead?" the boy says from somewhere atop the distant mountain range.

Ferrell moves his arms and legs, and everything works fine. He touches his cheekbone where the swelling has already closed his eye. With his tongue, he seeks out the place where his teeth have cut his gum, the blood metallic and harsh, like he runs on some bitter fluid and not the salty red wash of most.

"If this is heaven," Ferrell says, "I want to go back and do things a little different."

The boy stalks off toward the house, slamming the gates shut behind him.

Ferrell finishes the sheep himself, which he knows he should have done straight out. He finds Levon on the porch with a beer, though it's seven o'clock at best.

"Are you going to drink your breakfast?" Ferrell asks, looking at the boy through his one good eye. His cheekbone feels like someone stuffed a grapefruit beneath the skin.

"Shut the fuck up."

Ferrell shrugs. On the ledger sheet of their lives, the boy believes there are debts to settle. Levon raises the can and his throat works down beer.

"If it helps, I don't know why I laughed," Ferrell says. "It was some kind of archetypal thing. Like Charlie Chaplin or classic Stooges."

The boy glares, and Ferrell knows he's not helping things. The Stooges reference was a big miscalculation.

"Let's not get all schoolteacherly right now," Levon says. "I always hated that shit."

"To be frank, I hated it too. Talking always gave me a headache, like I was yanking thoughts from my head with a pair of needlenoses." After his days in the classroom ended, Ferrell returned to the language of his rural youth, the words plain and unadorned, few and far between.

They stare too long at each other. The look runs the gamut of emotions, before Levon backs down and glances off. As if on cue Ferrell hears a horse clopping the dirt road, and here comes Moonbeam bouncing in the saddle, her blonde hair whipping about her head.

"The cavalry," Ferrell says, "come to save our wretched souls."

Moonbeam sits the horse, sizing up the situation, Ferrell can see. She looks from Levon sulking on the porch to Ferrell with his shut eye and puffed-out face. When she hops from the saddle, her jeans ride so tight Ferrell wonders how she's not caught in some kind of special ecstasy. Her tank top is pastel blue, and she's all natural underneath, her nipples staring like a second set of eyes. He is reminded she's a well-shaped woman.

Without a word, Moonbeam walks to Ferrell and slips her arm through his, surprising him with the sudden closeness. She leads him across the space to where Levon sits on the porch, then guides him to the other chair. She places her palms on his shoulders and pushes down until Ferrell does as she wants. She sits cross-legged on the porch boards in front of them.

"When I was a little girl," she says, "my mother would have me sit down when I was mad. She'd tell me to see my anger in my head, to visualize the hostility on the movie screen of the mind, first in colors, then in shapes, and finally in words."

She levels a look at Ferrell that stills his tongue.

"I know you think I'm a flake, but you don't seem to have things under control right now, and it won't hurt to listen."

"I'm not the one playing Ali."

"Clam it," Moonbeam says, and he does.

"Now you two have put yourself in a place where there are no words, but *you've* gotten yourselves in this position, and it's your responsibility to find them. You must reach into that swirling cauldron of feeling and tell me what you see. Describe what's there."

Ferrell's about to tell the woman to head back to whatever planet she's from when Levon clears his throat.

"I see a black so black it shines," the boy says. "Like a big hunk of obsidian, all jagged and sharp on the broken edges, black razors waiting for flesh to tear."

Moonbeam nods. She reaches out and pats Levon's knee. She turns to Ferrell and smiles with such honesty he feels compelled not to send her packing. He closes his eyes and tries to make something up, but beneath his eyelids comes a nest of brown-and-dun copperheads from his boyhood. The snakes look young, maybe a week old at best, and there are so many they cover the bottom of his mind. When Ferrell looks closer, he sees the snakes are not copperheads but rattlers, their tails not yet hollow and dry.

He tells them what he sees.

Moonbeam leans forward and takes his hand, then slips her other palm into Levon's. When she joins him to the boy, Ferrell feels something bleak course his veins.

"We've got to channel this negative energy away," she says like she read his mind. "We've got to give this rage a place to go." She squeezes Ferrell's hand so hard he fears he'll cry out. "Open your eyes. Let all the bad stuff flow out your sockets, into the void of the sky."

Ferrell opens his lids and all the anguish of his life pours forth, out his head and gone. He feels the sky cloud with the black emotions they're setting free. He imagines the heavens have turned storm dark, but when he glances up, the world is still baby blue.

"Now, close your eyes," Moonbeam says, "and trap the good feelings inside your head."

Ferrell shuts his eyes and waits. "What next?" he asks.

"Now we talk," she says. "Now we make the words that cannot be made."

And so they do.

When Ferrell was newly a high school grad, bartending nights at the High Spot in Dundee, he used to hear the stories. Women are this, he'd hear night after night. Marriage is that, the bitter veterans of divorce would chant, whiskey fumes in his face. Ferrell tried to disbelieve, knew he and wife Larissa had something different going in the privacy of their second-floor walk-up.

But then one night a man in Harley chaps and a purple bandana sat down at the bar. Toward last call, and half wild from a long run of rum and cokes, the man leaned over the luster of the bar.

"Being married," he said, "is like paying someone to hit you over the head with a shovel, each morning and night, for as long as you live."

Ferrell quivered in his boots. From around the man's neck swung a metal lump that looked like honest-to-God gold.

"Wedding rings, melted down," the man said when Ferrell asked. "Five of them."

Forty-some years later, Ferrell believes that's about the size of it. Rilla'd been his third wife, after Larissa ran off with a software salesman from Canton, and Lindsi, his second wife, annulled their five-day marriage when she woke to say she couldn't stand Ferrell grunting over her. She said he didn't spend time in the lower gears—that he just went full throttle from the green flag and that full throttle wasn't enough. Ferrell said he'd change, do better, learn what she

wanted, but Lindsi would have none of it. She said the ways
of love could not be learned, said either you were born into
knowing how to be a man or you lived in Neanderthal darkness all your years.

"Lovemaking isn't something you can get from your
books, Ferrell," she said, sitting on her suitcase to get the
thing closed. "This isn't something you can read about, then
plod on through in that calculated, methodical way of yours.
You're not blessed in the sorcery of seduction, and you can't
turn a turnip into a stone."

Ferrell had to laugh at that last one. He thought she was
on a pretty fair roll, was laying it to him good, a real slash-
and-burner on his manhood, his character, the simian workings of his suspect heart, but then she brought out her dumb-
ass turnip line, and he knew he wouldn't mind Lindsi being
gone.

He'd reunited with Rilla at Tom Decker's fortieth birthday party. A dozen years before, Rilla had graced another
of Decker's famous parties, this one a raucous all-nighter to
celebrate his and Ferrell's master's degrees from Kent State.
Rilla was eighteen back then, and Ferrell was twenty-eight,
but they were inseparable all that summer. When Rilla went
off to college in the fall, the curtain dropped on their one-
act love.

At the birthday party, Rilla was like a rose blooming in
an empty field, her petals trembling with dew. She wore a red
sleeveless vest and green stretch pants that let Ferrell imagine
every muscle and tendon in her legs. Rilla was a short woman, not even topping five feet, and when they slow danced
her cheekbone was hot-welded to his chest, like she was bur-

rowing into his heart. Decker thought the two of them might rekindle some of the old fire, but not turn gaga like they did and marry at month's end. Ferrell had beat Decker to forty by six months, and Rilla had just made thirty, with a three-year-old son at home named after a song by Elton John.

Ferrell wanted to love the boy as his own, but the boy wouldn't have it. Levon knew his real father, his *bio-dad,* as he called him, was out there somewhere, though neither the boy nor Rilla knew where. He was pretty good about not throwing the you're-not-my-dad stuff in Ferrell's face, but sometimes he'd let something slip about his *real* last name that would drive a wedge into Ferrell's heart. Over time Ferrell couldn't sustain something that wasn't there, and the boy became another of his students, a student who stayed in his home and ate his food and left clothes strewn in each room of the house.

Weeks pass in the furnace heat of summer. The sun rides its white-glare arc, then drowns in wild red seas at day's end. Levon takes to joining Ferrell on the porch during eventide, and Ferrell grows not to mind the boy's presence. They're both still reeling from the morning Moonbeam did her thing, and they move about the house warily, like they've seen each other buck naked and want the sight erased from their minds. At first they sit and sip from cold cans of Coors, but then they talk some, not looking at each other, but staring into the immense bruise that is the horizon.

Tonight they're doing just that, confessing things to the sky as if God hid behind the afterglow curtain, listening with ears the size only God would have.

"I've never liked my name," Levon says and tilts the can to his lips. "I don't even like Elton John."

"My name's no winner either."

"Your name's got stud power."

"I always thought it was too feminine. When I was a kid I used to get my ass whipped over it."

"Tell me about it."

"I am."

Levon sucks the can dry. He crushes the aluminum in his fist in a great show of strength, then tosses the can into the front yard.

"I met my father," he says.

"What?"

"My bio-dad. I tracked him down."

"Where?"

"Los Angeles. That's why I went."

"How was he?"

"Not happy."

"I'm sorry."

"It's really how I hurt my ribs. When I knocked on his door, he thought I was the pizza delivery guy. After five minutes we was yelling and screaming. He said he didn't remember my mama. Said he'd never even been to Ohio. We started wrestling in his living room, both drunk out of our minds. He body slammed me into his end table."

"Quite a reunion."

"Tell me about it."

In the first years of marriage Ferrell had ridden the flood waters of Rilla's love, buoyed on the heat of their bodies at night, on her touch during sunlit hours. What he'd done wrong with Lindsi he now made up in spades, spending hours trailing fingerpads along Rilla's sleekness, taunting her, teasing her. Outside their bed Ferrell remembered to hold her and kiss her graceful neck, remembered to voice his love. During these years his cells would literally ache for her, like her touch lingered somehow beneath his clothes. He would stand at the blackboard and *feel* her cheekbone against his chest, recalling that slow dance at Decker's, when his heart burst like sparklers on the Fourth of July.

But no matter how much he gave, it wasn't enough—he was always a dime short, a day late, when it came to her needs—and some automatic survival mechanism kicked in. He was watching an infomercial late one night, and the shrink said men needed to go off to their caves, needed to clear the space around them. Ferrell knew that's what he needed or he'd smother. He saw Rilla as a black hole in the silent space of love, a negative force that sucked to her dark center all that came her way. After that something broke in his head, and Ferrell slowed his soft murmurings during the day, his marathon reveries in the night, the special things his tongue did under stifling sheets. Without these outward signs their love turned invisible, and since Rilla couldn't see it, she didn't think it was there.

During their final years of marriage, Ferrell learned the true meaning of being alone. He'd never have thought acute loneliness could fester with a woman sharing his bed, or sitting at their three squares, but there it was. He and Rilla kept on in the sustaining power of habit and routine, raising the boy to give them something to do. At night Rilla would shed her clothes in the dim bedroom, and he'd catch the shadow-shapes of her breasts, the dark patch between her legs, her pale skin offering its own light, then she would slide beneath the covers and turn from him, his manhood tingling at the remembrance of what sweet slick warmth lay inches from his reach. To Ferrell nothing was as hurtful as Rilla's back looming opposite him in the bed. He felt something shut down inside his heart, felt the lights go out and the plugs get pulled, imagined he was an empty vessel nothing would ever fill.

When Rilla and he would have the odd tumble in the hay—out of nostalgia more than anything, he supposed—he almost believed his own touch contained more truth than his wife's spread thighs. When Rilla looked off as he spent his love, Ferrell felt something he could only describe as his own death, come a little bit at a time.

Ferrell's in the barn when he hears the commotion. He steps from the door to see Cole red-faced and bursting, forked veins in sharp relief across his forehead. Cole rams his bulk against Levon, pinning him to the log wall of the cabin.

"You've been screwing my wife," he says, like it's news to Levon.

"We're just friends."

"In the middle of the goddamn night?"

"She likes to look at the stars."

"On her back," Cole says. Then he's done talking. He wraps his hands around Levon's slender neck and starts in. Levon's eyes bug like he sees his own fate. His face goes from red to magenta to purple.

When Ferrell cocks the shotgun, he's surprised how

good it sounds. He put his double-barrel in the barn the day Moonbeam handed the boy her card. He wishes he couldn't see things coming from so far down the road, wishes his fears didn't so often come true.

"Let go of the boy," Ferrell says.

He levels the barrels at the man's broad backside. Cole turns his head like he's forgotten where he is. When he sees the gun, he seems to remember.

"I get all twitchy when I get nervous," Ferrell says. "You best move your ass in reverse."

Cole's hands loosen and slide free. Ferrell sees bright finger marks on the boy's skin.

"Now don't overreact," Cole says. "We're all under control here."

"I'm about to piss myself. I don't think I'm in that much control," Ferrell says.

Cole eases back from the boy. His eyes never leave the barrels of the gun. When Ferrell clicks the hammers, Cole breaks into a dead run. He gets the pickup on the road in no time flat, its dust churning high into the morning air.

In the end Ferrell couldn't bring to life what Rilla craved, couldn't muster the energy and will to play her a midnight symphony. It was like he'd gone into an ice age of his own doing, as if gigantic glaciers were creeping down the floe field of his heart.

Ferrell didn't understand how far he'd gone till he flew to an annual teachers' conference in Tucson. He'd boarded the plane on time—always punctual, a fussy man if nothing else—and found his window seat aft the wing, as he'd requested. When the plane was about to taxi, a young couple not out of their teens dove into the vacant seats beside him, the kids out of breath from running. From the minute their asses hit the seats, the two couldn't quit each other. Ferrell tried to keep turned to his scratched Plexiglas portal, tried to interest himself in the in-flight mag, but he'd cast a side-long glance and see the kid's hands on her thighs, her bare freckled arms, her bright red hair. The hands would roam south to Mexico, then turn north to her breasts hanging like something ripe and edible. Her hands were into the fair-trade agreement, covering the boy's length until Ferrell was surprised she didn't yank off his boots and run finger magic over his toes.

In midflight, when the movie began its hazy flickering down the long tube of the hull, the couple worked into a kiss that put chills down Ferrell's spine. Ferrell was sure they'd go oxygen-deprived and need the yellow masks. When he looked, he saw their hands down each other's jeans, buried deep in their sacred places, and without thinking he unfurled his tiny blanket across their laps, the two of them not miss-ing a beat, not knowing he was even there, or that they were on a plane somewhere above the U.S. of A. As the cred-its scrolled the screen, the girl let out a moan that curdled Ferrell's blood, a low primal howl from deep in her interior, then the boy's jaw clamped shut, and Ferrell smelled the cop-pery scent of desire.

Ferrell sat with his back to the lovers while charged par-ticles swarmed his blood. Rilla's skin was under his fingers once more, and he remembered with startling clarity being inside her—how she'd grip him there so hard he couldn't fig-

ure how she accomplished such a thing. His mind flung back
to Rilla shouting his name like he had not almost crawled inside her. For years they lived one breath away from the bed,
the carpet, the countertop, but then barely shook hands for
an entire presidential scandal.

The lights flickered on, then the plane changed speed for
its controlled fall to the runway. As the lovers buckled and
zipped, Ferrell wept for the first time in as long as he could
remember.

By week's end the dust has settled, and Ferrell can see
well enough to assess the damage. His neighbor, he decides,
won't talk to him for a long while, but it's not like Ferrell
moved to the desert for companionship. He's sad, though, to
watch the acres of trees turn brown beneath the sun. Cole
has shut off the water to his trees.

Ferrell takes a cold one to the porch and parks his weariness. He's moved the other chair inside now that Levon's
gone, and he has to admit he misses the boy. Toward the last
Ferrell got used to having him around, had liked spooling
out words for the first time in his life, chatting about nothing
and everything that ever was. For the first time in months he
thinks of calling Rilla, whispering sweet nothings into her
machine, perhaps telling her direct about the ice age thawing
under the Idaho sun. He feels something down below that
doesn't feel too darn bad.

Ferrell sips from the can and stares across land that won't
end. He'd like to see a coyote out there, to see a pair of them
pounding up dust, leaping the clumps of tumbleweed and
sage, but knows that would be too perfect and knows life

doesn't ever work that way. He'll see the coyotes when he least expects them, some morning when he thinks they'll hide forever and can't be found, and he'll raise his beer to their fleeting shapes, watch their bushy tails recede down the chaparral.

Ferrell recollects he once told Levon to keep his lust in his pants, but he'd been wrong, flat wrong, and he knew that now. Your lust was what kept you going, gave you the itch to face the day. You had to keep your nerve pathways wide open, keep the currents flowing, or things would cool too far down. You get out beyond the reaches of emotion, he understands, you might never come back.

Above Ferrell the hawks hit the noon thermals, and he watches the easy drift and turn, the circling up the tunnel of the sky. He's so giddy he is up there with the redtails, looking down on his speck of a place in the lost desert land. From up high he thinks he can see Levon and Melody in the boy's beat-up Saturn SL, crossing into California and the miles of trees. He wishes them luck, blessings from above, oceans full of saltwater love, the Dalai Lama's regards. He knows the two of them are doomed, knows their love will run dry. Without fail they will wake from their foggy dreams, but for now Ferrell wants only the best for the lovebirds—Godspeed and all the rest, America the beautiful, from sea to shining sea.

The King
of Infinite Space

Ferrell's on the porch when he sees the dust. With dramatic flair a low sleek foreign car emerges from the haze, an alien space pod come to scout his lonely world. The car finishes the lane and parks beside his pickup, then idles like nothing good can step from its dark interior. Ferrell drinks his beer and works the creaky runners of the rocker. He can't guess who waits inside, but after Levon's recent visit nothing can fluster him. The devil himself could waltz from the car with his curved pointy tail, and Ferrell swears he wouldn't even blink. The door swings wide and out steps his ex in all her glory, looking utterly transformed. Ferrell feels his heart go supernova in the dark matter of his chest.

Rilla stands magazine-posed in the yard, backlit with the setting sun. She's lost some weight, he sees right off, and put things back in order somehow. Her hair catches the dusk light and glows bright as flame. To Ferrell's eyes she looks like the Second Coming—if Jesus were a fifty-year-old woman with hair as red as the sunbeams slanting down just for her.

Ferrell sips the crisp evening air. It strikes him that God

must be a junkie for unmitigated irony. Here Ferrell has finally settled into the habits of the solitary and the resigned,
has only now gotten the feel of living on his lonesome after
years of rough starts, and in comes Rilla like there's no past
and no tomorrow either.

His ex walks to the front porch and stands there shining.
Rilla Gabriella Swan—horsewoman virtuosa, Tai Chi devo-
tee, on most days his intellectual and emotional superior, his
equal in all other departments, physical or otherwise. Rilla
came of age the Summer of Love and, unlike most of her
fellow flower children, she never went establishment, cor-
porate, or any other way. The most popular crisis counselor
Ohio's troubled teen network has ever known, she has kept
herself young, Ferrell believes, by working with the youth
of the new millennium. She can talk and walk with the dear
children, can deal as much toughness and love as the kids
need. In short, a whole lot of woman in one small package.

"Cat got your tongue?" she says.

"Out here it'd be bobcat," he says.

"You look good, Ferrell. Kind of like a mountain man in
his twilight years. A Jeremiah Johnson in retirement, living
the sweet life."

"It's good to see you, too."

Rilla seems to size up his mood, her X-ray eyes beamed
into the neurons of his head. "I mean it, Ferrell. That compli-
ment was honest and true. I'd hoped to find you all withered
down to nothing, and here you sit as healthy as they come."

"You look a bit revamped yourself."

"Vitamins," Rilla says, walking up the porch steps. She

stands at the rail with her back to him, facing the coming night. "Plus lots of superb Tai Chi."

"Indeed."

Rilla turns to face him, the sheer silkiness of her dress inches from his reach. Without warning they've run out of words and the silence hangs. Ferrell samples his beer to give him something to do. He stands and the rocker creaks on without him. His arms become two foreign appendages he has just now grown.

Rilla stares as if he's a puzzle she can't figure. She takes his face in her hands. She kisses him hard on the mouth, her tongue seeking out places he's forgotten were there. When his tongue catches up with hers, his skin goes to flame in the chill of the night.

The first few days pass like a honeymoon redux. He and Rilla break in the futon he bought in Boise, then christen the living room couch, the shower, the flat cold length of the kitchen counter. Ferrell feels his youth humming through his veins, as if he's been reborn in the fire of his nether regions. In the midst of their sweat and toil he wonders if his old ticker can stand the strain. He knows it doesn't matter in the least.

At dinner, Rilla sits in one of his red flannel shirts and nothing else. Her hair competes hard with the red of the cloth. "I've got to admit this cabin business had me going, but it's not half bad," she says.

Ferrell had bought the log kit out of Montana, then hired a local crew to raise the place. On the phone, he'd kept Rilla updated as the house took shape. He'd tried his best to describe the dovetailed fit of the logs, the open interior beams, the sunlight like glazing on the blond wood floor.

"Thanks," Ferrell says. "I think."

"No, I mean it. I was seeing dirt floors, wind whistling between the logs, rain puddles on the bed. I saw Honest Abe huddled by the fire. Danny Boone all smelly in his coonskins and leather."

"I like the solidness of the place. I like the way the past feels close at hand."

Rilla butters cornbread he made fresh that morning. "How can you want the past when we are into a two and triple zeros? The crappy new century and all that?"

"All the more reason, I guess."

"Well, if you want to do the homesteader thing, what's up with the wide-screen TV?" She sits cross-legged on the chair, her bare knees bright as moons in the light. "Mr. Boone didn't get pictures from the sky."

"I'm a high-tech homesteader."

"You're a bullshit-steader, Ferrell. It doesn't matter you've moved to the middle of God-knows-where if you've brought all the junk of the world with you. You've got to trim back here. Lighten the lifeboat, streamline the operation."

The next day, Rilla has his truck most of the daylight hours. When she returns, the pickup bed is filled with all sorts of things from his father's upbringing—oil lanterns with curved glass bellies, the black hulk of a wood-burning stove, an antique flatiron like his grandmother used to use. In the passenger seat rides a scarred oak spinning wheel, the same kind he'd shown students on field trips to the Frontier

Days at the county fairgrounds, or the history museum in Cleveland.

This is not what Ferrell expected. He figured Rilla to pull him back from the brink of his own brand of retirement survivalism, to talk him out of his Idaho retreat. But here she is pushing rather than pulling, sending him further down the path. He'd wondered what it was like to live to the far left of center, and now Rilla is standing there, pointing the way.

The following morning Ferrell can feel autumn in the air, a hint of ruin tucked into the last of summer's heat. Even at noon the coming cold is there, hovering like an unspoken threat. He notices for the first time the trees by the creek have started to turn. Soon the chill will leach into his bones until he can't get warm no matter what.

In the irrigated pastures the sheep sense the coming change, eating to stubble the last of the sweet grass. Ferrell shovels out the barn stalls, where the animals spend the worst of the winter storms. Last month he bought hay from a rancher in Murphy, and now the stacked bales reach the rafters. When he enters the barn the heady fragrance unlocks time. He breathes the scent into his chest and a thousand childhood days stir through him.

Within three days of her trip to town, Rilla's got her new purchases in place. The woodstove broods in the corner of the kitchen, vented out the south wall, and near the back porch stand thirty cords of wood. His new ax leans against the stack. Around the house Rilla has put oil lamps of various shapes and sizes, some with handle loops, to carry light through her self-imposed darkness.

As much as she can, Rilla shies from things electrical. She and Ferrell cook on the wood-burning stove, his range and microwave unplugged and gathering dust. At dinner they eat by lantern light, an intimate glow Ferrell doesn't mind. The light takes the harsh edges off things, softens his perspective in pleasing ways. He imagines them young once more, their wrinkles and creases erased by the flickering flame.

"How's this for the past?" Rilla says after dinner one night.

They're in the living room, their maple rockers before the rustic fire. For the fireplace and mantle, Ferrell had three loads of river rock trucked from the Snake. The round stones remind him of rushing water, of movement held in place. When he closes his eyes the fire crackle is the splash of the current, that cold push shaping the stones smooth.

"This could be 1800, sort of."

"Not quite, Ferrell, but at least it's not the future."

Ferrell gazes at the bright orange coals. Rilla has the electric baseboards off, and the flame heat feels like a blessing on his face. Beyond the firelight the house lies lost to him, the rooms dark as primordial caves. He looks into the dry burning until his eyes ache.

"You want to go further into this?" he says.

Rilla mulls over what he's said. She gets the rocker going—working up an answer, he imagines.

"You're onto something here, Ferrell. At first I thought you were doing some grumpy loner thing, hanging out in the Wild West with your sour bad moods. But this place is pretty harmonious, and I haven't seen Butch or Sundance yet."

"So what's next? You want to stalk jackrabbits for food?"

Rilla stops her rocking and stands. She wraps her wool blanket around her, then totters over in tiny steps. He knows she is unclothed beneath the wool.

"You got a gun?" she says and sheds the blanket like something being born.

That night Ferrell wakes to the cries of the netherworld, a revolt from the caverns of Hades and beyond. The shrieks pour through the window screen—a yip-yap full of taunt and glee, something more than a little crazed.

"What is it?" Rilla asks from the dark.

"Coyotes," Ferrell says, only now figuring it out. He has never heard this many this close. He imagines they are in the room, tumbling in the dark air around his head. His heart takes a stutter step, as if the chambered beast itself wants to abandon him, gliding with the coyotes beneath the moon's cool cascade, past tumbleweed and sage and their attenuated shadows.

"They sound like they're dying," Rilla says.

"Or living," Ferrell says, as close to the mystical as he dares get. He remembers dumping dinner scraps against the fence line—not a smart thing for someone with dozens of sheep—but he would do it again to hear what he's hearing. Hell, if he could, he'd invite the devils into the house for tea.

In the last days of living in his prospering hometown, Ferrell felt the frustrations of the planet channeled daily through his tangled nerves. It seemed the *piss-offs* came hurtling his way—a no-brainer his colleagues couldn't see, some screw-up times ten with the phone company, the garbage man riding his stinking truck like he'd earned the right to fuck with you. For ages Ferrell thought it was him, maybe he was just one fussy citizen. But the more he thought about things, it seemed no one gave a damn anymore, yet he still did. He didn't want the stars and moon, for godsakes, he only wanted things done right, didn't want his garbage can left to roll in the street, or his electricity to shut off during dinner, customer service reporting no outages in his area as he stood in the dark.

The last straw was Ohio Power ringing his doorbell one fine spring day. They had to stand some new poles along his yard, they said, had to cut down the row of oaks that had stood for seventy-plus years—even though the trees *were* on his property and it *was* still America, home of the free. The young punk engineer had maps and deeds and copies of easements from 1915, and said that *yes* it was Ferrell's land, but the power company had their long-ago-granted-but-heretofore-unused easement to relocate the lines.

"Why move the poles?" Ferrell said, feeling the heat sizzle down his arms.

"It's those new homes where the old Snyder farm used to be. They need the volts and lots of 'em."

"Why not put the poles over there?" Ferrell said, pointing to the bare fields across the road. "Angle them."

The engineer shook his head. "Our numbers worked it out this way. On this side."

"Your numbers?"

"Our ratios. We use ratios to decide."

"Did you punch seventy-fucking-year-old trees into the fucking ratios?"

"Do you have to swear?"

"Goddamn right," Ferrell said, letting loose a tirade that left the poor kid shrunken and pale.

In the end, after paying a lawyer who couldn't do a damn thing about anything, Ferrell sat in the house with Rilla and watched them cut down his fifteen oaks with their leaves haloed in the sun—trees Levon used to climb, trees Ferrell and Rilla would have picnics beneath like scenes from sappy movies, where he and Rilla did so much more when night fell and the fireflies sparked like magic dust thrown from above.

And so Ferrell decided to take early retirement and park his butt in Idaho, a place he knew nothing about other than its fame as retreat from the world. Let them put power lines around his land, he told Rilla, or build shopping-mall battlements along its edges, and it would matter not at all because he would have, would outright own, endless acres of air and sun around him, the fenced lines of his property borders no others could cross.

But Rilla didn't care about his plans. She'd already filed divorce papers at the courthouse in New Philadelphia, her patience with Ferrell long since depleted.

After the night of wild howling, he and Rilla take up coyote watch in the yard, though they both want to hear the beasts more than keep them from the livestock. In the side pasture, the late lambs bleat for their mothers in the squeaky voices of old cartoons. Rilla sits bundled in his down jacket, and Ferrell wraps a quilt around his shoulders.

Night after night they sit before their kingdom of sage

and chaparral, of amaranth and Russian thistle. Past midnight the blackness deepens until the star points are in their hair, until they're up among the white lights of the heavens. Some nights he and Rilla stay out till dawn, staggering into bed as the sun hikes the sky. Soon Ferrell has been up more than he's been down. He wears his fatigue like billowy gauze over his eyes, moves through daylight hours that are slightly skewed.

Tonight the full moon over his head hangs battered and bruised, a testament to staying afloat in the clutter of space. It's bright enough to read in, and that is just what he does, turning the pages of a how-to on making solar panels. At his feet lies a book on the eleven vocalizations of the intermountain west coyote. His coffee grows cold, but he sips it anyway, feeding the wakefulness into his brain.

"I'd always wanted to die young," Rilla says, coming off a spell of wordlessness. "But now I can't."

"But you're *only* fifty," Ferrell says, then regrets his words. It sounds like he's pointing out there's still time to do herself the big one. Before them the air shimmers bright as false noon, the tumbleweeds throwing black pools across the land. He waits for that first lone howl from the silvery world. He pictures the silhouette of a coyote, pointed nose to open sky, from those double-feature Westerns his father loved.

"You ever feel old, Ferrell? I mean in your head, where it counts. Or your love places, where it counts even more."

"My head still thinks I'm twenty, and my pilot light's still burning most times. But there's something else inside me these last years. A kind of sadness on slow drip, seeping into my blood."

"You've always been a moody SOB. There's nothing new to that. You act like collecting sadness is a hobby worth your time."

Ferrell holds his tongue. He knows better than to explain. Words, he's forever understood, are at best rough approximations of what goes on behind his eyes. When he does send a thought into the air, it never cuts close to the original.

"My father died, Ferrell. He passed right before I left. Seventy years old plus a day."

Ferrell halts his cup on its way to his lips. He'd met the man once when Rilla was eighteen—a hard-nosed drinker, harmless despite his rants and raves.

"I'm sorry," he says for lack of anything better. He studies the shadows slanting off their heads and shoulders. He imagines the shadows are the shed skins of their former selves.

"That's the problem," Rilla says. "I'm not sure I am."

Ferrell waits until her words rise high into the night. When he turns to Rilla at last, the moon lies doubled in her eyes.

"I wanted to tell you the first night here, but couldn't somehow. You looked so damn peaceful on that porch of yours."

Ferrell settles his cup with care on the ground. In the space between them he feels something other than the air. Rilla stares at him with those twin moons hung in the blackness of her eyes.

"I've missed you, Ferrell."

As the shiver traverses his spine, the coyotes take up chorus in the dry wash to the north. He figures them a good mile distant, but the air is still, and the yipping travels direct

to his ears. Rilla sits with her head bowed as if the howling sets a buzz going in her ears. The coyotes settle down,
then comes a frenzied answer from somewhere to the south,
a different arrangement of notes weaving through the lus-
trous light, tangling, straightening into extended riffs. To the
southwest another pack starts, then yet another in a chain re-
action across the moonscape night. Many minutes pass until
the last wailing cuts short and fades, and he and Rilla sit for
a while recovering, feeling they've just returned from their
caveman past.

"Jesus," Rilla says, and Ferrell can do nothing but nod.

An Indian summer runs its course in blazing afternoons
of sun and sky. Along the river the trees burn in perpetual
flame, while higher up the redtails slip their shadows over
the ground. When Rilla does her daily Tai Chi in the yard,
Ferrell naps in his shorts and bare skin, the sunglow a nar-
cotic in his blood. Stretched on the lawn chair, he believes
he won't ever move again. He pretends he is a fat tabby gone
slack in the sun.

One night at supper Rilla starts to fast. She sits at the
table with her empty plate, the delicate light turning her into
an ascetic or high priestess before his eyes. She doesn't eat
the next day either, puts together a string of days without a
crumb. Ferrell feels odd man out, so he skips some meals,
too, then goes cold turkey but for the pots of chamomile
Rilla brews on the stove.

After three days his head has gone light. He can feel the
rhythm of his blood go awry, feel clarity drain from the flim-
sy folds of his brain. He and Rilla have stayed out late for

weeks, their ears attuned. It occurs to Ferrell they're on some Native American visionary quest, though he can't muster much introspection beyond that.

In the shrinking light of October, in the leaves doing their withering act on the trees, Ferrell embraces a melancholy beyond words, a piercing arrow of sadness that hits square his bull's-eye heart. All those years of living apart from the downhearted, looking from afar at those trapped in their glorious castles of pain, in their private dungeons of hurt and despair, and here rode Ferrell like a king, impervious to the sickness and frailty of the common folk. And now he is old and drying up, exiled from the kingdom, and he has the blues, feels there are endless tears to shed for a life so hard to bear.

One evening Rilla's at the spinning wheel, feeding carded wool with her fingertips into the whirling spool. Her foot works the pedal with a steadiness that hypnotizes if Ferrell watches too long. The living room is dark but for the firelight and the radiant oil lamps, and the effect is striking—she looks like an apparition, an angel sent to protect him from himself. He believes she's some lost treasure from the dusty attic rooms of his mind.

At her feet sits a basket of wool she washed and ran through the teeth of the carder. At this stage the airy wool reminds him of white cotton candy. He is surprised Rilla has thrown herself with such vigor into the ways of their ancestors. She plans to knit him a pair of socks, after she spins enough wool, then move on to a sweater of blended wools. She has never held knitting needles, far as he knows.

"You catch on fast," he says from the rocking chair. The cardings twist before the spool, and his gaze trails back to the intricate play of her fingers.

"I don't know what I'm doing yet, but I will."

"You could have fooled me."

Rilla keeps her eyes on the take-up almost filled with yarn. "That's something, Ferrell. You used to be hard to fool. You used to be hard to please."

"It's all this Spartan living. I'm getting easier by the day. More hungry, too."

Rilla lifts her foot from the pedal and the big flywheel stops. When she looks over he knows something serious is headed his way.

"You don't mind me here, do you?" she says. "I mean you had quite the recluse experience going for three whole years."

"But we were married seventeen."

"I don't want to be a habit of yours, Ferrell. A comfortable couch you're fond of because I'm soft and broken in."

Ferrell can feel his Rockwell moment slipping past. "I like having you here," he says, his voice taking more edge than he'd hoped. "More than not, if you must know."

"That's encouraging."

"Look, Rilla, you're spoiling the damn pastoral interlude we've got going. I've not been missing our usual bickering routine."

She's out of her chair on that one. He knows he has sunk too low. In their married days this was the moment when they did the most damage, tossing out words to hurt and maim, to shoot the spirit down. He feels too old and ragged to take up the battle.

Her eyes catch light, and he knows she is fighting tears. Ferrell leaves the chair and takes her in his arms. She holds on as if a windstorm has blown into the room.

Toward midnight, while Rilla sleeps unburdened from her thoughts, Ferrell rises from the futon. He dresses in the dark and navigates the stairs to the living room, where he lights each oil lamp in turn. He hikes out into the night, crossing the yard and then beyond, moving into the scrub. It's a new moon, and the darkness presses from all around. Ferrell walks with a purpose he can't name, tripping in his boots, listening to the magnificent noise of his heart. He breaks a sweat and doesn't let up till he reaches his far pasture fence. He likes the thought his land keeps going—all those acres spreading out north, south, east, west. Ferrell turns to see what he has come to see. In the distance his cabin rises from the inky black, its first floor windows pale with light, a small ship at anchor in the divine emptiness of the sea.

Days pass and Ferrell feels his winsome youth return in brilliant movie-screen snippets. The morning sun in the dusty barn, Sam Cooke on the transistor radio, the twist and drift of leaves to the ground, and Ferrell's got visions in his head, a random scattering of moments he lived decades ago—his mother's profile in filtered barn light, his father humming "You Send Me" at the breakfast table, an autumn morning as the yellow school bus brakes beneath the red trees. For brief instants Ferrell is stunned by these old emotions churned anew in his chest, pumped like liquid fire through his squiggled veins. He senses the momentary order in the drawn-out run of his years.

One night Ferrell crosses the border from sleep and hovers there, his mind suspended above the bed. He lies still on the futon, a white static in his ears, an electric thrum he finally understands to be rain—a heavy hard rain pounding the metal roof. Ferrell lifts his head, and the room smells of sage and sand gone too long without storm. The scent is redolent as incense, and it seems like the first rain in all the world.

Ferrell gets up and stands at the screen. He listens to the dark drumming. There is a rustling and Rilla stands close. She has left her clothes on the bed.

"The rest home called when he started to fail," she says, including him in some private conversation already under way. "I got there right after."

Rilla brushes a bare shoulder against his own. "He was still warm, Ferrell, like he was sleeping, but I knew he wasn't, and I didn't feel a thing. I mean, I was trying to churn up what I should have felt—loss, grief, regret—but I couldn't muster the right feelings."

"Maybe you were in shock. That's common."

"They wanted me to write the eulogy. The pastor said to recall the good times, to focus on some pleasant memory of my father." Her fingers grip his bicep, holding him fast. "I just kept seeing the bad—the drinking and the womanizing, the typical, boring stuff that goes with it. It was like my mind was poisoned or something. The more I thought about it, the madder I got. It's like he was a damn caricature from some daytime talk show. Like he was Oprah's wretched guest of the week."

"Was he really all that?"

"Of course not, but that's all I could remember. Did you know he once bought Christmas presents for the kids of his mistress and not for us? That he once took us to play with her children, while he did her in the bedroom. Can you believe?"

Ferrell pries loose her fingers, draws her near. He wants to say the man probably had reasons, but knows that's as lame as it gets.

"This is weird, Ferrell, but when I was writing the eulogy, I understood all the good things I could have written about you. What a good man you are." Rilla presses her ear to his chest, as if listening for stirrings within. "The morning after the funeral, I woke and had the leave-of-absence papers filed before noon, got all my kids reassigned. I rented one of those happy moving vans and put our stuff in storage, then rented the house to a nice Vietnamese couple from Newcomerstown. I got this car and was on the road before I knew I was headed your way."

"And you didn't turn around?"

"I put the pedal down, Ferrell. I stayed the course."

"You want to keep on here?" he says, as if the idea hasn't roamed his mind dozens of times before.

"Damn straight," she says, then pulls his boxers down to his ankles.

Ferrell steps from the shorts.

"Come on," she says, taking his hand.

"Where?"

"A symbolic cleansing. A washing away of our trespasses and all that. We can't pass up this sensational Hollywood rain."

Before Ferrell can protest Rilla has led him from the house. She tugs him to the center of the yard and releases him, the rain much colder than he ever imagined, needling his bare scalp, his shoulders and back, numbing his mind. The downpour roars in his ears, seems to be filling up his head. Rilla is a blur before him, a ghost spirit in all that rain, dancing to some beat of her own making, and Ferrell starts moving too. He throws his arms around some, does a forgotten shuffle step he learned in high school. He feels chilled through, but his inner furnace keeps him going, his heart a dark star throwing heat.

Come morning the world's gone white. An inversion layer, the radio says, cold dense air trapped on the ground, the humidity off the scale in some freak global-warming way. The fog stretches a hundred miles in each direction, covers the state and beyond.

On the strung lines of barbed wire, on the bare branches of the trees, the fog feathers delicate white crystals. The end of the world, Ferrell thinks, despite the radio reports, an ice age revisited, the earth plunged into darkness and cold. For days on end it stays below freezing, and he trucks boiled water out to the animals, their water buckets frozen to the core. In the frigid air the sagging power lines creak and moan, then snap somewhere along their long run to civilization. Rilla has so many things electrical shut down, it is the unlit fridge that finally reveals the outage.

"We're free, Ferrell."

Rilla stands bundled in flannels and sweaters, a quilt around her waist. She skips around the kitchen without much enthusiasm, while Ferrell stares into the darkened fridge.

"We've cut the umbilical," she says, finished with her mock celebration. "Or rather the humongous hand of God has reached down with big old wire cutters and cut us loose from those wicked city ways."

"What about our food?" Ferrell says, feeling too much the whiner, the reluctant child not willing to play the game. "You know I like my cow juice cold."

Rilla gives him a look that says his brain is running low. "Have you gone outside lately? It's cold enough to freeze your man-thing off and keep it fresh till spring. The pantry's the same temp as the fridge, and we'll keep our frozens on the porch in the ice chest."

"I guess it'll serve till they get us hooked up."

"Ferrell, my sweet but slow-thinking man, we'll tell them to keep their power. Keep their juice. We'll give them back the big proverbial finger."

"What about come spring?"

"Propane fridges," Rilla says and smiles a smile to refire the sun.

Over the next days he and Rilla stay the course of fasting and late hours, huddled in the night fog, their wool blankets damp in the wet air, their faces cool and slick. Ferrell feels something at work in his veins, as if his blood runs clear and pure, the solution charged with particles of comets and meteors, with minerals from the high deserts of the moon. He stumbles when he walks, and his arms and legs work out of time, but his head gains strength while his body grows weak. Some noons he rides with the hawks winging the winter sky, his vision keen and true, the house and barn adrift in miles upon miles of nothing at all.

On Thanksgiving morn, Ferrell opens his eyes to Rilla hunkered on the futon in her clothes and boots.

"Get dressed," she says.

Ferrell does as he is told, pulls into his long johns and flannel shirt, his insulated canvas pants. His clothes hang like a bigger man's borrowed for the day. When he pulls his stocking cap onto the smooth dome of his head, he notices Rilla holds something in her arms, a large blue vase with delicate handles.

"What's that?" he says.

"My dad."

Ferrell sees now it is a funeral urn, though he can't recall being close to one before. He wonders where the thing's been hidden these last months. He feels a strangeness in the room, an off-kilter vibe, as if the old man has joined them. Ferrell rubs both hands over his face, hoping he is not quite awake. He decides he needs to eat today.

"What are you going to do with the man?"

"Follow me."

Rilla leads him down the stairs and out the front door. She heads into the scrub at a good pace, and he struggles to keep up. Tracks run out ahead of her, footprints in the snow, and she follows the path someone else has set down. The fog hangs near the ground like fallen clouds.

Ferrell looks back and the house is a charcoal sketch. His boots tangle with a brittle tumbleweed and he crashes through. Up ahead Rilla has stopped near a gathering of boulders. When Ferrell reaches her she is crouched in the snow, the urn cradled against her jacket as if to keep her father warm. In the billowy white Ferrell makes out what she has found: a coyote den tucked beneath the embankment of the dry wash, sheltered by the rock. Dried grasses have been trampled down, and small white bones lay scattered about. The den looks downright cozy, and Ferrell considers crawling inside.

"I found the place this morning, Ferrell. I got up and just started walking, like I was a divining rod and some force was leading me straight here. When I saw this place I knew it was what I'd been searching for all along."

"I didn't know you were looking for their dens."

"I wasn't."

Rilla gives him the eye, and he holds his skepticism in check. "Don't try to figure it, Ferrell."

Ferrell hunkers next to her in the snow. Rilla lifts the lid from the urn, carefully handing him the small glass disk. With her teeth she pulls off her mittens and lets them fall. Before he can voice his wonderment she tilts the urn and takes ash into her palm. It seems the surrounding boulders are bearing witness, their silence an act of supreme will. Rilla studies the ash in her cupped hand. She makes a fist, then opens her hand flat, some of the finer powder lifting into the stillness. She casts the handful before her as if throwing seed, shadowing the snow. In her actions Ferrell sees ritual and the demands of ceremony, though this is surely the first time she has ever done this.

Rilla tips the urn and takes another handful. She brings it to her nose, both eyes shut tight, cheeks blushed from the cold. Ferrell knows what's coming next though he doesn't

know how, and she brings her palm to her lips, touches
tongue to ash, then offers some to Ferrell.

"We'll make him a part of us, as I am part of him," she
says. "He'll live a better life within us."

Ferrell has his pulse in his ears. He feels the cold pass
right through him, as if he has lost substance and can offer
no resistance to the world. He does as she wishes and holds
the bitterness on his tongue, a private sacrament to a woman
whose past is intertwined with his own.

Rilla rises and carries the urn to the shelter of the den.
She upends the blue glass and shakes loose ash and bone,
powders the dried grass where the creatures sleep with the
full moon in their heads. She bows her head a moment, then
takes Ferrell's hand and leads him back through the fog. All
around them the whiteness is absolute: a clean slate nothing
bad has ever touched, a place as undisturbed as the plains of
distant stars.

The Mistress
of the Horse God

In the bright spring sun, Ferrell and his ex hike the rocky hills behind the cabin, up along the ridge where the world falls away. To each compass point the land stretches without end, enough to dwarf his skinny frame beneath the huge scary sky. He knows Rilla wants to reach the top out of breath and shaking, wants to deserve the view before her, all that air and nothing to stop her eyes. She especially likes the ridge on the rare days after rain, when the air is clear enough to make them both weep. She says there's no space between the moonscape below and where she stands, as if she can touch the distant buttes with her outstretched hands.

"I never get tired of your backyard," she says at the top this pristine morning. "The whole place changes with each angle of the sun, with each shadow the clouds put down."

Ferrell studies Rilla without comment, amazed her temporary stay has now reached seven months, a fact neither of them speaks.

Rilla is still huffing from the steady hard climb, her chest heaving beneath her *Ohio Is for Lovers?* T-shirt, sweat like cut diamonds across her brow. "I feel like jumping out of my skin, Ferrell," she says. "I feel I could truly fly." She gathers her light red hair into the ponytail of her youth, twists in place a thick rubber band. When she wipes her face with the hem of her baggy shirt, his blood quickens at the unexpected flash of belly.

Ferrell walks the ragged spine of the ridge and takes a physical accounting. Due east, across a hundred and fifty some-odd miles, the postcard peaks of Sun Valley stand dirty white in the sun. A few degrees south and a hundred miles closer, the long runways of Mountain Home Air Force Base lie hidden amidst the desert sage. From the ridge at night he often watches the runway lights glitter like strung Christmas bulbs. Now and again a handful of lights will detach and glide upward, a night fighter off to patrol the hostile world. Sometimes when Ferrell is out walking, pairs of space-age jets wheel low over his head, visitors from the future, he imagines, come for the day. He always wishes them well with what they'll find.

Rilla comes to stand beside him, a silent companion to his clamorous thoughts. Without explanation she draws her shirt over her head. In a practiced motion he knows by heart she unhooks her bra and hands both pieces of clothing to him. Her nipples tighten in the breeze, a lovely event Ferrell has never ceased admiring. Rilla unbuckles her walking shorts and slips them over her boots, then does the same with her white cotton undies. She gives these things to Ferrell as well.

"That's better," she says. "I feel way less held down. Now maybe I *can* get airborne."

Though he's seen Rilla naked more times than he can

count, Ferrell feels weak in the knees watching his ex in hiking boots only, her skin smooth alabaster in the sun, a fine sweat sheen between her bare breasts. In all this open air she seems naked as she's ever been, as naked as she can ever be.

"Wow," he says. "You do all right for your age."

"I do all right for any age." Rilla fluffs herself down below, works her fingers through the tiny tangles. "I've never understood the big deal over this puff of hair. There isn't a whole lot to admire."

"It's where the universe begins and ends, Rilla. It's the portal to immortality. The secret fountain of eternal youth."

Rilla frowns out of feminist obligation, but he can tell she's not displeased, accustomed as she is to the serfdoms of his mind, those lowly places where his thoughts chug ale in bawdy roadhouse inns. "I'm not a portal to anywhere or anything, Ferrell Swan. And that fountain thing is just plain weird. You'll need to stave off death in some other way."

"There isn't any other way," he says, but she doesn't seem to hear.

Rilla raises both arms skyward and twirls. She jumps up to challenge gravity's hold, but her boots raise dust as she lands. She faces the grand spectacle of the Owyhee Mountains, looming just fifteen miles distant, as if to rival their natural beauty.

Ferrell tries to study those craggy peaks of granite and pine, but the years he's known this woman, his acute knowledge of her, occupies all the space inside his head. He looks to the south, away from Rilla and the Owyhees rising like a monument to violence. The land in the distance seems to take on the curve of the earth—more land than a man could cross in a week, a month, a life. Sometimes he believes he is not meant to see so much at once, not meant to stare at this many miles, to understand the planet's actual size. Here Ferrell has gone off to the desert for his forty days and found Lucifer wasn't there—just sun and sky and rocky earth, just his own head and its scattered electrical workings. It's more than he bargained for: rattlers in the kitchen, coyotes at the door, heat that wants the air to burn. He had wanted retreat, he knew that much, but the price for exile runs high.

"Let's walk the north forty," Rilla says, hiking into the ravine, opposite the way they came.

Ferrell starts down the backside of the ridge, away from his cabin and barn and the civilized world. On this side of his land he could be in the days of the Hole in the Wall gang. He thinks about his years of boring ninth graders in the lessons of American history, how he always wanted to live out his days beneath the overwhelming sky, to ride with the spirits of every misfit and outcast come before him. Sometimes he can't imagine how all that kid teaching was accomplished with just books and blather, can't imagine he taught about something he didn't truly know.

Ferrell watches the globes of Rilla's fine bum, her smooth back with its taut flexing, her long red hair released from its rubber band. He tries to remember the first time he saw the hidden parts of the female form and decides it was Missy O'Connor, out behind the Little League dugout. He guesses they must have been ten when Missy dropped her one-piece just for him, his interest in baseball gone before it could even begin.

Fifty years, he thinks, *and still amazed.*

At the bottom of the ridge rests the complete skeleton of a wild mustang, the wildness still there though the bones don't move. Ferrell discovered the skeleton when he first hiked his land, astonished at the bright white skull and its dark eerie sockets, at the curved hoopwork of ribs, the long leg shafts tucked as if the animal still might rise. He knows the place possesses a sacredness that never diminishes over time.

To his surprise, Rilla kneels before the bones. She rolls the enormous skull over, and the lower jaw falls free, leaving in one piece the cranium with its long snout and toothy upper jaw. Ferrell can see the underside of the cranium is broken. Rilla lifts the partial skull from its resting place and holds the thing in front of her. From where Ferrell stands, she seems to slip the skull over her head, her fingers gripping the snout.

Ferrell grows loose in the knees for the second time that morning: a horse skull atop the body of a naked woman, some ancient creature from folklore, some monster from dreams born of desire and fear. He stares into the skull's shadowy sockets.

"I am the mistress of the horse god," she says, her words in the voice of someone else.

"Lucky god," Ferrell says, more unsettled than he wants to be. He feels his reality too altered right now, feels they've changed from who they were when they left the cabin an hour before.

"You dare to mock the horse god?" Rilla says. "You dare to look upon his mistress with lustful eyes?"

Ferrell stands sweating beneath the hot sun. He doesn't know why the moment has turned so creepy so fast. He wants to say he's spooked, but can't utter a word. He suspects that soon she may be gone, headed back to that red brick house from their past. He pictures his cabin without her, the small rooms again just rooms and nothing more. He thinks to tell her something important about their lives, something that will make her spring into his arms, but he knows each insight is lost when spoken aloud. To his relief, Rilla lowers the skull before he can answer.

"You lost your chance there, Ferrell. I hear horse women can make a man beg."

"Or worse," Ferrell says and smiles to hide his fears.

They hike a good ways into the open scrub, leaving behind the skeleton with its skull returned. In time they plot a wide circle back toward his place, picking their way along the low lunar hills with Rilla in the lead, her bare back glistening with sweat. Her shoulders and neck take on a reddish hue, and Ferrell rubs sunblock from his daypack on his nude ex-wife. As they reach the edge of the dry wash, Rilla stops short.

"What's that?" she says, pointing.

Ferrell sights along her outstretched arm to find the air vent of Din Winters's underground bunker, before them as if an illusion. A former EMT from San Francisco, Winters had bought his parcel before Ferrell bought his, and buried on his land three gasoline storage tanks bought at the salvage yard in Kuna. He said they were unearthed when a gas station was torn down, and he cleaned and treated and painted their curved inner walls until the gas stink was a pungent memory. With a rented backhoe, he reburied the ten thousand gallon tanks in a T pattern, joining them tight with welds that took him weeks to get right. He brought in power underground for a quarter mile. When Ferrell got the tour, he was astounded with the roominess of the underground complex, but this surprise was tempered by the sharp feeling he'd been buried alive.

"It's just one of your neighbors," he says, hoping to downplay the secret he's kept from her since she arrived. He hadn't wanted to burden Rilla with the knowledge of a man who lives beneath the sand. She'd always been skeptical about Idaho, its shady reputation as outlaw sanctuary.

Rilla gives Ferrell the eye. She doesn't bother to ask for explanation, just waits for him to fess up.

"Okay," he says. "He's from California, and he lives in real big gas tanks down below."

"Is he one of those hatemongers?"

"Far as I can tell, he's a refugee from hate. He says he left the general populace when he couldn't take the abundant anger. He's kind of gotten into a reclusive mood."

"Let's go visit him," Rilla says and starts walking.

Ferrell catches up and takes her arm. "He doesn't really like company. That's the idea." He nods in her direction. "You're also naked."

Rilla reaches for the clothes he has kept bundled in his arms.

At Winters's buried home, Rilla stands wordless with her hands on her hips. Except for the scores of footprints, and the short pipe sticking from the ground, the place is nothing but rocks and silver sage.

"He really lives in the ground?" she finally asks. "Like those crazies you hear about in the news?"

"That's where he got the idea."

"How's he get down there?"

Ferrell points to a metal trap door painted the color of the sand, its curved handle barely visible.

"Jesus," Rilla says.

Ferrell picks up a rock and walks carefully to the trap door. He pounds the metal twice, pauses, then raps two more times. Against his will comes the sensation he's waking some beast better left alone.

"What was that?" Rilla says.

"The signal he said to use."

"You been here before?"

"One time," he says. "It gave me the willies."

As Rilla readies her answer, Ferrell hears clanking below, then the door lifts an inch, a wedge of darkness in which Ferrell sees not a thing.

"That you, Swan?"

"In the flesh."

"Who's with you?"

"My ex-wife."

"Thought you two lived in separate states?"

Rilla steps to the edge of the trap door. "Not right now," she says far too loud, as if Winters might be out of practice with the spoken word. She gets down on her knees, peering into the thin black space between the door and the metal frame. "Are you going to come out into the light of day?"

The door clangs shut like a rifle shot. Ferrell listens as the noise sails off to the hills and returns to them changed. He's not in the mood for the neuroses of others, given how many of his own he needs to bear.

"Now you've done it," he says.

But the trap door swings open until it rests on the ground, a gaping mouth into the belly of the earth. Din Winters climbs out with unexpected enthusiasm, blinking at the bright like the mole he is. His hair is cut shorter than Ferrell remembers, and he's wearing his old EMT jumpsuit with *San Francisco County* stitched over his heart. Winters pulls a pair of sunglasses from his breast pocket and puts them on.

"I don't get visitors," he says.

"So I'm told," she says, reaching out her hand. "Rilla Swan from Ohio, as the shirt so proclaims." She holds her palm steady until Winters shakes her hand.

"I'm Din."

"All right then," she says. "Nothing like a little civility in the wilds to bring folks together."

"What now, Rilla?" Ferrell says.

He watches Rilla and Winters scrutinize each other. They seem to be searching their past lives, trying to figure if the other is friend or foe. Before Winters can save himself, Rilla steps forward and hugs him. He stands with his arms pinned to his sides, his eyes asking Ferrell what the hell he has brought his way. Ferrell only shrugs.

"Sorry 'bout that," Rilla says. "You looked like you needed a big dose of love and affection."

"I'm not a people person."

"You don't exaggerate, either."

"Well," Ferrell says, "we just came by for a friendly spell. We've got to be going."

"Don't let him fool you. I came to see your underground fortress," Rilla says, her hand touching Winters lightly on the elbow. She stands between Ferrell and his hermit neighbor, a woman used to people whose hearts can't find a proper place to hide.

"Then so you shall," Winters says and bows stiffly from the waist, already under Rilla's spell.

Midnight departs and Ferrell and Rilla still sit on the comfy couch, their host holding court from a white leather armchair. All night Ferrell has meant to ask Winters how he got the furniture down the damn ladder, but he hasn't had the chance. The revelry began at dinner, when Winters broke out some California red, a ten-year-old bottle of his best pinot noir. The man has kept the wine flowing ever since—merlots, cabernet sauvignons, zinfandels—a regular stockpile of his favorite Napa wineries, hoarded below the earth against unnamed catastrophe. With the wine inside him Winters turned chatterbox, he and Rilla sharing stories like buddies from ages past. Ferrell has been happy enough to soar with the wine.

"After my wife left me to study batik in Bali, I lost my zest for the day to day," Winters says.

"Forgive the counselor in me, but didn't saving people help counter your loss?"

"Oh, hell, saving people is highly overrated. The ones you save get all indebted to you, like they love you and not the thing you just did for them. Most people adore themselves way too much, and feel this great rush only because you've handed their asses back to them."

As if forgetting his guests, Winters holds his glass to the

glow of the nearest oil lamp, swirls the wine in a colorful display, takes a sip. "But what pulls you down," he says without missing a beat, "is the daily carnage, the gazillion knife wounds, gunshot wounds, ice pick wounds, Bic pen wounds. The blunt trauma, the remarkable things a fist can do to a human head. Blood pooled at your feet like spilled paint, so bright and incredibly red, fluorescent really, so much death you think it's the way to go."

"Goodness," Rilla says. "That is one gloomy outlook."

Winters stands and pulls the cork on another bottle. "It's zero visibility, for sure." He hands the cork to Rilla, who gives it a dainty sniff and nods. Winters pours wine into everyone's glass, filling each to the brim.

"Aren't we supposed to have just a smidge in here?" Rilla says. "Enough to simply wet our palates?"

"We're fast tracking, honey. We're on an express route to Shangri-la and I'm your conductor. You let old Din here show you the way."

"Men cannot show women anything."

Winters looks at Rilla as if he's been slapped. "You sound like my former wife."

"A smart woman."

"Now, don't get me started on that particular topic. Don't forget the full story here—she left me."

"You see, in their hearts and minds, men leave women first," Rilla says, serious now despite the wine. "We just break the physical connection. We basically finish what you're too weak to finish yourselves. We end the misery for all concerned."

"That's not how it felt to me," Winters says. At once he looks sad beyond belief, a man set back on his heels by his own history.

"It's a kind of death," Rilla says, as if talking only to her soul. "At his funeral this summer, Aunt Ruth said my dad died thirty years ago. She told me his divorce from Mom was the real funeral, the same damn thing with a different name." Rilla finishes her wine and looks around for more. "He just changed one day when he was forty-two, like the life went out of him. Ambition, courage, love of family, common decency—all gone like he'd used up those things."

"What happened after the divorce?" Winters says.

"Oh, the Jerry Springer stuff—he went through the rest of his life with his pecker leading the way."

Ferrell studies Rilla as if he's never truly seen her. She's speaking some hard-won truths here, insights earned during their nightly coyote concerts on the porch, those starry hours when he knows she is searching the caverns of her heart, the cold dank places only pain can help you find. He understands they're both orphans now.

"The world's turned upside down," Winters says, oblivious to the revelations swirling the room. "The weather's all back-asswards. People have lost their minds. There are signs daily in the firmament. The night I moved here I saw a meteor burn like a rocket across the sky. The thing was so close I could hear it roar, white fire sparking and crackling all around. I thought it was my very own death star, coming to blast me to tomorrow."

With his eyes turned dark, Din looks straight at Ferrell.

"You know," he says, "my wife left me without so much as a good-bye and fuck you. I didn't even know where she was until I got the postcard from Ubud."

Rilla glances at Ferrell and he knows it's time to leave, that she's done with this sad pale man with the broken heart. Ferrell nods slightly, the signal they used to use when it was time to leave some faculty social at the school, or some fundraiser for the crisis center, when one of them had had enough of wasting their precious lives. They stand at the same time.

"You guys leaving so soon?"

Rilla squints at her watch as if the numbers are hard to decipher. "It's one something in the A.M.," she says. "If we don't depart, we'll turn into pumpkins."

Winters stands with an empty bottle in his hand. "The grape juice is almost gone," he says. "We sure made a dent in my stash."

"You can always get more vino," Rilla says. "Take a trip back home, load up the trunk."

"I'm never setting foot in California again," Winters says. "I'm here and this is where I intend to stay. Hell, when I die I'll already be under the ground."

Rilla slips her palm into Ferrell's, squeezes hard. He feels her tremble beside him. She reaches for the ladder and starts to climb.

When they reach topside, Ferrell is surprised it has rained long and hard, the sand drenched, the air delicate perfume. Above them the night stars glint and shine, while to the south lightning tears up the horizon in long spidery streaks.

Huddled together, shoulders touching, the three of them seem to Ferrell to be members of a tribe long past, watching the showy indignation of their god.

"Damn," Winters says. "That looks nasty."

"Or beautiful," Rilla says, rocking on her heels.

"You know," Winters says, "humans make great conductors, our inner fluids sloshing around. We each throw step leaders toward heaven like personal glowing calling cards. Like our auras spin into a single rope for God to yank us home."

Ferrell knows this to be true. He remembers old Leonard Schwartz, the science teacher at Dover High, explaining over many cafeteria lunches the intricacies of lightning strikes.

"Lightning," Winters says in almost a whisper, "has been known to travel twenty miles or more, seeking people whole towns away. A man once got killed off his mountain bike in the Haight with nothing but blue above him."

"Can that happen?" Rilla says, stepping closer to Ferrell.

"Anything's possible. You can get blown out of your shoes holding the handle of your fridge, or zapped off the crapper while reading the news."

"On the commode?" Rilla says.

"I had a dozen calls for lightning strikes during my time. Oddest thing you've ever seen. Saw a woman once with her clothes shredded off her. The lightning left these tiny forked veins across her chest, like a perfect miniature bolt emblazoned on her skin." Din spreads his arms before them. "Lightning can fix you dead without even touching you, can stop your heart with just its electromagnetic field. They find hikers in the mountains all the time, young and healthy and dead, not a mark on them."

"You make it sound like lightning *tries* to get us," Rilla says.

"Oh, hell, if it wants you bad enough, lightning will hunt you down. There was a forest ranger in northern California struck seven times. The human lightning rod, they called him, a chosen man."

Ferrell wavers where he stands. He's three sheets and then some, the wine pumping through him like new blood. From somewhere atop the ridge a coyote yips at the night, and he closes his eyes to let the sound be all there is—no billion stars to distract him, no ex-wife he still loves, no lonely underground dweller wishing to die. The cry rises on the air, a fevered improvisation of short barks and longer yowls. When the coyote finishes what it needs to say, Ferrell opens his eyes to find Winters watching him.

"They are called God's dog, you know?" Winters says. "The Navajo named them that."

"I bet they did," Rilla says, her hand upon Ferrell's arm.

Winters rubs his palms over his face. "Little buggers drive me to the edge. All that full moon foolishness. I swear some nights they are taunting me, pointy-nosed bastards, mocking my choice to live among them."

"Some believe coyotes created the world," Ferrell says.

"Well, I'm glad I live beneath the soil where I can't hear the ridicule, night after freakin' night."

"Maybe they are cheering you on," Rilla says. "Maybe they are saying, *Din Winters, you the man.*"

In what little light surrounds them Winters looks stumped, his brain unable to make the turn Rilla has put before him. "I saw you up on the ridge," he says. "I saw you butt naked with my field glasses."

"How was I?"

"About half an inch tall," Winters says. He looks in the direction of the fiery storm, his shoulders slumped, defeated in a battle he did not want or choose.

"I'm off to bed," he says at last. He hugs Rilla longer than he should, his face unreadable in the thin starlight, then shakes Ferrell's hand, the man's palm a cold soft thing, part of a creature who dwells beyond the sun.

"You come back soon," Winters says.

"You bet," Ferrell says, knowing he won't.

"For sure," Rilla says, but Ferrell hears she feels the same. The man is a certified doomsayer, and black clouds hover above him, bathe him in shadow wherever he goes.

Ferrell stands in the coarse sand, his toes within his boots like roots spreading down. Above him the stars drift loose in the sky, some breaking free to fall in smoky streaks. Rilla tugs him into motion, and he follows her on the long trek toward home.

Ferrell stumbles through a night made otherworldly after his time below. He feels released from something, set free—a submariner, perhaps, surfaced after months beneath the black sea. The land tilts and rolls, wobbles like a moving deck, the tumbleweeds rising on the swells. Ferrell watches the brilliant flashes career along the rim of the earth. He knows every fifty yards or so a new step leader is born, the strike jagging in a different direction, angling ever toward that negative charge. At times the bolts hammer the desert plain, but most scatter lengthwise across the low sky, the clouds flaring for miles in each direction. Now and again he hears the faint roll of thunder, a rumble so deep it seems to tremble the unstable ground.

Ferrell and Rilla hike through aromatic sage, guided like sailors by the bright map of the stars. Rilla gets out ahead of him, inspired as she is, and Ferrell works up a head of steam to keep from losing her. Soon he comes across a batch of compact shadows on the ground and fears the worst, something on the order of vengeful rattlers waiting in the dark, Rilla lying somewhere with venom loosed within her.

When Ferrell reaches down, he expects the hot jab of twin fangs. He finds instead the warm softness of Rilla's abandoned clothes—the heavy canvas walking shorts and cotton underwear, her sweaty damp socks. He wonders where her boots have gone. A few feet ahead he spots the pale dimness of the *Ohio Is for Lovers?* T-shirt, the white coiled bra, and then Rilla lies before him in the sand, her dark outline as if his own shadow has been thrown to the ground.

Ferrell becomes a giant in the desert night. He knows the wine and the potent loneliness of Winters, radiating off the man as a beacon of loss—plus the horizon ablaze like fate approaching—have them both randy as wild cats, their desire risen to the surface of their skin. He pulls free of his clothes, slips from his boots. He stands in the sleek indigo breeze, caressed as if by a loving hand, his nerves tingling like they've been exposed to the air.

"Hurry, Ferrell," Rilla says. "Get down here before I cry."

Ferrell drops to his knees in the wet sand. He thinks, oddly, of the mistress of the horse god, expects to touch that giant skull when he seeks her with his mouth, but it's only Rilla's tender cheek against his lips, her hands upon his shoulders.

Ferrell feels his body awash in negative ions, feels the barometer of his heart plummet off the scale. He slips inside her as cold rain pelts his back. He imagines their own neon step leaders reaching from their crowns, rising ever skyward. His scalp begins to tingle, the few hairs he has left standing on end.

"You don't just stop, Ferrell, till I say you can, you hear? You don't just leave me alone in all this fucking space."

Ferrell tilts his face into the falling rain. He prays he'll last as long as she needs, beyond her every desire.

Swan's Song

When Rilla heads to Jackpot to bail out her son, freedom's thrill doesn't hit Ferrell like it should. After nearly three seasons of playing man and wife, Ferrell isn't sure about returning to the pleasures of solitude and retreat. Before the dust of her car can settle, he has bad visions in his head: his queen-size futon too big, the dinner table half bare, a solo coffee cup on the porch in the quiet wake-up hours. He can't imagine having no one to hold when the coyotes go crazed.

As for Jackpot, Ferrell has seen billboards but never been. He pictures some two-bit casino town seventy miles due south, across the Nevada line. For the time being Levon is dealing blackjack at a place called Cactus Pete's. Ferrell wonders how many lovers the boy has left in his wake. He wonders what kind of mess Rilla will find when she arrives.

Ferrell rises from the rocker to stand at the porch rail. In the glaring noon his hundred acres look forsaken, a physical depiction, he imagines, of his wasteland heart—sheep sorrel and ghost fern, bunchgrass and Russian thistle, silver sage. Abruptly he feels the need to move, to orbit someone's personal space. Harrison Cole would be the obvious possibility, but Levon's visit last summer put the skids on neighborly relations. The twosome didn't last, it seems, but when Melody didn't return after things were said and done, now several months and counting, Ferrell felt bad. He realizes with a start he hasn't spoken to Cole since he pointed the shotgun his way.

Ferrell casts a long gaze eastward, toward his neighbor's land. Every so often Ferrell sees Cole amongst his now-dead trees, a tragic figure in all those trunk husks, the twisted branches reaching like withered hands—a hell of a painting, Ferrell thinks, if he were inclined to paint. He misses that block of green in the midst of endless scrub.

"Well, shit," Ferrell says and heads off down the road.

Cole doesn't answer the door, but his black Dodge diesel stands sun-dazzled in the drive, so Ferrell heads into the trees. It's creepy in there, surrounded by all that tree death, and Ferrell is reminded of the black-and-white vampires of Sunday matinees. Beyond the treetops a gorgeous redtail floats the neon sky, its fanned silhouette corkscrewing down.

Ferrell searches each row as he wanders around, but there are acres of trees and just one of him, and he soon gives up. He turns for Cole's house, then realizes he has no idea which direction that could be. Ferrell checks the sun and figures his east-west line. He's about to set off when something clamps onto his shoulder. He spins to find Cole standing there, sunken-eyed and pale, a self-made ghoul to fit his Gothic woods.

"Jesus, Cole," Ferrell says, "you've taken this abandonment thing way too far."

"Why are you in my trees?"

"I'm looking for the dumb-ass ranger who did them in."

Cole eyes him up and back. The man's an emotional wreck of spectacular proportions, and Ferrell isn't cheered. Visiting his neighbor wasn't the best idea to take his mind off Rilla, and he works up an excuse to get himself home.

"It's easier without her, you know," Cole says in his best zombie improv. "She was tough to keep on an even keel. She was hard work."

"Amen to that," Ferrell says, though he wouldn't know one way or another.

"So why am I so miserable?"

"Can't live with 'em . . ." Ferrell says and shrugs. He wonders if he can get free without more melodrama.

"Melody had this thing with her tongue," Cole says, "not a real sex thing, not like you're thinking." His eyes glaze and go blank. "She'd put her tongue in my ear and work it around like there was no tomorrow. I never liked it, but now I miss it."

Ferrell nods, at a loss for what else to say. He has never been good at male bonding rituals. He wonders if he is supposed to offer Cole something about Rilla's vigor between the sheets.

"You ever hear from my wife?" Cole says.

"I think she split with the boy a while back."

Cole looks down his planted rows. "I sacrificed my trees in her name," he says. "I shouldn't have done that. Now everything's dead."

"You can grow new ones."

"It takes them awhile."

"Are you going somewhere?"

Cole turns his sad eyes onto him until the fault lines shift in Ferrell's heart. "Rilla stopped by this morning," Cole says. "She said she was going for awhile, that we should look after each other. She said she was sorry her son took my wife."

"She means that, Cole. Her Levon leaves a path of destruction wherever he goes. The boy's a calamity magnet, always been. He's neck-deep in some trouble right as we speak."

"What'd I do to him?"

"It wasn't about you."

"It is now," Cole says and walks west, toward where his house must be. Ferrell lets him get a good lead, then follows behind.

The next morning Ferrell rises before the sun. He rocks on the porch as light comes, watching the desert dark shape itself into tangible things—the dense clumps of sagebrush, the spindly halos of tumbleweed. On the wind rides something blooming. He has forever loved first light, when the coming day could be any day from his adolescence—some morning, perhaps, long before he screwed up his life in ten thousand imaginative ways.

The horizon brightens, and Ferrell finds himself staring down the road at Cole's defunct tree farm. Where the trees stop, the chaparral takes over, oddly green from the meager spring rains. As Ferrell sips his coffee, a radiance commences inside his head, right behind his eyes. He knows what to do before the cup is empty.

In the barn, Ferrell hoists his shovel and rake and heads into the scrub. He moves with a purpose he hasn't felt in a good while. In the crisp morning air, in the touch of the worn handle shafts in his palms, Ferrell feels his younger self return, a special guest star from days gone past. He welcomes the vigor thrumming his veins.

At the first dead tree Ferrell stops to gather his wits. He is standing at the far side of Cole's property, along the boundary to his own land. He chooses the conifer in the near corner of the twenty-acre square, then sites down the trees marching off in Cole's straight rows. He glances toward his own house, where porch and rocker await, then drops the rake with the tines pointed down, as his grandfather had taught him. He hefts the shovel, reassured with its familiar weight. He studies the roots spreading from the base of the trunk, then sets the shovel point and pushes his bootheel down.

Past noon the sky clouds, and Ferrell is thankful for that little mercy. He has dug out seven trees and dragged them to the edge of the property. In the way he's lined up the trunks, he sees victims of some terrorist act, though it was just Cole shutting off his drip lines that did in the trees.

Ferrell stops to take a good lean on his shovel. He can feel the work between his shoulder blades, a dull ache that'll be full-blown hurt tomorrow. His low spine is talking too, at the place where he flattened some disks bucking hay when he was young. His soaked shirt clings like a second skin. All in all, he feels reborn.

"What the fuck?" Cole says from behind him.

Ferrell wrestles a smile onto his face. "You must have

been a ninja in a former life," he says and turns around. "I can't hear you coming for the life of me, and you such a big man to boot."

"What the fuck?"

"Now, Cole, don't get yourself in a state. What we have here is some constructive thinking at work. We've got to give God a hand."

"God?"

"We can plant ourselves some seedlings and restart this miniature forest of yours. It'll be like Arbor Day times ten. God's got to love the little trees, don't you think?"

Cole stands squinting, and Ferrell can tell the circuits have jammed. He didn't mean to bring God into the discussion, but he needed help fast. Cole closes his eyes, sways slightly on his heels. Ferrell worries a systemwide failure is on the way. At last Cole opens his eyes and stares right through him.

"You'll help me, Swan?"

Ferrell lifts the shovel like it's some special prize. He sinks the point into the ground. Cole's question sounds too all-encompassing, but Ferrell will take what he can get.

"Damn straight," he says.

He steps forward and reaches out his hand. Cole studies the hand a moment, then slides his rough palm into Ferrell's.

Sometimes when sleep won't come, Ferrell aims his old pickup down the road, his tunneled high beams the only light for forever and beyond. Above the curve of his windshield the stars cram the sky, so many it scares him if he looks too long. As he drives he carries his one secret truth deep in the marrow of his bones: his failure at life has been fantastic and complete. Sure, he's given himself some good moments in the classroom, times when he was speaking pure poetry and knew it, but in all areas that truly matter—sonhood, husbandom, fathering—it's been multiple strikeouts for his team, big wild swings and nothing but air.

He tunes his mind to the only station he gets out here, an oldies station from Boise. In the depthless dark, with the world thrown only as far as his headlights, the songs put him behind the wheel in 1965. He likes the lonesome numbers best—an Otis Redding, say, or some Diana and the Supremes—melodies that uncover the places where he hides his youth. He cranks his window down, and in the blowing dark feels the old notes to the tips of his toes, his nerve pathways primed for what cannot be again.

When the songs cut too deep, Ferrell twists the dial to nothing but static. He once saw a show about astronomers hearing big bang tracings in a radio's empty crackle and snap. He is not sure if he's listening to echoes of his cosmic past, or to the whispers of God himself, but he pushes the truck hard just the same, rockets himself into the black velvet night.

Ferrell wakes the next morning still in his clothes. When he lifts his head he senses with absolute clarity every ligament and tendon he owns, each muscle sheath and its exact location. There's an anatomical chart alive under his skin, and he pictures the workings of his musculature in great detail. He stands and his back flares into heat, then his shoulders sing their individual praises. Despite this world of hurt, Ferrell is one happy man.

In the kitchen he spends a good long while staring at his boots. He lifts his coffee mug, and the intricate bandings in his hand burn fiercely, his fingers and palm swollen from the shovel handle. The brutal ache is a direct line into his past, and Ferrell feels haunted once more by his teenage years, when summers were hundred-acre fields to bale and load. He recalls sweating through the endless hours, witness to the sun rising from one horizon, falling into another. At the time his grandfather would have been in his sixties. Brimful of piss and vinegar, the man whose name Ferrell bears worked like it was the last day on earth, and he wanted things right when the angel trumpets came blaring down.

It was these hours of toil that had chased Ferrell from honest work, had sent him off to Kent for his two history degrees, then onward to the classrooms of the young and distracted. Even years later, standing between the desk rows of his homeroom class, he would imagine the old man in the buggy fields, the white-hot sun as if to burn out his mind, and Ferrell would be thankful it wasn't him. Sometimes, while the kids were watching a film on one war or another, Ferrell would put his feet on his desk in the flickering dark, just because he damn well could.

But now, retired to his own land, Ferrell hears the curious call of hard labor. Yesterday, he had actually enjoyed the urgent thomp-whomp of his heart, had liked sucking breath into his lungs. When the salt sting burned his eyes, he wiped them with the muddy hem of his shirt and kept right on working.

At last Ferrell pushes himself from the chair. For the first time in a long time he has found something worth doing.

Here he is, a man who lived his life in the glorious cathedral of his head, a man who wore ironed slacks and shirts, and paced a path within four classroom walls, and now, at least for the fragile moment, he is craving the life his grandfather had. In the days to come he wants his bright blood to surge through the complicated run of his veins, his mind only on the task at hand.

On the porch, the morning cool could be imported straight from heaven. Ferrell soaks the chill into his bones, stores it there for the noon heat to follow. He drains his coffee, the motivation slipping straight into his brain, then creaks down the steps, his soreness epic in its implications. He pulls air deep into his chest and holds it, savoring what there is.

By week's end, Ferrell has slipped into the routines of a working man. During the day he and Cole labor like men possessed. They head down the row without much said, digging out the trunks one shovelful at a time. When they yank loose a tree, the dust drifts from the wiry roots like smoke. Ferrell tries not to race, but feels the keen edge of competition nevertheless, Cole's huffs and puffs spurring Ferrell into his own bursts of effort. At times they both stop as if a buzzer has sounded, and Cole stands there wild-eyed and panting, the sweat raining down his sorrowful face. Ferrell strives for words but nothing comes, and he just holds Cole's gaze. We're okay, he tells him with his eyes. There isn't anything beyond this.

Toward Saturday dusk, he and Cole reach the end of the first three rows, seventy trees in all. Ferrell drags over one last conifer and sits on the rough trunk. He has come to love this moment of the day, when he is drained beyond himself, depleted to some elemental core, and all he can do is sit and watch the light show above the Owyhees.

Cole staggers over and sits in the dirt. Ferrell waits for the world to swing them around into the dark shelter of space.

"I feel like there's nothing left inside," Cole says, as if robbing Ferrell of his thoughts. "It's like all that was inside me is burned up and gone."

Ferrell only nods. He doesn't want to spoil the purity of what's been said.

Cole turns from the fiery sky to stare in the direction of the trees. "Took me two years to plant all these. I planted every one like it was a child of mine."

"You ever have kids?"

"I never was married till Melody came along, and she didn't want any. Before her, I lived out alone in the national parks. I've done time in almost every one you could name."

From above comes a high shrill shriek, and Ferrell looks to see a redtail winging for home, its feathers black against the violet air. The hawk passes overhead and aims straight into the burning horizon, a sneak peak at the apocalypse.

"I couldn't help but note you had a few years on the girl," Ferrell says, when the hawk moves beyond the reach of his eyes.

"Twenty years my junior."

"How'd you get that started?"

"She used to come camping with her family every year at Yellowstone. I watched her grow several years straight, then she hit eighteen and came alone that summer. She kept showing up on my rounds through the park, and we'd cross paths a dozen times a day.

"Before I knew it, we was doing things around those geysers that wouldn't have pleased her daddy. I thought I'd discovered the Holy Grail, the lost city of Atlantis, all the rest. I thought love was something we just invented."

There comes a silent stretch that Ferrell knows isn't good. He thinks he hears muffled gasps escape into the air. When Cole stands in the faint light, his shoulders hunch as he grapples with the demons of gloom.

"Shit," Cole says. "I done sweated her out of me today, and now she's taken back all the space in my head."

Ferrell bites his lip, understanding he's raised Melody's specter. He knows women aren't ever gone once you let them inside your skull. Here he made Cole open the door, and in came his wife with her suitcases and trunks and overnight bags. Cole has been condemned to a bad sleep.

As if he wished it on himself, Ferrell wakes when the night is not half done. He does the toss and turn for most of an hour, then gives up and takes a beer onto his porch. No sooner does he get the rocker going when the coyotes start their moonlight rituals. First comes a lone yapping from the dry wash, then an extended mournful howl like something from a fever dream. The devil cries never fail to crawl beneath his skin—as if, it seems, he's listening to some personal invitation from the guardians of Sheol.

During sleepless nights, Ferrell has shaped his own beliefs about the coyote. He has come to believe the beasts aren't even around in sunlit hours, that in the first stirrings of dawn they cross a clandestine border, gone entirely from the physical world. At sunset they return with news of what they've seen.

What he hears now, he's convinced, is their nightly update from the cramped caverns of Hades. It's a vital truth delivered in a language he cannot understand, a coded message just out of reach. If he listens hard enough, he will one day translate these strange announcements. When that happens he promises to keep the secrets to himself of what lies on the other side.

For the next month, he and Cole stay the course of work and bone-weary sleep. If this were a pilgrimage, Ferrell thinks, they'd be far along the route, their hearts closed against the world. Over the weeks, their skin turns the color of saddle leather, and Ferrell's muscles tighten and grow thick. In the hours of labor he melts off the softness in his body and his head, distills himself to an essence he'd almost forgotten was there.

At siesta one late March day Ferrell decides that Cole, not a man given to easy gabbing, is more silent than usual. On his porch, Cole sits in a rocker and doesn't rock, just stares into the bright like he's seeing visions there—his wife splayed beneath Levon's sweaty self, or some such troubling image. Though Ferrell has never been keen on prattle, Cole's stilled tongue unnerves him.

"Are you napping in your head?" Ferrell asks. "Sleeping with both eyes open wide?"

Cole gets the rocker moving, which is better than no response at all. Ferrell will take what he can get.

"I woke up this morning," Cole says.

"A good way to start the day," Ferrell says, trying to take
the edge off what is coming. Cole gives him a look that could
fell a tree.

"I just made my eggs and buttered my toast and spent
some time figuring what kind of juice I wanted, orange or
apple. It wasn't until I got a look at all those killed conifers that I remembered there was a Mrs. Melody Cole somewhere, trucking my last name around."

Ferrell waits for a few beats, then breaks into a round of
handclapping. He reaches over and slaps Cole on the knee.

"What the hell?"

"You threw the woman out of your mind. Next you'll
start housecleaning up there. You'll dust off those memories
of who you were before you two met."

"I'm not sure I remember who I was. I'm not sure I could
ever be him again."

"Oh, hell, you won't be. You'll be new and improved,
stronger in all the hurt places."

Ferrell sips his diet soda but wishes for something more
potent. He's talking total hooey here, acting like words can
change perspective when he knows they can't. Whatever's
in Cole's head will stay put till time runs down, and Ferrell
could quote Freud and Kant, Buddha, Gandhi, and the
Prophet Muhammad, and it wouldn't mean a thing. Hell,
Jesus himself could whisper sweet nothings in Cole's ear
and the man would probably shrug. Your thoughts stay put,

Ferrell knows, no matter what, and he's only talking to pass the noontime hour.

"My problem," Cole says, slipping deeper into the tar pit of introspection, "is how guilty I felt for not remembering her. If I can forget her so easily, does that mean I didn't really love her? I could have sworn I felt happy this morning eating my little breakfast there all alone."

Ferrell stands and leans on the rail, his favorite pose for thinking things through. If he smoked, this would be when he lit one up, blew dramatic smoke rings into the hot, still air. Instead he goes inside and gets two beers from Cole's fridge. He stares at the boom box above the sink and grabs that too, then heads back to the porch and hands a bottle to Cole.

"What's all this?" Cole says.

"We need to slow down that mind of yours before you hurt something."

Ferrell sets the boom box on the porch rail and adjusts the knob, fine-tuning the oldies station. He keeps the sound low until he has something clear, then cranks her up and out pours "Dock of the Bay."

"What's the year, Cole?"

"2001?"

"No, buddy boy, it's 1968 and you're where?"

"Yosemite, in '68."

"That's the ticket," Ferrell says.

With his feet on the rail he draws hard on the bottle, the beer so icy his teeth throb. He waits for some Jimi to come next, or maybe another hero from the battalions of the rock-and-roll dead. He's going to drink more than he should this afternoon, and he'll regret it in the morning, but for now things are just fine, and these days that is all he can ask.

In the night, under the damp sheet, Ferrell's own touch opens the floodgates of despair and he stops. He lies there tingling and raw-feeling in the barren space of his futon, lost in the electric need shooting through him. He recalls how pleased Rilla used to be to find him waiting in bed for the starting gun, night after festive night. She and Ferrell could be high schoolers, she would say, desperate enough to steam the windows. He wonders about the wisdom of missing his ex-wife after all that's come to pass, wonders why his heart won't leave the rest of him the hell alone.

When sleep at last comes, Ferrell dreams of the sound of loneliness, of emptiness wrought into the wonders of pitch and timbre. His mind fills with a howl sustained on the night, a cry haunted with the ghosts of pain and loss, of grief and unmitigated woe. It's melancholy made manifest, all the suffering in the world piped directly into his head. In his dream, the wail ignites all the hurt Ferrell has ever felt, proclaims his sorrow to anyone who will listen.

When the sound threatens to consume him, to reach a flashpoint of his incendiary emotions, Ferrell opens his eyes. He lies in the lingering mists of sleep and dream, listening through the screen to a coyote in the scrub. The beast must be near the front door, standing close to where Ferrell likes to sit—the closest he's heard one in months. Without the muting of distance, the coyote is loud enough to consecrate the entire night, the whole world, all that ever was and ever would be. Ferrell shuts his eyes tight, knowing the song is meant just for him.

With Easter approaching, Ferrell and Cole plan to miss the observances, too tired to bother with much else but food and sleep. For weeks Ferrell has had those final rows in his sights, and he has pushed Cole to keep the daily routine of shovels and sun. At the border of their properties stands an enormous wall of piled trees, which Cole plans to chainsaw for the winter cold. Where the trees had been, the open acres sit ready to plant, and Ferrell hungers to wrench that last dead trunk from the ground and dance upon the spot.

On Easter the day clouds at noon, then cools as rain pocks the dust with fat silver drops. In the chill Ferrell works harder than before. He feels as if his heart will never throttle down, as if he's driven beyond what he can physically do. He wonders if desire alone is enough to sustain.

When twilight moves in, the men sit in Ferrell's yard for the nonfestivities. The rain has scrubbed the sky, and now the sage blows strong off the land, filling his lungs with something close to hope. At their feet he has built a fire to ward off the sharp nip the rains have brought. Despite the day's hard efforts, Ferrell still has something left in the tank, and he can tell Cole does too, his feet tapping out some Morse code of his own making, a private message sent into the dark cool.

"It's not enough tonight," Cole says after an hour of saying nothing at all.

"I know."

"We're just two old men digging their asses off for no reason under the sun, other than to forget their women."

"That's one way to look at it."

"What's another?"

"We're planting some trees."

"I'm feeling it tonight, Ferrell." Cole drains his beer and tosses the bottle into the darkness. It hits something and clinks softly in its breaking. Cole turns to him and shrugs.

Ferrell drinks from his own bottle, but the beer goes metallic on his tongue. He's remembering Rilla and the extended sadness of their last years together, all those days of waking in their separate lives—how a stretch would pass of sharing meals, paying bills, wrestling on occasion beneath the covers, then over television one night she'd review his amazing shortfalls as a husband, how he didn't know any more about being a companion than a fence post did.

"You only know the past, Swan," she would say, the words scripted over time until he could recite them, "but it's jack-diddley about the present, and lord knows what you think of the future."

"We share the present," Ferrell would say, his own line in the play it was their fate to perform without audience or acclaim. "We talk. We make love."

"We chit-chat, Ferrell. We fuck. There isn't much beyond that."

Ferrell would sit in the television's blue glow until deep in the night, listening to Rilla lay waste to all that was his life, to every way he conducted himself through the day—a seek-and-destroy mission that left little to rebuild. And yet rebuild he would, rising from the ashes to put on his clothes and drive to school, where he would stand in tatters before the kids and pretend one *does* truly learn from the past, pretend one studies what has come before in order to improve what will happen tomorrow. He didn't want them to know they were all doomed.

Ferrell walks to his truck for the whiskey bottle he keeps under the seat, then squats at the fire. Near the edge of the flames, some of the branches he snapped into pieces aren't burning. He lifts the longest branch he can find and pours whiskey on the broken end. He pokes the tip into the coals and sparks bounce and swirl upward. He raises the flaming tip above his head, the guiding light of caveman days. When he waves his arm, tiny embers leap forth, showering Cole's feet.

"What are you doing?" Cole says, but Ferrell can hear more curiosity in his voice than anything else.

"Getting the Lord's attention," Ferrell says. "Letting him know we need some help down here."

Ferrell tosses the branch into the fire and sits down. He lifts the whiskey high in the air, offers a toast to the white chaos of the stars.

When Ferrell wakes sometime in the night, stiff from having fallen asleep in his chair, he believes the world has gone to flame. In the moonless dark burns a great conflagration, a shifting mass of orange and red and black—the sun fallen at last, he thinks, the end of all that has come before. With great abandon the flames reach far into the sky, reckless and wild, arduous in their burning. It's a color plate,

Ferrell decides, from a leather-bound Dante, or perhaps some textbook depiction of the Druids in action, maybe a routine night of Viking pillaging. In due time Ferrell understands Cole's colossal brush pile is on fire. Cole is nowhere around, his chair empty by their little fire, now just spent coals.

Ferrell leans back in his chair. He tries to reclaim his thoughts from the whiskey sloshing in his head. Even at a distance he can hear the terrible whoosh and draw of the flames, the scaled-down explosions as wood bursts into heat. Above the fire, heat has distorted the air, the haze-light shimmering in garish colors, a surreal dawn. As Ferrell watches, a small tongue of flame separates from the rest and hovers low, then moves into the remaining trees, flickering among the dark branches. With striking urgency, one of the trees erupts into flame, then another tree goes to fire.

Against this bright raging Ferrell spots Harrison Cole—phantom of the unholy night, caretaker of an inferno of his own design. The man sprints down the rows, pausing only to light each tree in turn. Ferrell debates if he should play a role in the climactic scene Cole is acting out. He considers holding Cole in check, preventing him from burning up the reach of their land, but decides the most the fool will burn down is his own house and barn. If he does, it'll give him something better to worry about.

The rogue flame separates from the trees, and Ferrell makes out Cole running toward him, his torch held high. He stumbles to where Ferrell sits, then stands there sucking wind, speechless and crazy-eyed, as if he has moved beyond language and can't recall the ordinariness of words. His face is wet and glistening, streaked with dirt and ash. In the weak flame light Cole looks demon or mystic, Ferrell can't decide.

"You can't miss this," Cole huffs, finding words at last.

He holds the torch out to Ferrell, and in the action he sees the pact they've just formed. Ferrell rises from his chair and grips the flaming branch in his right fist. Cole grins hard, his teeth white in the charcoal of his face.

"Let's do this thing," Ferrell says. He sprints to where the trees blaze like monumental candles in the night, a sign to those watching from above.

In the morning he is lying in the powdery dust of his driveway, soot-streaked and reeking of smoke. What was inside his skull has shriveled and now floats free in the whiskey bowl of his head. When he opens his eyes the harsh noon light slams home. He struggles to his feet, then manages his front porch, where he sits and contemplates what the night has wrought.

Across the road, thin white spires rise from the black trees. What remains of the brush pile crackles as it settles down. Near the barn Cole lies spread-eagled in the weeds.

Ferrell tilts an ear to a distant engine hum. As if summoned, Rilla's car glimmers on the road like a mirage. She takes his long lane slow, her dust rising to curl with smoke from the smoldering trees. When she parks beside his truck, out steps the whole ragged crew—Rilla and Levon and Melody Cole herself, a regular family reunion of the new world order.

"Jesus, Ferrell," Rilla says. "You were supposed to just wait quietly for my return. Maybe weed the garden or something."

"He's just livin' large," Levon says, happy, it seems, not to be in jail.

Melody stands shy behind Levon, looking a little worse for wear from her ordeal, but otherwise intact. Ferrell can't get a good look at her, but she seems to have put on weight. She spots her husband in the shade of the barn.

"Is he dead?" she asks over Levon's shoulder.

"Not even close," Ferrell says.

"Levon," Rilla says to her son, "you help Melody get Cole home, then you come straight back. Do not mess around."

"No worries there," Levon says. "I do not intend to be around when that dude wakes up."

Rilla takes Ferrell under his arms, helps him to stand. She wets a fingertip and rubs his cheek. She smells hotel clean, fresh as flowers blooming, like morning time in the throes of spring. She looks like all that is right and true in the big bad world.

"Come inside, Pyro-Man," she says, winking with false exaggeration. "You come tell Mama what you've been up to."

With the women returned, Cole and Ferrell loosen their male bonds. Cole works alone around his place, and Melody keeps herself indoors, the curtains drawn like she's seen enough of the world. Mornings, Cole plants saplings ordered from tree farms back east. He kneels in the powder of his fresh-plowed rows, his daily progress barely visible to Ferrell's watchful eyes. By noon Cole is gone from the land as if he's never been. Ferrell knows he is mending Melody in the familiar rooms of their big Victorian. He pictures rough

palms blessing pale smooth skin, as if touch alone can say all
there is to say.

As for Levon, the boy hung around the place for a handful of hours, then sped into the dark after supper, borrowing Rilla's car without bothering to ask. He had Boise in his
crosshairs, the nearest place with enough people to lose himself among. Rilla doesn't think he'll return anytime soon.

Weeks unfurl and Ferrell's at a loss to know what to do.
He's gotten so used to the ways of the working man, of sweating beneath the morning sun, that he wakes each day fired up
with no place to go. He stands all twitchy at the window, sipping coffee like he needs even more edge, and stares at Cole
crouched before his saplings. In the clarity of morning light,
Cole is etched in bold clean lines. Ferrell swears he can read
the stitched *Yellowstone* on Cole's baseball cap, despite the distance that separates the two. He ponders giving himself his
own jobs to do—hand dig postholes in the sunbaked ground,
stretch some angry barbed wire—but nothing quite suits the
magnitude of his desire.

And then one wild dusk he's out in the yard while Rilla
does her Tai Chi routines. He watches her through dragon-
sweeps-its-tail, then looks to where the horizon flares like an
explosion without sound or speed. Amidst this fanning light
come his neighbors, walking side by side.

Cole and Melody stop at the edge of the yard. Ferrell
glances at Rilla with her underwater moves, then back to
the Coles. Melody is walking toward him with the greatest of care. She's big as his barn, and Ferrell flips through
the calendar in his head—she and Levon commingling in

the midnight desert, Levon's potent seed taking root in the dark fertile places inside her. It's no wonder she hid behind Levon when they first came back, why she's avoided Ferrell ever since.

Melody stops before Ferrell and waits. He goes a moment without words because he must. Behind her, Cole nods and heads toward Rilla, who watches them from across the yard.

"I'm soon to be a grandpa?" Ferrell asks.

"Why I'm here."

Melody steps closer to him, her enormous belly leading the way. She looks beyond mortal health, as fresh and vibrant a woman as any man could paint.

"You're beautiful," he says.

"I'm radiant," she says. "I feel like I'm competing with the sun."

"And winning."

"Kicking ass even."

On the porch, Rilla and Cole talk in hushed voices. Melody gives Ferrell a look that speaks a language he can't understand.

"Levon?" he says.

"He has some fool idea I'll run off with him again, have his boy in a motel somewhere, I suppose."

"Cole?"

"Harrison's converted his den into a nursery. He acts like this is the event of the ages."

Ferrell nods, hoping the gesture says whatever she wants to hear. In the dusk light pouring over them she seems otherworldly indeed, someone who knows more than he ever will.

She places her hands over the baby, rubs perhaps a shoulder or a knee. He knows it is gift or burden in there, depending on the moment and the direction of her thoughts, and he prays for all of them at once—for Rilla and Harrison, for Levon out there running from his soul, for Melody and her little one, and for himself as well, a makeshift grandfather in a makeshift family.

When Ferrell opens his eyes, he's surprised they have been closed. Cole stands before him, his baseball cap tilted up. The women sit in the rockers on the porch, talking in conspiratorial tones. Ferrell smiles and reaches out his hand. Cole slides his palm into Ferrell's, their callused hands still strong from the handles of shovel and rake. In Cole's face Ferrell spies every emotion, then he sees only fatherhood in all its impending fear.

"You all set for this?" Ferrell asks.

"Damn straight," Cole says, letting loose, at last, of Ferrell's hand. Rilla calls for them to come inside.

Ferrell turns to what is left of the sky. The sun has spun beneath the horizon, trying one last time to set the world on fire, and Ferrell understands he'll have a few things to tell this new young Levon, this child of fiery night skies and coyote howlings.

Cole waves at him. "You coming?"

Ferrell gives him a shrug.

That night Ferrell rises in degrees from the black depths of sleep. Most of his brain stays down deep, but a single rope runs to the surface, pulls a lone thought up like a bucket from a well. When he reaches the top he lies in the pitch-dark and listens for what has waked him. In the distance comes the bark of Cole's beagle, relentless and hoarse, urgent in its message. Ferrell rises naked from his bed, where Rilla sleeps the sleep of the blessed. He stumbles, then navigates to the front door.

When he steps into the yard, the blue-black night blazes with swirling galaxies and suns, a celestial storm raging not too far above his head. Ferrell stands stunned beneath the wild enthusiasm of the sky, as if the heavens have gone too vibrant for his eyes. Or maybe, he decides, he has stepped into some dimension other than his own, into a place where things seem the same, but are not. His skin prickles at the thought. Ferrell raises both arms, in defiance or embrace he knows not which. He reaches far into the heavenly zeal, takes handfuls of planets and stars into the sanctuary of his fists.

Something makes him look down, and he knows what is there though his eyes can't see. A dozen yards out a pack of coyotes stands mute in the dark. He can feel the heat of their eyes upon him, can almost hear the breath leave their lungs. If he listens hard enough he believes he can hear the steadiness of their hearts, those ruby-red miracles caged in the jailhouse of their ribs. Tonight they will not speak of what they've seen.

The Bones
of Hagerman

Late in the afternoon Ferrell and Rilla stretch and yawn, finished with another peaceful siesta. As Ferrell lifts his jeans from the hardwood floor, he thinks how greatly his retirement has improved since Rilla's return. It's been a tenuous truce, to be sure, but somehow each dusk they manage to count small blessings, drinks raised to the dropping sun. He knows his life could be a whole lot worse.

Clothed, he and Rilla step onto the porch. Miles from his cabin, lazy white smoke billows on the air, obscuring Ferrell's panorama. He can smell the routine scent of burning bunchgrass.

"What's on fire?" Rilla asks.

"Each April farmers and ranchers burn their ditch banks and fields. Gets rid of the weeds."

"Don't people have to breathe?"

Ferrell only shrugs. Over the course of her extended visit, Rilla's love affair with his adopted state has been rocky at best. While struck deeply by the rugged land and its host of wild things, she's found fault with what she calls Idaho's nineteenth-century ways.

"So what now, Ferrell? We've taken our morning stroll, eaten lunch, napped for hours. What's left for the day?"

As if God wants to answer personally, Ferrell hears something he can't make out: a faint rumble, a hollow thudding, small and almost lost on the air.

"What the hell?" Rilla says.

"I have no idea."

To the west, from out of the haze, Ferrell spots a gathering of smoke, hovering low. He realizes it's not fire, but the drift and rise of dust. He squints hard into the horizon, excitement like helium in his veins. Cole has always claimed mustangs roam the adjoining public lands, but the only proof Ferrell's seen has been the solitary skeleton on the ridge. *Ghosts*, he says when Cole mentions the herd. *Spirits of the purple sage.* The roiling dust grows closer, and the ground begins to tremble—as if, he imagines, doom itself bears quickly down.

"Speak, Ferrell," Rilla says, her voice more than a little concerned.

"Mustangs," he says. "Coming fast."

As if formed from the dust itself, the horses take shape: wide white eyes and flared nostrils, flying manes. Their forelegs blur as hooves reach and drive, and Ferrell pictures those big hearts clanging in their sweat-dark chests, that old Spanish blood churning hot. The mustangs gallop straight for the cabin, but veer right at his outer fence, changing direction with a single mind to run lengthwise past the porch. They're ruffians, Ferrell decides, not scraggly drifters like he expected. These brutes are bulky and stout, their necks and flanks scarred from hooves and teeth, tails and manes a tangled mess. It's not freedom he's watching but something other, as though these beasts rush toward their own deaths and can't wait to arrive. It isn't grace at all, but a scene from Revelations.

The last stragglers blister past, blown breaths audible above their pounding hooves. Ferrell takes a final glimpse at sinewy flanks and streaming tails, then can see only dust in the air, the whole thing ending the way it began.

"Good Christ," Rilla says, the air still reverberating though the mustangs have gone.

"More like the devil, I'd say."

Ferrell leans both hands on the porch rail, spent after witnessing his first horse stampede. Behind him Rilla sits in her rocker, too stunned, it seems, to offer further comment. He hears the helicopter before he spots it, the thing coming low and fast, blunt nose angled down. He understands why the herd was running.

"What's going on, Ferrell?"

"Bureau of Land Management."

"Tell me they're not shooting them." Rilla shakes her head. "I swear this place is in a time warp. Why don't they just kill everything and get it over with?"

Ferrell has to side with Rilla on this one. He himself has never quite recovered from last month's coyote massacre, the drone of the small white plane as it scanned the public lands, the sharp report of the rifle. When the plane had gone, he and Rilla hiked the desecrated ground, kneeling at each dead coyote they came upon, offering meager prayers. Up close, the animals were more beautiful than Ferrell could bear, and Rilla cursed openly the concept of shoot on sight. "Fuck the fucking ranchers," she shouted. "This is public land, and I'm part of the public too." Before bed that night she wrote three dozen protest letters, mailed them next morning to state and government officials, knowing she might as well have asked Ferrell to piss into a gusting wind.

Cole's Dodge diesel growls from the road, sun glaring off the polished black. The truck pulls fast into Ferrell's drive, as if Cole's been out chasing mustangs himself, and skids to a stop.

"Ghosts my ass," Cole yells, jumping from the cab. "Did you see them?"

"They were hard to miss."

Ferrell watches Melody ease from the high passenger seat. Before he can offer to help, Rilla is beside the truck. Ferrell knows Melody's due in five weeks and two days, with Rilla set to serve as midwife, but wishes, as always, he didn't know the rest.

Cole takes the porch steps three at a time. "Damn, that was something," he says and gives Ferrell a bear hug worthy of its name. "I bet there was sixty of those sons of bitches, maybe seventy."

"What was that helicopter?" Rilla asks, escorting Melody up the steps. Rilla guides Melody to a rocker and helps her sit.

"Once a year, BLM officers round up mustangs and cull the herd. It's part of their management policy."

Ferrell bites his tongue. He cringes whenever the term *management* is used with nature. In his time out west, he's seen the BLM *manage* public lands via blanket grazing permits to ranchers, seen cattle and sheep eat the chaparral down to nothing, leave behind trampled desert and muddied streambeds.

"What do they do with the ones they cull?" Rilla asks.

"There's an annual mustang auction, up near Boise. Most go for a couple hundred bucks."

"Let's buy a mustang, Ferrell," Rilla says. "Let's bring one home."

"But you haven't ridden in years."

"But I rode *for* years, Ferrell. It's not like you forget."

Ferrell gazes across the unexplored miles stretching from his porch. He sees himself tall in the saddle, riding the range like outlaws of old. It's never dawned on him to *buy* a horse, to roam at will the vistas he so dearly loves. From the cobwebby shelves of his mind comes Ferrell's long dead father, how the man watched every cowboy matinee ever shown, all those TV Westerns where heroes drew first and bad guys died without bleeding. His father, despite his fascination with horses and the West, never once climbed into a saddle.

"Well, Ferrell?" Rilla says. "Will you buy a girl a mustang?"

"Can you teach a boy to ride?"

As for bloodlines, whole generations of Ferrell's people were farmers, tough men who worked brutal hours, their bodies busted up. In high school, Ferrell's father chose the vocational route, figured standing at a drill press or lathe beat hustling butt on the farm, beat bucking tons of hay, or plowing from first light to good dark. But his father was a flesh-

and-blood contradiction, and despite his denial of the farmer's life, he dreamed daily of the West, of cowboys riding
beneath the high hot sun. At the time, it was beyond Ferrell
how the man could transform a cattle drive into something
other than days of heatstroke and an aching ass.

"At least a tractor won't buck you off," Ferrell said once
at dinner. "A John Deere won't kick you dead."

"You don't understand the way of the saddle."

"And you do?"

"I've learned much from the old boob tube."

"You're romanticizing those stupid shows," Ferrell said, a
recent concept from his ninth-grade literature class. "You've
seen too many Roy Rogers flicks."

His dad looked down at his plate. "You'll have dreams
someday," he said. "You'll understand what sustenance they
provide."

Five days after the mustang roundup, Ferrell drives the
hours to Boise with Rilla at his side. Having his ex in the
truck returns Ferrell to that torrid summer before she left for
college—cruising those gravel back roads, Rilla against him
on the bench seat, her fingers teasing the back of his neck.

Near the airport, Ferrell turns east across the sage flats
and follows the handmade signs to the auction. He parks
among the other trailers, and Rilla leads him to the formi-
dable holding pens, rough-hewn planks bolted onto eight-
by-twelve railroad ties.

"I guess they don't want them escaping," Ferrell says.

Rilla peers between the slats of the first enclosure. "Oh,
damn, Ferrell, that breaks my heart."

On the far side of the pen, dozens of horses cluster to-gether, looking remarkably less wild than the last time Ferrell saw them. Up close the mustangs seem even larger, capable of doing harm to his rickety self. Most of these horses look like the prisoners they are, defeat glazing their eyes, but a few still snort and prance, refusing to believe in the fence between them and the open land. All have big black numbers dan-gling from their necks, and Ferrell spots the corresponding numbers on posters nailed outside the pens. He also notes the letters B–L–M freeze-branded onto the neck of each horse.

The next hour's spent wandering pen to pen, Rilla nam-ing the strengths and weaknesses of the horses, pointing out stifle joints and gaskins, fetlocks and cannon bones, pasterns and the rest. As he studies the mustangs Ferrell recalls the fossil beds of Hagerman, those first nomadic horses now pre-historic bones behind dusty glass. At the last holding pen, five minutes before the silent auction closes, Rilla grabs Ferrell's arm.

"That's ours," she says.

"Which one?"

"The silver sorrel."

"The what?"

"That deep red mare, with the gray mane and tail. Between the buckskin and the paint."

Ferrell finds the one in question, the horse looking much like the other hundred or so he's just seen. "What's so special about her?"

"See how she moves, Ferrell? See how her withers line up with her back?"

"That's good?"

"That's great."

Half an hour later Ferrell is a new horse owner, his rented trailer backed against the loading chute, the horse driven up the ramp and in. He and Rilla shut the gate and climb into the cab.

"Your daddy'd be proud, Ferrell."

On the drive south, Rilla naps against his shoulder, the radio picking up the strong signal of Boise's oldies station. With Rilla dreaming the miles away, and the bygone songs shearing time and space, those strange days of Ferrell's childhood fill his head.

When his father took to wearing cowboy garb, Ferrell's mother started to worry, telling Ferrell to be ready for anything. At breakfast one Sunday, his father clomped from the coffee pot to the table, his cowboy boots scuffing the linoleum. He set his white Stetson beside his plate, ran fingers through his mussed hair. When Ferrell's mother put down her fork and stared, Ferrell ducked in his chair.

"What?" his father said.

"You know."

"They're just boots, Merle. I like the way they feel."

"Is it me?" his mother said, boldly upping the ante. "Is it your son here? Are you tired of us?"

Ferrell's father scooted scrambled eggs around his plate. "I could count myself the king of infinite space," he said, "were it not I have bad dreams. Or something to that effect."

"You're reciting poetry now?"

"It's from *Hamlet,* Mom," Ferrell said. "Dad's been borrowing my English book."

"Well, your father's not a king of anything."

"Nor an outlaw." Ferrell's father sipped his black coffee. "I'm just wearing western gear."

"People are talking, Maynard. The Hardings saw you at Beueler's last weekend, pushing your cart down the aisle all decked out. They asked me if they could come ride Trigger. Dobson was very amused."

"Let the bastard laugh. Old fart could use it."

"Ferrell, honey, tell him what your friends are saying."

Ferrell moved his own eggs around. In the past months it seemed the household alliances had shifted, that new loyalties had formed within his family, the hierarchy upside down. In this curious reordering, Ferrell and his mother were in command, his father the one to be brought into line. "J.R. wondered if Tonto was bunking in my room."

His father put his fork down. "Sticks and stones, son. But I'll tell you what. A man has to do and say what he damn well wants. Otherwise he's not a man."

"For godsakes, Maynard, is that from one of your stupid movies? Or are you babbling Shakespeare again?"

With studied deliberation, his father reached for the Stetson. He rose slowly and ambled across the kitchen to the back door. As he turned the knob Ferrell studied the familiar profile, in sharp relief against the window, and for those few heartbeats he saw a stranger passing through town. His father put the hat on his head and stepped into the brilliant Ohio sun.

At dawn, Ferrell follows Rilla to the barn. He cradles the new English saddle in his arms, the oiled leather smelling sweet and good, while Rilla carries the halter, bridle, and wool saddle pad. Ferrell's favorite procurement has been Rilla's tight riding britches, her rearside view stirring his blood in pleasing ways. Despite the years, she still has the keys to unlock his safe.

"Oh, quit staring, Ferrell," she says without looking his way.

Toward the farms in Melba, Ferrell sees the ditch bank fires going strong. In the rising light, smoke spirals here and there like signals from lonely tribes. To Ferrell's dismay, his Owyhees loom as faint ragged cutouts.

"Distant war," Rilla says. "Battles rage."

Inside the corral, Chroma stands watching. Rilla named the horse for her silver mane and tail—like chrome adornments, she said, against the red. Chroma pivots on her hindquarters, lopes to the far corner, faces them once more. Rilla climbs the fence and calmly crosses the sand. During her childhood, before abandoning his family for parts unknown, her father owned a string of horses, and Rilla grew up in the saddle, taking dressage lessons from the time she could hold reins. At eighteen, Rilla was junior show jumping champion of northeast Ohio, a beautiful sight out in the ring, such a slender slip of a girl atop her airborne stallion. From the stands, Ferrell had shouted as she cleared each jump, willing rider and horse to stay in one piece.

For the last three mornings, Rilla has worked her magic. Through diligent groundwork Chroma has learned who's in charge, Rilla becoming lead mare of their herd of two, the new sheriff in town. Before Ferrell's eyes a wild mustang has turned into an attentive pleasure horse, her ears not back but forward. Now Chroma responds to a raised finger, to Rilla turning her shoulders, dipping her head. She's melded minds with the mare, he thinks, his own little horse whisperer of the Owyhee rangelands. His whole life Ferrell has never exerted that much influence, never had any living thing pay him such mind.

After patient minutes to saddle Chroma, slip bridle and bit in place, Rilla is ready to climb aboard. Ferrell holds the reins, feeling small beside the strongly muscled chest. The sparkling bridle headband transforms the mustang into royalty come to visit their lowly ranch.

"She looks like a princess, Rilla."

"Oh, she is," Rilla says, leading the horse in tight circles. She sets the reins in place and nods his way. "Look out, Ferrell. She'll probably move the second my butt hits the saddle. I'll bet she just *loves* to go."

Rilla slips a boot in the silver stirrup, and drum rolls play inside Ferrell's head. Then she rises to the saddle, the horse takes off, and Rilla is an angel with her wings restored. Ferrell resists going romantic, getting too darn sentimental, but he can't fight it off: Rilla *is* goddamn beautiful up there, and violins have begun to play. She signals to the horse in some way Ferrell can't see, and Chroma gears up into a canter, practically floats around the corral. His ex circles him in a wide orbit, her flying ponytail a miniature version of Chroma's own. Rilla's face flushes with joy, the mare's flanks shine with sweat, and Ferrell stands in the center as a fiery sun.

In the months before his departure, Ferrell's father built himself a room in their concrete-block basement, opposite the tidy workbench. He started one night after supper, hammering away like he fought some dungeon monster, and the room was framed and drywalled when Ferrell left for school in the morning. By the time the bus dropped him off, his father had the door hung and locked, and his mother was nowhere in the house. Ferrell didn't know what else to do but knock. His father answered the door with paint specks in his hair.

"You seen Mom?"

His father gaped at him, as if he didn't quite know of whom Ferrell spoke. "She's at your grandmother's," he said at last.

"Did she say when she'd be back?"

"When hell grows cold and frosty."

His father turned back into the room, and Ferrell followed before the door could close. Inside he found white walls and pale blue shag, an army cot and portable television. Left of the door, their red ice chest sat beneath the folding cardtable with a hot plate and toaster. The room smelled of paint and new carpet and his father's potent sweat.

"Want a beer?" his father said.

"So you're living down here?"

"I wouldn't call it living, but this is my new abode."

"In the basement?"

"Safest place in the house. Come a twister I'd haul ass to my room, no doubt."

"How long do you intend to stay down here?"

"I haven't thought that through, son. I just got the idea at supper last night."

"But what will my friends say? What will Missy think when she comes over?"

"She'll think your old man can build a hell of a room. She'll say he's got a way with his hands." He switched the television channel and played with the silver antenna ears. "Besides," he said, fishing twin Rolling Rocks from the ice chest, "you two can bonk like bunnies in here when you're older."

Ferrell took the offered beer, but drank the cold dripping bottle in his room upstairs.

Toward dusk the big Dodge grumbles into the drive, spooking Chroma with its clanking diesel drama. From the porch Ferrell watches Rilla jump the fence to calm the trotting horse.

"That thing's louder than a damn bulldozer," Ferrell says as Cole climbs down.

"Uses gas like one too."

Cole helps his wife from her side of the cab. Melody stands shielding her eyes from the low sun, her belly swollen more than seems possible.

"Wow," Ferrell says. "You're enormous."

"Way to go, Ferrell," Rilla says, coming back through the gate. "Make a girl feel pretty."

Together the neighbors line the corral, elbows on the top rail. Chroma faces the foursome, her ears forward and listening, then she comes over and nuzzles Rilla's outstretched hand. In the ruby light, the horse looks as fine an equine as Ferrell has ever seen.

"You've done wonders, Rilla," Cole says. "I didn't think you could even get close to a mustang for weeks."

"Rilla's got a way with animals," Ferrell says. "She could train coyotes to fetch the morning paper."

"So why hasn't it worked with you?" Rilla says.

Bored, Chroma walks off and nibbles the remains of her evening hay. Rilla leads Melody to the rocking chairs on the porch, where they sit like frontier women from ages past.

"So how's it going?" Ferrell asks.

"Aside from not speaking, we're good."

"That bad?"

"You ever spend time with a pregnant woman?"

"Levon was three when Rilla and I got together the second time, after our practice marriages to other people. I missed those tender experiences—pregnancy and birth, breast-feeding and diapers, teething."

"Lucky you." Cole slips a Skoal can from his shirt pocket. He renews his chaw and spits a dark streak into the dust. "So you were stepdaddy to that boy for close to fifteen years?"

"I did all I could."

"Think it was enough?"

"Not by a long shot."

"But you still made a difference?"

"Does it look like I did?"

Cole studies Ferrell with his frank, searching gaze. "Surely it seems worth the effort? Looking back, I mean."

"I'll tell you what, buddy," Ferrell says, wondering how much truth to offer. "My father left my mother and me when I was in junior high. I never forgave him for that. At least I was there for Levon."

"You think he'll try to see the baby?"

"Levon's run from responsibility his whole life. I wouldn't expect him to change now."

"But didn't *any* of your influence stick?"

"Like water on a duck's ass."

"That's reassuring."

"Ah, don't listen to me, Cole. I find fault with a sunny day, you know that." Ferrell watches the sun dip from sight, a final winking out of the world. "I believe it's cocktail time," he says and leads his neighbor toward the house.

When the tormented man headed west, Ferrell found himself mostly relieved. His father ended up in Los Angeles, not the open range as far as Ferrell could tell. He found a job at Lockheed in tool and die, his days spent beside his trusty lathe. In rare letters home, his father would scribble about plans to visit Death Valley, or to spend his vacation at a dude ranch in Nevada, but the closest he ever got to the West of his dreams was Anaheim, where he strolled the phony streets of Knott's Berry Farm. That Christmas he sent Ferrell a picture of him wearing a sheriff's getup, silver star pinned over his betraying heart.

Another dawn and Ferrell's in the corral. It's been weeks of training sessions, hour upon hour of Rilla taking Chroma through her paces. The pair have learned much about each other, leaving Ferrell odd man out. "Can't we take a day off, Rilla?" he says, his voice whiny to his ears. "This seems too much like work."

"Today's *your* day to ride."

Ferrell feels a sizable jolt of fear. It's been one thing to watch the proceedings, but to climb his fragile bones atop a half-ton animal is indeed another. "Why didn't you tell me sooner?"

"And give you a chance to worry and fret?"

Ferrell wants to protest, but changes his mind. He rarely wins with Rilla, even when she's flat-out wrong. In too few minutes Rilla has the saddled horse before him, the spot he needs to sit a ways off the ground. He hears the goofy chortles of herons, and spots a dozen birds high above, headed haphazardly for the Snake. When Ferrell first heard their weird croaking cries he was surprised such humor issued forth from the long sleek flyers. Today the great blues seem to be laughing directly at him.

"Okay, Hoss," Rilla says, "foot in the stirrup, and swing on up."

Ferrell moves before his mind can halt what he's doing. His leg arcs over the horse's back, and the rest of him follows until he's on top, thighs hugged to the mighty curving ribs. He looks across the corral, amazed at the unexpected height, at the perspective from his horsetop view. Rilla stands far below, smiling like he has done a truly good thing.

"First time on a horse ever," he says.

"I bet you thought you'd run out of firsts." Rilla rubs Chroma along the sweeping neck, whispers into her ear.

"Hey, no secrets down there," Ferrell says.

"Hang on."

And then the complex musculature awakens beneath him, a tremendous flex and release he feels through the saddle. The horse clops across the corral and Ferrell turns giddy. In some dreamy physical memory he is on a merry-go-round at the fair, laughing with pure kid glee at the lift and drop of the brightly painted pony, the wind against his face, his father blurred with rushing movement.

Rilla leads Chroma across the dusty corral, each step signaled back to Ferrell in that fantastic interplay of muscle and bone. He remembers not to slouch, his reins held off the withers. He looks over the horse head guiding him through the world, the ears like radar searching. Before them is a western landscape of distance and sage, of mountains hulking in the smoky light. He narrows his eyes to take Rilla and her lead rope out of the picture, and he is for once and all time John Wayne, off to save the world.

When his father's heart quit at age sixty-two, Ferrell was home grading papers. He'd wanted to outwait the old man, to see if his father would care enough to visit him and Rilla, and he was still waiting when someone named Charlene called him. The woman said his father had collapsed halfway across Sepulveda Boulevard, his life finished before he hit the ground. Ferrell held the phone like he was supposed to do, heard the words being driven into his ear, but he was hollowed clean through.

"He's dead," the woman kept repeating, as if Ferrell didn't understand her simple message. "Your father is dead."

Ferrell hung up with her still insisting that he know.

The funeral was small, his father gone so long from his birthplace few remembered him. Except for his mother and his uncle Walt, Ferrell and Rilla were the only ones at the lonesome grave. Even the pastor, a man accustomed by trade to burying the unloved and neglected, looked disappointed. Ferrell knocked once on the lid of the coffin, his eyes scalded with tears, and marched swiftly to the car.

In the days after the funeral, Ferrell would be in class when the words would hit—*He's dead. Your father is dead*—and strike him dumb, a stoic schoolteacher wanting to cry out. Acutely, he felt his loss everywhere he went, as if his own threadbare heart had worn too thin. Some nights, sitting in his den, Ferrell would look up from his papers and stare, his old man keeping beyond the pool of lamplight.

Like most things in his life, that first ride was pure beginner's luck. In the weeks that follow, Ferrell earns his share of bruised butts and bruised egos, entering into a squally love-hate fling with Chroma that changes by the minute. For brief stirring moments he rides at one with the mind of the horse god, then he is on his ass with nothing but blue above. He falls off to his left and he falls off to his right, and during one difficult moment Chroma rears like high-ho Silver, sliding him down into that hazardous place of horseshoes and hard ground. But he survives the batterings, and the days finally amount to some measure of horse savvy and skill. Soon Ferrell knows enough to ride out alone and come back alive. His favorite place to go is the BLM, those hundred thousand acres unchanged since Jesse and Frank James rode through.

One blustery morning, Ferrell rides into this dazzling world, already tired and the day not half done. Last night his dreams ran too fitful to suit him, and now his mood's gone south on its own fast horse. He gallops through the sharp clean air, Chroma's hooves kicking up powdery dust.

Sagebrush reaches for his legs like withered hands, and the distant Owyhees call his name, cast as they are in such odd storm light. Despite himself Ferrell wishes his father could see him now. Here he is breathing air almost fifty years from the day his father left, and he's still waiting for the man to return, but now it would be from the grave and not just Los Angeles.

As Ferrell rides beneath the leaden sky, he feels the stinging hurt of not uttering a word to his father for dozens of years, how his headstrong ways kept him from picking up the phone, those squandered hours jet-streaming past: Ferrell rushing to make the morning bell, Ferrell trudging home with ungraded exams, Ferrell and Rilla in brief sweaty embrace, the ticking alarm clock a time bomb to his fleeting dreams. Entire decades a jumbled blur, his forties, his fifties, those years raising Rilla's wayward son an entire career. Home repair and shaggy lawns to mow, parent-teacher meetings without end—there was always something to steal his days, to suck away time. And while his father sat out in L.A., tan and wrinkled in the fabled California sun, Ferrell, stubborn in his pride, drove Rilla and Levon to vacations in every direction *but* west. If his father didn't want to see him, well then screw the selfish bastard. It was his father who left Ohio, not him, left Ferrell and his mother as if blood ties were cumbersome bonds to break.

With the day turning dark and ominous, Ferrell rides the ridge above the cabin. Over his head towering clouds slide heavily past, some gray-white, others black and swollen, one nasty storm invading his skies. With speeding heart, Ferrell reins short of the sheer drop-off. He feels purged in body, if not in spirit. Over the tremendous space below a redtail rides the strong currents, eye level to Ferrell and the horse on the ridge. The hawk glides for a spell, then draws hard against the air, its wingstrokes the most graceful thing Ferrell knows. Dipping a wing, the redtail slides into a hard banking turn, then holds itself in place against the wind, its fierce eyes and hooked beak pointed straight at Ferrell Swan. If he were Nez Perce he'd believe he was seeing a reliable sign, an omen from the Great Spirit about the tricky hours to come. Hell, he might as well think so anyway, his Anglo blood be damned.

Ferrell tucks his head and rides, buffeted by the wind. He leans into the gusts as if invisible hands push back. At the mouth of the ravine he guides the horse down and the wind dies. As he descends the trail, steep slopes rise on either side, menacing sage and strewn rocks, an alien world where he doesn't belong. In this forbidden place he thinks of Melody's child, fatherless, not even born, then thinks of Levon, his own father run off while Rilla still carried him inside. And what about Rilla, her father gone when she was a girl, or Ferrell's taking longer but finding the door like the rest? For the moment the world seems crammed with sons and daughters but no fathers. He imagines men everywhere disappeared from villages and towns, from outlying homesteads and packed cities, an entire gang of slackers and bums, riding the badlands while their families soldier on.

Ahead Ferrell spots what he's come to see: the bleached bones of the lone mustang, his pilgrimage when he needs to be restored. The skull's dark sockets watch Chroma approach. Ferrell dismounts and leaves the horse to graze the cheat grass. He kneels at the bones, a confounding collection of leg shafts and arching ribs, pelvis halves the size of hubcaps. He skims his fingers along the smoothness of the skull, picturing when Rilla filled that vacant realm with thoughts once more, how she wanted him for untame purposes.

Now Ferrell himself lifts the skull from its scattered bones. The thing weighs more than he imagined, dense as stone in his hands. He looks straight into the sockets as if wise eyes will be looking back. He raises the skull the way he thought Rilla had done, but it doesn't fit his head. Maybe she hadn't worn the skull that strange day, but had *become* the creature she claimed to be. In this supercharged air, anything seems possible.

When he lowers the skull to his chest, Ferrell hears the shaking of thunder, then spidery lightning threads the dark wisps hung from the clouds. If Ferrell wasn't already a believer in the supernatural, this would be when he started. He kneels in the sand to make the horse whole again. He points the snout westward, aiming those hollow sockets toward the rough country below, where somewhere in the rain-blurred miles its companions still run.

When the phone rings, Rilla lies curled into Ferrell on the futon, their sleeping selves as loving as ever. Rilla tromps to the kitchen to quell the jangling, while Ferrell pulls her pillow against him and drifts back down.

"Let's go, Ferrell," she says, standing above him. "Melody's dilating like mad. It won't be long."

Ferrell drives Rilla the pitch-black mile and parks beside Cole's truck. He walks with her to the door, the stars flashing messages in arcane code. "A good night to be born," he says.

"Any time is a good time to be born."

"It beats dying, that's for sure."

Cole answers the door in a bad mood. It takes Ferrell a minute to understand that simple truth has hit Cole between the eyes: another man's child is about to be born. Seeing his wife sweat and moan, caught as she is in the intimacy of birth, Cole must be reminded of what she and Levon did in the seclusion of the sage, halfway between this house and the cabin. To Ferrell's relief, the baby slides easily into the world and howls at what he finds.

With the baby shivering at his mother's breast, Ferrell hands Cole a cheap cigar. The men lean against the far wall, clumsy oafs without a clue. Ferrell feels witness to an act ancient and private, and he humbly averts his eyes.

"You boys head out under the stars," Rilla says, shooing them from the room. "This is mommy time."

Ferrell leads the stunned Cole onto the porch, a fifth of Jack Daniel's in one hand, two glasses in the other. He holds a match to Cole's cigar, then lights his own, his first in forty years. Anticipating the event, he bought Swisher Sweets at the gas station in Murphy, but the celebration now seems a briar patch of emotions, none suited for a Hallmark card.

Ferrell pours their whiskey and puts a glass in Cole's hand. "How're you feeling?" he asks.

"That looked more like dying than being born."

"I won't argue."

"You have any advice for me now?" Cole asks.

"None yet."

"The father's not here," Cole says. "I'd begun to feel it was me, but tonight I'm no more father to that boy than the coyotes on the ridge."

Ferrell sips whiskey until the amber glow reaches his head. "But you're the one here."

Come morning, Ferrell wakes a troubled man. All night long his lost father wandered his dreams, his physical presence as real as the room into which Ferrell opens his eyes. He wants to tell the sleeping Rilla of his haunted hours, of spending company with a man reduced to dust. In his dreams his father looked as he had the day he left, young and full of swagger, his home and its crushing obligations standing between him and the wild frontier.

"I need to light out for the territories, son," his dreamfather said, straightening the cowboy hat on his head.

"But you're a machinist," Ferrell said, somehow his own age in the dream and not fourteen.

"Well, I'll build me some horses then, make them from polished steel."

Ferrell looked down at the work boots on his father's feet. "Will I see you?" Ferrell asked, knowing he would not, his dreamself possessing knowledge of the years to come.

"Sure as shooting, son. Hell, we'll grow old together, buddies to the end."

"But that's not true," Ferrell said. "You'll die before we ever reconcile. You'll return to Ohio in your coffin."

"Well, then you'll visit me out West, son. You'll come ride with me, side by side, our hats pulled low."

"I'll not," he said.

His father shook his head. "For a youngster, you don't have much good to report."

Remembering these conjured words, Ferrell climbs from bed, careful not to disturb Rilla. He dresses in jeans and boots, slips into his western riding shirt, the buttons shiny as coins. He gets his Stetson off the nightstand, pressing the hat firmly on his head. Downstairs, the kitchen radio reports of flames racing unchecked across the BLM, near Murphy and Oreana, Ferrell's corner of the world. Morning gusts have fanned a burning ditch bank into wildfire seven hundred acres and growing.

Outside blackish smoke hangs thick as fog, his fence lines mere traces, the sun a cool white star. With pocket binoculars he locates flames and churning smoke, the whole ugly affair like an advancing evil horde. Swinging his glasses along the fire's leading edge, Ferrell comes upon the mustang herd, not a mile from the blaze. Some of the horses stand guard, their heads raised toward the flames, while others circle nervously about, eager to bolt. Ferrell glances at the house, then looks to Chroma pacing in the corral. The idea strikes him as preposterous, even as he knows it's what he'll do. In fits and starts Ferrell saddles the horse, coaxes the clanky bit into her mouth. He ties his red bandanna below his eyes and climbs into the saddle.

Beyond the gate, Chroma canters without Ferrell's asking, heading toward the herd as if magically drawn. His blood heats up, and Ferrell wonders what he's doing, riding as he is straight into a raging wildfire. Near the mustangs, smoke and dust swirl over Ferrell and darken the sky. His eyes sting and water, and he labors to breathe through the bandanna.

Chroma drops into a slow trot, then abruptly stops, blowing hard. Her ribs heave beneath Ferrell's quivering legs. She
whinnies once, twice, sidesteps in alarm. He senses the herd
in the dense smoke ahead, but can't see a thing. Chroma
whinnies yet again, louder and with more fervor, and next
comes a whinny from somewhere to his right. A second horse
nickers in the opposite direction. When Ferrell looks this
time he finds them in the haze, more mustangs than he can
count, edging closer to where he sits the horse, tossing their
heads, tails raised. For one peculiar moment he believes the
horses of Hagerman have been resurrected from the flames.

A buckskin stallion cuts near Chroma, and she throws
her head, gathers under Ferrell as if to rear. Another stallion, this one nightblack and lathered, wheels close in the
smoke and is gone. Soon mustangs circle them until Ferrell
goes dizzy with the swirling mass, as if he's inside a fantastic
cosmos. The horses understand one of their kind has finally
returned, Ferrell's lanky figure a figment of their dreams.

Ferrell holds Chroma in check amid the skittish herd. He
closes his bleary eyes to the pounding hooves, to the snorts
and squalling cries. He thinks of the mustang skull alone on
the ridge, thinks of his father's bones beneath the ground, as
useless as the bones of Hagerman. When he looks again, his
father hovers not ten feet away, mounted atop the black stallion. The man's dressed in his finest cowboy attire, a white
Stetson on his head. He touches the brim of his hat, and
Ferrell does the same. Without a word his father turns the
horse and disappears into the smoke.

God's Dogs

After winters of record drought in southwest Idaho, Ferrell wakes to a blizzard coming down, ragged flakes swarming the dawn sky. Ferrell bundles in his Carhartt and wool cap, wakes Rilla with news of what the night has brought. On the cabin porch his high desert looks pristine, the tumbleweeds haloed in white. Rilla joins him with her steaming coffee mug, slow to wake in these months of cold days and bitter nights.

"Damn, Ferrell," she says. "Your scrubland looks almost worth something."

"It could be Ohio."

"I guess, but for the distinct lack of people and trees and most everything else."

Today Ferrell ignores the needling about his desolate land. Lately, her thoughts circle Ferrell's decision to retire early to the West, to *buy* so many acres of nearly nothing. Ferrell tries his best to shoulder the responsibility for their divorce, but some days the load makes him tremble.

"We'll hike the high ground when she lets up," he says. "Look for coyote tracks in the snow."

"Now that's a date, honey."

Ferrell takes Rilla's hand, their fingers intertwined. He ponders their deep desire to see and hear the beasts as often as they can. It's something that strikes Ferrell as altogether inexplicable, this affection for an animal most of Idaho shoots on sight.

Near dusk, the snow abruptly stops. A blurry sun breaks beneath the swirling clouds, spotlighting the ridge where he and Rilla trek. Coyote tracks crisscross the top of the ridge, meandering into the ravine, angling down the steep slope to his fenced pastures. It's almost as if Ferrell can see the loping beasts themselves in the tracks left behind.

Rilla kneels in the snow, a latter-day Sacagawea. "Lordy, Ferrell, this place is coyote central."

"It somehow makes things right, at least for the here and now."

In the waning light, he and Rilla follow a set of tracks into the ravine, investigating places where the coyote had done the same. Ferrell finds holes dug through the snow, comes across icy blood sprinkled about, the swift end of a vole or pocket gopher, most likely.

Up ahead, Ferrell's property line cuts sharply north, boundary to the secluded habitat of Din Winters. They haven't visited Winters much this last year, deciding his company is best taken in small doses.

"Think Din is okay?" Rilla asks.

"Snug as a bug, I'd bet."

"It's like being buried alive."

"Din still claims he's alive because he *is* buried. He says the world's too far gone."

"Poor sap."

Back on the ridge Ferrell peers through the dim light, checking on his other neighbor. Lights galore blaze in Cole's Victorian, a remote castle in the frozen landscape. As crystal flakes spiral down, Ferrell follows Rilla along the trail to their cabin.

In the night, snow rushes wildly from the sky, piles high before the cabin and barn. Ferrell stacks extra split wood in the kitchen while Rilla stokes the woodstove and fireplace. She and Ferrell nestle down in the living room, the back rooms of the cabin chilly and dark.

"This is an adventure from ages past, Ferrell."

"That's the way you like it."

"You're the retired history teacher," Rilla says. "You know living something's better than reading about it any old day."

Ferrell studies his ex in the flickering firelight. After years of sharing their thoughts, including certain opinions uttered during the divorce, there isn't anything they haven't aired.

"Sometimes reading about a thing is even better than being there. It's like dreaming while you're awake."

"Not even wet dreams can beat real life."

In the crackling silence that follows comes a knock on the door. It's a sound Ferrell can't recall hearing in his cabin, a christening of sorts. Rilla looks as if she's heard the strangest sound that ever was.

"Who in the world?" she asks.

"Could be Mormons, out recruiting through sleet and snow."

"Oh, now, even *they* don't think God's in this forsaken place."

Another set of knocks, louder this time, more urgent. Ferrell stares at his solid door, wondering how much trouble lay on the other side.

"Go on, Ferrell. Someone could be hurt."

Ferrell carries an oil lamp to the door and turns the knob. In the steadily falling snow stands Din Winters himself, subterranean dweller come up for air.

"My feet are numb."

Ferrell steps to the side, his lamp held high. Winters hurries into the room, a short, scrawny snowman in a torn parka and tennis shoes. He brushes snow off his shoulders and sleeves, then shakes out his navy stocking cap, a tiny blizzard sent Ferrell's way.

"What's the occasion, Din?" Ferrell says when things settle down.

"Power's out."

Winters sheds his coat and hands it to Ferrell, then pulls his feet from soaked tennis shoes. To Ferrell's amazement, the man isn't wearing socks.

"My place got real cold real fast. I don't have a woodstove or fireplace like you do."

Ferrell wants to comment on the wisdom of living so far from the nearest town without alternative energy, but Rilla steps between them with a lamp of her own. In the burnished light her red hair seems to glow, as if her womanly charms radiate outward.

"Come and sit," she says, "warm up. You can stay here till the power grid starts flowing again."

"Rilla," Winters says, the single word containing a host of impure thoughts.

Within minutes Winters is ensconced before the fire, out-stretched toes looking toasty warm. In his hands he clutches a tumbler of Ferrell's cherished Lagavulin, sipping the single malt with reverence. Owing to their neighbor's violent shiv-ering, Rilla made Ferrell open his stash of sixteen-year-old scotch, Winters needing to be warmed from the inside out. Ferrell hates to see such treasure wasted, but knows to keep his mouth shut. Of the suffering souls she has sought to save, Rilla finds Din Winters to be her greatest challenge.

"Good hooch," Winters says, glass raised to the fire-light.

"None better," Ferrell says and tries to smile.

Rilla returns from the guest bedroom with a folded wool blanket, which she unfurls over the man's skinny legs. "Comfy?" she says.

"I tell you people," Winters says, "this is heaven. One min-ute I'm freezing my ass off, and the next I'm all peaceful and cozy and drinking good scotch."

"So how've things been going?" Ferrell says, hoping to switch Winters from the topic of his prized liquor.

"As good as ever."

"Which is?"

Rilla gives Ferrell a scolding look, but he only shrugs.

"Which is not very good at all," Winters says.

"So what do you do with yourself?" Rilla says, ever the counselor, guiding wandering conversations to the promised land.

"Well, I lie in bed a fair amount. When I can't stand not knowing any longer I turn on the cable news, wondering if the carnage will be great or small."

"You get cable out here?"

"I got satellite TV last month, beamed from the stars into my very own living room. Haven't you guys seen my new dish?" Winters gulps the scotch left in his glass, causing Ferrell a final pang of regret. "I tell you people I die a little each hour on CNN: young ones snatched off the streets, whole families taken from their homes. Snipers shooting commuters on their freakin' way home. It's like a death lottery out there, and you waiting on your number to be called."

"Oh, there's more good than bad," Rilla says. "That's always been the case. You know the news just distills each day's evil, feeds it to the public in concentrated form."

"Well, I'd watch 24-7, if I could. It's like a bad traffic accident you can't turn away from. It breaks my heart all day long."

"Why don't you get out more, wander the BLM? Rilla and I were out tracking coyotes this morning."

"You know coyotes spook me. Those bastards'll eat anything that moves."

"You talk about violence, Din, you look at the coyote. Here on this land first and regularly shot, trapped, poisoned, gunned down from the air, often on taxpayer money.

They've gone nocturnal 'cause they can't walk the light of day without us slaughtering them, guilty of anything or not. You know coyotes mostly eat the little rodent critters ranchers don't want? They've never once bothered my sheep, but Cole'll shoot 'em without thinking twice."

"Okay, Ferrell," Rilla says. "Off the soapbox there. You're scaring our guest."

"I'm just saying Mr. Winters should sympathize more with his desert neighbors. They live the persecuted life he only imagines."

"I get scared easily is all."

"You've got to buck up there, son. What are you, thirty-five? Forty?"

"Thirty-one."

"My god . . . ," Ferrell says, but another look from Rilla shuts him up.

"We all get shaken," she says. "It's what makes happy times all the happier."

"I've been in counseling, Rilla. I've heard the namby-pamby stuff before. But even *you* can't deny God is up there smiting us down. It's misery upon misery, you ask me."

With that dire proclamation someone else knocks on the door, spooking Ferrell. When he once again opens his home to danger, he finds Harrison and Melody Cole on the porch, the baby wrapped in a blue blanket in Melody's arms.

"No power?" Ferrell asks.

"Power company says none for days. A week maybe."

The Coles stamp snow from their boots and step inside. Rilla comes and takes the baby while Melody slips off her coat, the women, as usual, not needing words. Ferrell looks at Harrison and strains to smile.

"Scotch?" Ferrell says, reaching to shake Cole's hand.

During dinner, Ferrell sits at the head of a crowded table. After years of eating alone, or sharing meals with Rilla, it's strange to have his neighbors gathered before him. He had to add the extra tableleaf, and use almost every dish and piece of flatware he owns, but they've managed to seat everyone. His grandmother fed much of Tuscarawas County during her generous life, her evening meals big and raucous. Stopping to visit near suppertime meant a place at the table. Ferrell glances out the window, where snow hurtles against the glass. He wonders how he acquired his hermit tendencies, this profound preference for privacy.

"Think it'll stop?" Cole says, knife and fork petite in his hands. Ferrell recollects when those thick fingers once throttled Levon's throat.

"Boise weatherman says a whole series of storms," Winters says. "It's a freak weather pattern from Canada, a hint of what's to come."

"Oh, hell, Din," Cole says, "everything isn't a sign of the end of life as we know it. Sometimes it just snows."

"I've lived here ten years and have never seen this."

"A decade's a blink of the eye down here. You know that."

Rilla raises her wine glass, having poured everyone a California merlot. "Here's to neighbors," she says.

Ferrell sips his wine, pondering the ragtag group assembled at his table—misfits and outcasts, himself included, seeking refuge in the stark Owyhee rangelands. The random circumstances and ill-thought-out decisions that have brought them here boggle his mind. He downs his glass, urging on that fuzziness that brings with it benevolent love for mankind.

"I hope the baby sleeps a while longer," Melody says, tucking her blonde hair behind her ears. "I wouldn't mind eating a meal all the way through for a change."

"How is it being a parent?" Winters asks.

"Tough," Cole says.

"Amazing," Melody says. "Like there's a direct link from little Harry straight to my heart. It almost hurts for real, like physical pain."

"The pain of not sleeping," Cole says. "Of never having a peaceful damn moment, morning, noon, or night, ever again."

"You think you'll have kids?" Ferrell asks, gesturing toward Winters with his glass. He may not be a professional, but he knows when to change the subject.

"Last time I checked you need a female partner to consider such a thing. I've not dated since I moved here."

"Wow, that's a lot of you," Rilla says. "You must be darn good company."

Winters lifts his wine glass to his neighbors. "The best I know. I've never let me down."

After dinner Winters offers to wash the dishes, and Melody takes the baby off to nurse, Rilla tagging along. Ferrell pours two tumblers of scotch, and he and Cole retire to the fireplace. It's not quite brandy and cigars but close enough.

Ferrell watches the hardy flames to give Cole time. He

knows the man has something on his mind, something he needs to convey to someone other than his better half.

Cole looks down at his lap. "Me and Melody aren't doing so well."

"No secret there."

"We fight like blood-feud enemies, yell and curse and break things. We say things we know won't ever go away."

"Rilla and I have waged wars such as those. During the divorce we didn't hold anything back, yelled all measure of nastiness and spite." Ferrell swirls his scotch, watches golden waves break over jagged rocks. "Took me years to recover, after everything was said and done. To learn the magnitude of your failure as a man, of how you've wasted the best years in a woman's life and so on and so forth, well, that sets you back."

Cole nods his head in a sad and final way. "I used to think stuff said in anger could be written off, but I swear now when Melody lets loose it's like pronouncements from above."

"Hell, Cole, after our fights I was the walking wounded. I'd be twiddling to the bank and elsewhere, mundane errands on my list, and I'd feel like terrorists had invaded my head."

"So what am I going to do, Ferrell? I thought raising a kid would keep us occupied, divert our attention from our sorry marriage."

"You're asking me?"

"But surely you have some advice?"

"I do," Winters says from across the room.

Dishtowel over his shoulder, Winters waves from the kitchen doorway. He shuffles to the fire and warms his hands.

"My wife left me on Monday, August 10, 1992," he says. "I said good-bye to her, as usual, at 7:15 that morning, left for the hospital, and that was the last I ever saw of Rebecca."

Ferrell and Cole sit hushed in their rockers, drinks in hand.

"We'd made love that previous night, and she did things to me never done before. At work that day I sped around the city, from one mangled human to another, so much blood and grief, and I kept thinking how frantic she'd been, how she wanted me more than was possible, like she would up and die if she stopped. All through my shift I could actually *taste* her in my mouth. I thought somebody would flatline under my hands because I couldn't stop remembering.

"So I get these fucking roses on the way home, and a bottle of her favorite wine, and there isn't a sign of her in the whole house. Hell, I don't even know if she's alive or dead till the postcard from Bali."

Winters turns from the fire, staring straight into the eyes of Harrison Cole. "So what's your advice?" Cole asks.

"Pray to God that woman never leaves your bed."

When the houseguests wind down—Winters passed out before the fire, the Coles sharing the futon in the guest bedroom, snugged beneath extra blankets—Ferrell and Rilla gather coats and caps for the nighttime feeding. Rilla likes having the horse on three meals a day, hoping to thwart the demon colic. Ferrell's amazed at the fragile health of such mighty creatures, how a simple bellyache can bring them down.

Outside, a stout moon hangs in the fragments of the stars. Moonglow turns his pastures luminous and eerie, the snow awash with fine pale light. Ferrell spies pretty Venus about to set over the ridge, her bedtime early this time of year. He locates Orion and his belt, finds the Big Dipper on its handle, aimed toward the constant North Star.

"Winter wonderland, Ferrell," Rilla says, pulling her wool cap over her ears. "After all that chatter, I sure can use the fresh oxygen."

Ferrell and Rilla cross the yard, their footsteps marring the smooth perfect snow. "I was about peopled out," he says, "neighbors or no."

"Well, tonight I'm on your side. Inside we've got one man in such need he's dying a slow death, and a couple quietly tearing each other to shreds. I wouldn't even know where to begin."

"Strong words for a woman who used to save people from themselves."

"Maybe I've visited this place too often. Maybe your solitary ways are rubbing off. About halfway through dinner I wanted to tell the whole wretched lot to do less talking and more eating."

"Amen to that."

At the haystack, Ferrell scales up the side to the top. Late summer, a farmer from Melba brought ten tons of third cutting, over three hundred bales, enough to get his sheep and Rilla's horse to the pastures of spring. Ferrell tosses the heavy bale over the side, then stands perched twenty feet off the ground, scanning the incandescent pastures for slinking shadows, for those amber eyes reflecting the moon.

"Hey, up there. See any of our friends?"

"Not a one."

As Ferrell kneels to climb down, a coyote cries from the dark, close enough to startle him. He sees Rilla give thumbs up. Between them they've felt every emotion when the coyotes call, from awe to tingling joy, from utter loneliness to outright love. Tonight this single cry has made Ferrell afraid for no reason he can name, not fear for himself, but fear in its most ancient form. Before Ferrell can have another thought, the whole pack answers, a sudden filling of the air with low register barks and high-pitched yips and yaps, with classic sustained howls. He locates the pack against the snow, a dozen shadows clustered in his south pasture, their pointy snouts raised straight to God, calling down their master's wrath or blessing or both. The frenzy lasts for more time than Ferrell can judge, pinning him against the domed ceiling of the sky. He can't help but feel the beasts are singing for Rilla and him, a wild chorus for the miseries of the beleaguered human race.

And then the howling cuts short as if it has never been, and Ferrell watches the shadows dart across the snow, wildness spectacular in its freedom and grace. He climbs down without a word, shaky and weak. When his feet touch ground, Rilla takes him in her arms.

Over the next sunrise and sunset, Ferrell has a house full of need. He finds neighbors camped out all over his cabin, Winters eyeing the women too long and too often, the Coles locked in their secret struggles, the baby mostly happy to let the world pass by. To keep the brood occupied Ferrell gets out playing cards and poker chips, leaves books here and there like traps set. Without fail he ends up in a room *with* someone, has meandering conversations about whatever comes to mind, as if tired thoughts gain new gusto when shared.

On the afternoon of the second day, Ferrell's at the living room window, watching snow drift lazily from the sky. He picks out a single flake and follows its haphazard route to the ground, then starts anew, his entertainment needs scaled way back. Winters lies stretched on the couch, a pair of Ferrell's socks on his feet.

"Don't you have a radio somewhere I could listen to?"

"Batteries are dead."

"You know something real bad could be happening."

"You can bet on it."

"I mean real bad, like major cities in flames, giant asteroids headed our way. How can you live not knowing?"

"Would it help to know I'm doomed?"

"Who's doomed now?" Rilla asks, carrying the baby into the room. The sight of her cradling Harry, now eight months old, sends Ferrell hard into the past, a rending of time. Before him stands the Rilla of their early marriage, a young mother again. Ferrell peeks at the baby gnome as Rilla passes, so wise in his oblivion.

"We're just talking generalized destruction again, Rilla. You know, planet killers, dirty bombs, biowar, the usual fun."

Rilla settles onto the couch beside Winters. He sits up fast, smooths down his unruly hair.

"Ever hold a baby, Din?" Rilla asks.

"My ex's sister had kids, but that's been years."

Before Winters can protest, Rilla positions the child in his arms. She tells Winters where to put his hands, how to brace his arms, her directions matter-of-fact.

"He'll cry," Winters says.

"You're fine."

"You're doing this on purpose, Rilla. Hand a baby to Din and watch the bachelor hermit squirm."

"You're thinking too much, hon. Just hold that baby like you're his papa. Hold him like you are his protector and savior, like you will guide him into a future glorious and bright."

"But . . ."

"We're one big family here," Rilla says. "We're our own pack. Did you know the betas in a coyote pack help raise the pups? Males and females alike, keeping the babes safe."

"I can't even take care of myself," Winters says.

Rilla rests a finger across his lips. "Shhh," she says. "You let Harry nap. Don't wake him with your gloom and doom."

Winters looks at Ferrell, his eyes full of panic.

"I'd listen if I were you," Ferrell says. "Rilla doesn't take kindly to no."

As if to settle the matter Harry stirs, and Winters has no choice but to rock him to and fro. When the child has calmed, Winters leans carefully back and closes his eyes, beyond which distant cities collapse and burn.

Near midnight the baby starts to cry, waking the house with his distress. The shrill cries seek out every square inch of the cabin, filling the cramped rooms with misery and woe. Rilla lights lamps while Melody paces the living room with her child, cooing softly, to no avail. All three men line up on the couch, dejected and forlorn, their heads hung low. With the lamps beaming, Rilla runs through possible baby maladies from Levon's past, but comes up at a loss.

"Maybe he's teething," Winters says, surprising Ferrell.

"How'd you know that?" Rilla says.

"I was an EMT, remember?"

Ferrell puts on coffee, and the women and men tote Harry around, touring the cabin to keep him on the move. Come his turn Ferrell cradles the little guy to his chest, amazed how light and delicate he is. He imagines their two hearts beat off rhythm, one slowing with decades of wear, the other vital and strong. Ferrell thinks how he missed the baby Levon altogether. Had Ferrell held his stepson this way, then maybe things would have turned out different. Ferrell returns to the living room with Harry dozing in his arms. He eases across the squeaky floorboards to the couch. When Ferrell stops moving, the baby wakes with a vengeance, his vigorous cries renewed.

"Almost, Ferrell," Rilla says. "We were rooting for you."

Ferrell hands Harry to Melody, and he cries even louder, something Ferrell didn't think was possible.

"What now?" Ferrell asks everyone in the room.

"When Levon teethed," Rilla says, "I used to drive him around town at all hours, just the two of us cruising along."

"But the roads need to be plowed," Ferrell says. "We wouldn't get ten feet in the truck."

"We'll walk," Rilla says. "Head out under that full moon."

"But I'll get cold," Winters says.

Rilla shakes her head. "You can borrow a pair of Ferrell's boots."

In full winter gear, the crew steps out the door. They assemble in the yard around Melody and the swaddled baby, who falls silent in the sharp air. Halfway up the sky the moon burns like a bright white sun, the sage flats glistening, indigo shadows stretched on the snow.

"Where to, Rilla?" Ferrell asks. "You're the guide."

"Let's do the ridge. I've always wanted to be up there at night."

"Is that safe?" Winters says. "I mean, aren't there lots of things lurking out there?"

"We can only hope," Rilla says.

With Ferrell in the lead, the group tramps through the crusted snow, knees lifting high. At the trail to the ridge, Ferrell picks his way upward with patience and care, carving out solid steps with his boots. He is tribal elder, he imagines, leading his people to safety across a snowy pass.

"This is crazy in the dark," Winters says from directly behind him.

"Shut up and climb," Rilla shouts up to Winters. "It's bright as noon out here."

At the top the group stands sucking air, their breath clouds merging in the cold. The snow shines so brightly Ferrell needs to squint. He notes shadowy pawprints run across the ridge, but doesn't point them out.

Ferrell creeps to the edge of the steep slope. He searches

the glimmering snow field below for anything on the run. Melody walks over to him, with Harry fast asleep in her arms in his cocoon of blankets. "Wow," she says, "I feel like God's right here. Like if we jumped off he'd hold us up."

"Let's just *look* from here, okay?" Ferrell says, taking her firmly by the elbow. He turns and leads Melody away from the drop-off.

Ahead Rilla crouches in the snow with Din. Cole huffs and puffs in front of them, unable, it seems, to draw a decent breath.

"Our lights are on," Cole shouts, pointing north to where his house stands shining. "We can go home, forget this foolishness."

"I want to walk," Melody says. "I want to see what's out here."

"Then so we shall," Ferrell says.

The caravan traverses the ridgeline until the ravine opens on their right. Rilla glances at Ferrell and starts down, weaving around the pungent sagebrush, the scent clean on the cold air. Where the mustang skeleton lies beneath the snow, Rilla stops and raises her hand, palm out. She seems focused on the east side of the ravine, and Ferrell follows her line of sight until he sees them for himself: five or six coyotes, loping easily between the dark clumps of sage. Instinctively he looks over his shoulder and locates another half dozen shadows creeping down the western slope of the ravine.

"Surrounded, Rilla," he says softly.

"Yep," she says.

"Surrounded by what?" Winters says, much too loudly, given the circumstances.

"I'll ask you not to scare the coyotes." Ferrell gestures along the opposing slopes of the ravine. "We wouldn't want to startle them."

"I wish I had my fucking gun," Cole says.

"No," Melody says, "you fucking don't."

Ferrell hears the panting of the coyotes, as if they've run far to intercept these intruders to their midnight world. When one animal turns its head, eyes flash gold in the light, moving low and fast. Both sets of coyotes ease into the bottom of the ravine, converge noiselessly into one pack a dozen strong. Ferrell and Cole step in front of Melody and the child, while Rilla and Winters guard the rear.

"So close to home, and I'm going to be killed," Winters says. "I should have never left my place."

"You can still make a run for it," Ferrell says.

"Hush, you two," Rilla says. "No one's getting killed tonight."

And then there isn't anything more to say, just Ferrell and his band standing before a pack of curious coyotes, rival gangs waiting for what's to come, neither sure what that will be. Ferrell wills himself bigger than the night, those dozen sets of eyes like something from his nightmares. He wonders if he and Rilla have been wrong to champion the most successful predator on the continent, thirty-some-odd pounds of sleek muscle and sharp teeth, an intelligence equal to his own.

"Is *this* better than reading?" Rilla says to Ferrell.

"Ask me later."

Melody inches up next to Ferrell, shifts the baby to his near side. "Take him," she whispers and delivers Harry into his arms. She steps straight toward those glowing eyes, both arms raised out to her sides, as if sacrificing herself to spare her son. Cole starts forward but Rilla grabs his coat sleeve.

"Wait," she says, low and firm. "No sudden movement."

The baby stirs in Ferrell's trembling arms, wanting to be free of whoever's holding him. Ferrell peels the blanket from the miniature face. Exposed to the bright moon, Harry lets loose a sustained howl that would do any creature proud. The wail breaks the night like a siren. When the baby's breath runs out the coyotes answer the call, noses trained at the blazing moon, the most magisterial group-howl Ferrell's ever heard, an impromptu celebration of another day of not getting killed.

Halfway to the coyote pack, Melody looks back at her baby son crying in Ferrell's arms. She seems about to cry herself, her hands shaking uncontrollably, then she seems about to laugh at them all. Ferrell raises her child high to invite her return. Melody shakes her head, an expression on her face Ferrell can't decipher, and he lowers Harry back to his chest.

Melody turns to face the frenzied coyotes. She raises her mouth to the moon, throws her arms wide, and starts to howl. On his right Rilla follows Melody's lead, her shouts lost in the tumult, and to his left Cole stands dumbfounded, his mouth clamped shut. Winters glances at Ferrell and the women, stares at the pack with their heads aimed skyward. In the silvery light he lifts his chin and yells.

Ferrell closes his eyes to the clamor all around. He cradles Harry to his chest, the infant's little heart hammering like mad. He hears yet another howl and realizes it is his own, his voice somehow filled with as much defiance and cocksure sass as he's ever mustered, his own wild heart at last set free.

The Prodigal Son

In the first true heat of spring, Ferrell hikes the rocky hills above the cabin, a man reborn. He stops to watch Rilla riding in the corral below. Over the last year of horse ownership, Ferrell hasn't understood her fondness for ring work, not with his empire at her feet. While Rilla canters in perfect tight circles, he turns for the backside of the ridge.

For three rainy days, he and Rilla have been captive in the cabin. Ferrell heads straight to the ravine and starts down, eager to behold the outcome of warmth and rain. To his delight, patches of purple lupine and yellow arrowleaf crawl the slopes. Golden petals crown the sagebrush. At the mustang skeleton, bumblebees swarm above the skull like particles around a nucleus. Tender shoots poke through the sockets of the eyes. Ferrell picks up his pace, thrilled his vintage parts move like they should. Every spring without fail, he catches glimpses of the man he once was, imagines a chorus of angels in the blazing sky.

Near the bottom of the ravine Ferrell stops midstride, though his heart keeps racing. Three yards from his doubting eyes stands a huge coyote. The big male holds his ground, watching Ferrell watch him. The two lock into a gunfighter staredown in which Ferrell sees in the animal's eyes neither fear nor threat, simply that fabled cool intelligence. The coyote trots several feet, stops and turns broadside, exposing his whole length. Ferrell marvels at the red and tan and gray grizzling of the coat, the darker brown of the flanks, the splash of black on the tail. *Canis latrans*, he thinks, those elegant words he loved to recite when he taught the unit on the settlement of the West. He considers how far removed that noisy Ohio classroom is from this place, of the distance between those heavy textbooks and the living beast before him.

Incredibly, the coyote sits on its haunches, white chest squared to Ferrell, a faithful dog waiting on its master's command. Ferrell does nothing but stare into those amber eyes. He loses track of the minutes ticking past. He and this coyote are all that remain of this or any world.

As if their visit has concluded, the coyote rises to its feet, shakes dust from its coat, lopes off into the sage. Ferrell watches until the coyote reaches the top of the ravine and is gone. Since that moonlit night in the ravine, coyotes have become his personal saviors, his guardian angels, and what he's witnessed gives sanction to his day. He scans the miles before him, empty once more, and turns toward home.

From the ridge, Ferrell spots Rilla's car in the drive, beat-up and dust-covered, as if it's struggled to reach his outpost home. He surveys his intruded-upon cabin and barn, the riding pens and corrals, the pastures where the sheep spend their idle days. Rilla has finished riding and is nowhere to be found.

At the boundary to his irrigation rights, Ferrell scrambles over the split rail fence. He crosses the emerald pasture where his thirty sheep graze, the flock oblivious to those eyes spying from the ridge. He's lost nary lamb nor ewe to coyotes since he bought the stock, though Cole insists his luck won't hold. Once a pack samples his livestock, Cole had told him this winter, it's over and done. As Ferrell climbs the corral gate, the sight of his stepson on the porch stops him halfway.

"You always do stuff the hard way," Levon calls out. "It'd be easier if you *use* the gate."

Easy's been your problem, son, Ferrell wants to say, but holds his tongue. He knows to delay the fireworks as long as he can.

While Ferrell approaches, Levon leans on the porch rail, slouchy and loose-limbed, as has always been his way. But something's wrong in the way Levon cradles his right arm, with how his jaw seems set against some looming pain.

"What'd you do?"

"Didn't do anything, this time," Levon says, smiling despite the hurt. "Got it done *to* me for a change."

Ferrell studies this boy, now grown into a man, another year and surviving somehow. In the boy's defiant face, in the glare of his hard black eyes, Ferrell sees the Levon of all those childhood years—trouble reincarnate, made flesh and blood.

"Well?" Ferrell says.

Levon shifts his weight, stands as erect as he can. "The blade missed most things that matter, though part of my liver is no more."

"You got knifed?"

"Sliced and diced, more like."

"Christ, Levon."

"Oh, God wasn't near me that night."

"You lived."

"The doctors saved my sorry ass, not your higher power."

The screen door opens and Rilla joins them, a family reunion years in the making. Since the divorce, the three have not shared much quality time. Rilla stands at the rail beside her prodigal son, returned from afar. She looks wounded and hurting, a mother's pain. Ferrell knows she might as well have been stabbed herself.

Down at Cole's tree farm, Levon's son will soon mark his first birthday. Harry is the striking image of his father: inky black hair and pouting lips, eyes wanting everything he sees. Cole has done his best at raising the toddler as his own, a bittersweet struggle Ferrell knows too well.

"You're not planning any neighborly visits while you're here, are you, son?"

"Oh, you bet."

"Your mother and I think that might not be best."

"Not best to see my son for the first time? It's almost his damn birthday."

"You can't not say a word to Melody since his birth, then come sailing in expecting rights and privileges. Have you sent her a single dime?"

"Haven't had a dime to send."

Ferrell stares into the wide-open land, noon-bright and never-ending. He's reminded of a thousand conversations before, those times of trying to talk sense into the boy. Levon's always done whatever crosses his mind, as if living outside the boundaries and conditions that govern Ferrell's life.

"How about lunch?" Ferrell says, the western equivalent of a peace offering.

Come morning Ferrell and Rilla hike out before sunrise, climbing the steep, winding trail to the ridge in the faint light. At the top Ferrell stops to rest, no longer inspired, each of his years felt in every step. Rilla joins him on the ridge, breathing hard. On most hikes she's out ahead of him, blazing trail, but today she hangs close. Ferrell's shaken to see her so vulnerable and sad.

"Ready?" Rilla asks.

"You bet."

He and Rilla trudge along the ridge, their backs to the risen sun. From here Ferrell can believe he walks the roofline of the world, the land stretching to places he's never been. At the mouth of the ravine he heads down, Rilla at his heels.

"I saw him right there," Ferrell says, pointing ahead.

"Lucky man." Rilla studies the place as if to will the coyote into existence. She runs a freckled forearm across her brow.

"My son's home, Ferrell."

"That he is."

They walk on without saying more, heading due west as if never intending to stop. Before them the BLM acres lie uncharted, so much unpopulated land Ferrell feels forlorn indeed. He and Rilla loop back around, reaching the outer fence of his pastures, the grass vibrant from the rain. Rilla climbs the fence and Ferrell follows, but she doesn't move when her boots hit the ground.

At her feet lies what's left of one of the lambs. The small head is untouched, the eyes closed as if sleeping, but great violence has struck the torso. Torn flesh and bright red blood, scattered tufts of wool, some pure white, some stained pink, surround the lamb.

"What of your coyote friend now?" Rilla asks, surveying the ghastly damage wrought on so gentle a creature.

Ferrell knows to feel regret at the death of something so young. Or, at the very least, anger at the loss of his meager profit at the Melba sale yards. But these feelings don't arrive, only amazement a coyote has feasted on his bounty and fled like a thief into the hills. If he were a shepherd from Old Testament times, he thinks he'd be out of a job.

They leave the lamb untouched and cross the pasture. Near the cabin, Ferrell finds yet another vehicle in his drive, the morning going to hell in a big way. To his dismay he recognizes the black Dodge of Harrison Cole. It's about the last thing Ferrell wants, a far cry from the peaceful breakfast with Rilla he desires. Without comment, she leaves his side and heads to the cabin.

Cole climbs from his truck in cowboy boots and an ebony Stetson, his wrangler getup. Last fall he began raising Black Angus on half his property, seventy fenced acres nourished from the Snake. With his thousand evergreen trees, and his new hundred head of beef pasturing in the tall grass, with his two-story Victorian tucked among the leafy trees of the creek bank, Cole's place has become an oasis in the proverbial wasteland.

"We got a problem, Swan," Cole says.

"The boy won't cause you any harm."

"*Boy?*"

"Levon."

Cole braces at the name. He scrutinizes the battered car parked beside Ferrell's old pickup, then glances at the cabin. Across his face flits a host of unnamed emotions.

"He's home?" he asks.

"For a few days only," Ferrell says. "He'll leave without causing a single scene."

"In a pig's eye."

"So what's that problem you came for?" Ferrell asks, bummed to have tipped his hand about Levon's return.

Cole sways in his scuffed boots. He looks rattled to his toes, close to some moment of personal discovery Ferrell would rather not witness.

"Coyotes," Cole says with effort. "A sizable male, harassing my calves almost every night. Probably a loner, forced out of his pack and looking for new territory."

"Haven't seen anything."

"Sure you have," Levon shouts from behind them.

Ferrell looks to find Levon standing on the porch, having slunk out from wherever he was hiding. Ferrell wishes for once everything wouldn't go wrong all the time.

"You saw that big sucker yesterday morning," Levon says. "I heard you tell the old lady."

Harrison Cole faces the front porch, his back ramrod straight, his bulky shoulders squared. Before him stands the man who ravaged his wife beneath the icy stars.

"You've got no business with us," he says, his voice suddenly hoarse. "Melody don't want you around."

"Have you asked her already?" Levon says.

Ferrell watches the two stare each other down. With Levon's talent to provoke, it won't be long until Cole rushes the porch, his big strong hands once more on Levon's throat.

"You go back inside," Ferrell says to Levon in his voice of authority. He's daddy taking control, the years dropped away. To Ferrell's relief, the screen door opens and Rilla steps outside. She takes Levon's hand, hesitates, and leads her son into the cabin.

Cole turns pale at having met the demon of his nights. Despite what's happened, Ferrell counts Cole as a friend in these years of lonely living, and seeing him pained hurts Ferrell too.

"That coyote'll get your sheep, Swan. He's going to kill my calves."

"I'll keep watch."

"You'll have to do more than that. I bet he's in the ravine that runs off the ridge. That's on your property. You'll need to go after him."

"I'm not sure I want to kill something that belongs here more than you or me."

"If you don't," Cole says, "I will." He marches off toward his truck, looking stiffly over his shoulder. "And keep that home wrecker away from me, you hear?"

The next morning, Ferrell wakes so damn sad he can hardly bear up. Years of raising that boy and nothing learned. He rises before Rilla can surface from the depths of her dreams.

Outside, Ferrell discovers tranquillity on an epic scale. He stands on the porch with his coffee, willing the silence into his anxious heart. In his years of being apart from the world, Ferrell's come to worship such mornings of utter stillness, when Eden stands before his eyes. Yet today he views this peace unsettled. With the events of the past day, he's feeling too crowded, too pressed upon, his place cluttered with people and their relentless ideas, their loud chirping voices. He needs to put space around him, requires a nice stretch of solitude the way he needs air.

Ferrell heads up the steep trail to the ridge, his favorite morning absolution. Rilla, in her need to smooth her jagged thoughts, wanted to make love last night, and Ferrell was happy to oblige, but a pervasive sadness radiated from her skin, and when they were joined he felt the force of her sorrow enter him, as if his nerve pathways were linked to hers, as if their hearts had somehow merged. It was more of a union than he'd bargained for.

At ridgetop, Ferrell studies the tremendous desolation below. He strides with renewed purpose to the ravine and descends, toward the mustang skeleton and its eternal slumber. Something moves on the rocks above him. It's the big male for sure, perfectly outlined against the rosy sky, watching as if Ferrell's the guest. He half expects the coyote to lift a paw and wave. As Ferrell had hoped, his troubles shed free, his brain waves roll gentle and flat. Despite the native tales flooding his head—coyote as trickster, as crafty charlatan, laughing at the gullibility of man—Ferrell sees a wise monk on a mountaintop, waiting to deliver inscrutable answers. He bows from the waist out of respect, and when he rises the coyote isn't there.

When Ferrell gets down from the ridge, the sun has scaled

the sky. He sees the lambs before he reaches the fence, perhaps as many as five in the grass, desecrated and bloody. He
climbs the fence and walks among the dead, more carnage,
surely, than one coyote can accomplish. He hates that Cole's
prediction has come to pass, hates how often fate steers clear
of what old Ferrell Swan wishes for the world. He squats beside a moorit buck, the poor thing not six weeks breathing
air. With his fingertips he closes the staring eyes, then rises
wearily. He'll bury the lambs after breakfast, he decides, and
say nothing to anyone.

He finds Rilla on the porch with his cherished Lagavulin.
In her hands she cradles a tumbler of scotch, thinned with
water.

"A mite early for a nightcap," he says, "weak though it
may be."

By way of response, Rilla brings the glass to her lips. She
grimaces at the smoky taste, her eyes shut as if in prayer. In
his head, Ferrell sorts through shelf upon shelf of snapshots
such as this: Rilla knocked back on her heels by something
Levon has done.

"Did he go to Cole's place?" Ferrell asks.

Rilla nods, the movement slight but the meaning large.
"We fought right here on the porch, yelling like days of old.
Déjà fucking vu, all over again."

"You want me to go get him?"

"He's twenty-two years old, for Christsakes."

"And we want him to be twenty-three."

"Oh, Ferrell, he *is* the boy's father."

Now it's Ferrell's turn to nod. Rilla has always been the

more reasonable—those decades of kid counseling, case after case of tormented youth, more tribulation than Ferrell could ever have faced. It's been the central irony of Rilla's life, the wellspring of her deepest regret: an adored and highly praised counselor, unable to counsel her own.

"Is there something I can do?" Ferrell says.

"You can come up here, Ferrell. You know, companionship and intimacy and all that jazz."

Ferrell climbs the steps and moves behind her rocker, his palms resting lightly on her shoulders. Rilla places her left hand over his right, their years together contained in the simple gesture. In this fragile moment Ferrell senses why, despite divorce and disappointments too numerous to name, they keep trying to share the same roof.

He and Rilla are arranged like this, posed, he imagines, like some faded sepia picture of rural love and hardship, when Levon comes strolling down the road. As far as Ferrell can tell, the boy's still in one piece and smiling to boot.

Levon stops in the yard and studies the situation. "The two of you look darn sweet up there, all lovey-dovey and concerned." He falls silent, waiting, Ferrell guesses, for one of them to ask about his adventure, forever milking as much drama from his life as he can.

"Well?" Ferrell says.

"I hugged my son." Levon folds his arms to his chest, holding an invisible child. "Levon Jr., right here against me."

"That's not his name," Ferrell says, ever on guard to keep the record straight.

Rilla squeezes his hand, her signal not to hijack the conversation. "How was Melody?" she asks.

"Sexy as ever. Even as a mommy, that woman weakens my resolve."

"What about Harrison?"

"The old man went to Boise, some lawyer thing to stop me from interfering. Left the castle unguarded, just like before."

After breakfast Ferrell washes while Rilla dries, a calming ritual resurrected from their years of marriage. He knows she's recalling her countless counselor years, how good she was at saving so many, while Levon remained a rogue nation unto himself.

"Want to talk some?" he says when Rilla has stored the clean dishes in the cupboard. "Circle the wagons?"

"I'm going to ride, Ferrell. I need to burn off some negative energy here, get my mind settled down."

While Rilla saddles up, Ferrell heads to the shed. He shoulders his favorite shovel and slips quietly from her field of vision, putting the barn between his ex and the west pasture. At the spot of the kills, he studies the attitude of death each lamb has assumed, imagines those last terrifying seconds as the coyote bore down. He wonders, as he seldom ever does, about his own final ticks of the clock.

Ferrell sets the shovel point and drives his bootheel down. In his time out West he's buried more dead animals than in his decades in the heartland. Ewes and rams, yearlings and newborns, struck dead by heat or bloat or white muscle, killed by rattlers, by scorpions, by the wicked sun itself. He leans on the shovel handle, shakes his head free of dark thoughts clouding the air. He's got a fair amount of digging ahead to bury five lambs, wants to be done before Rilla finishes her ring work and brushes Chroma down. He gives himself over to the task at hand, finding a steady rhythm in the simple actions of the shovel, digging past the hardpan to where the dirt grows dark.

"Sweet baby Jesus," Levon says from somewhere over Ferrell's left shoulder.

Ferrell tosses a shovelful behind him.

"Hey, watch the shoes." Levon shakes dirt from one foot, then the other, makes a show of wiping off his pant legs.

"Didn't see you there, son."

"My ass."

"Shouldn't you be out causing more heartache for all concerned?"

"Looks like you found some of that yourself. Looks like that old coyote paid you another visit."

"Maybe so."

"Oh, it's more than maybe." Levon walks among the ripped-open lambs, kneels before a head torn clean from its body. He lifts the dainty head by one of its ears. "That big boy don't mess around."

"I need to get to burying them," Ferrell says.

"Mom know about these new ones?"

"No."

"Mr. Harrison Cole?"

Ferrell shakes his head. He lifts the shovel and begins to dig.

"That can be our little secret, Ferrell. You and me, keeping the world in the dark." Levon tosses the head into the hole Ferrell has dug. "I'm proud of you, really, breaking free from the burden of your honest ways."

"This secret won't hurt anyone."

"I believe our friend Cole might disagree. Melody says he's invested a hundred thousand in his herd. That's a lot of greenbacks to have between a measly fence and hungry mouths."

Ferrell does the math in his head. Registered Black Angus, each steer and heifer a thousand some dollars wandering the night as Cole sleeps. The boy, much to Ferrell's chagrin, is right. He shovels out the lamb head and sets it to the side.

"You got your own problems to concern yourself with," Ferrell says. "You leave me to mine."

"Sure thing," Levon says and walks away.

Ferrell returns to shoveling dirt, the hole growing deep and wide. He tries to cool his blood by making his heart beat faster. He's almost past the heat when he sees Levon returning, a shovel held like a shotgun in the crook of his arm.

"Come to help," he says when he makes earshot.

"I don't need any."

"Mom's brushing Chroma as we speak. You got fifteen minutes at best."

Ferrell gives Levon the eye.

"Trust me, Ferrell. I know the two of you like clockwork. You're playing my game now—stealth and invisibility. Doing stuff on the sly."

Ferrell can't deny such forthright truth. Throughout his

youth, Levon earned advanced degrees in snooping and co-vert behavior, his hawk eyes always casting about for some-thing that could benefit him.

Levon digs tentatively at the hole, skinny arms strug-gling. He flings three small shovelfuls in quick succession, his movements spastic and unfocused, his wound surely hurting. Unsure of what else to do, Ferrell tucks his head and together they dig.

In ten minutes, the hole is plenty large. Ferrell lays the first lamb in the bottom of the makeshift grave and Levon follows suit. When all five bodies are in the ground, arranged as though napping, Ferrell climbs out. He loads his shovel and throws dirt across the lambs.

"Aren't you going to offer up one of your special prayers?" Levon says, shoveling in some dirt.

"God didn't take part in this."

"You mean he didn't call these innocent babes back home?"

"If he wasn't around when you got knifed, the way you claim, he surely wasn't in this side pasture today."

As if the work is done, Levon stops shoveling. Ferrell finishes filling in the hole, then mounds the dirt for when the grave settles. He looks up to find Levon staring with an expression Ferrell can't identify.

"I never felt alone before that night," Levon says, the everpresent sarcasm absent from his voice. "I felt the knife go in slick as you please, real hot and tingling, and all I could do was curl up on that deserted street corner."

"Did you think you were going to die?"

"I wasn't sure I wasn't dead already. I felt as lost and for-

gotten as they come—like the entire fucking city was abandoned but for little me. I didn't see any white light or tunnel
like they talk about, everyone waiting at the other end to
throw confetti. All I felt was utterly and totally alone, a loneliness like no other, cold and scary and no damn comfort to
be found."

"God was there, if you'd called him."

"That's the thing—there wasn't *anything* there. I felt an
absence, Ferrell, not a *presence*." Levon drives his shovel into
the mounded dirt, its handle standing like an unfinished
cross. "As I shuffled up and down the hospital corridors, I
felt something had been taken from me. I felt broken beyond
repair, like a part of me was lost for good that night, like I'd
been shown something others can't see. I decided right then
to come and meet my son, before I can't any longer."

Ferrell studies his stepson and has no idea what to say.
The boy has spoken with more conviction over the last minute than Ferrell can remember in the previous dozen years.

"Tell me something, Ferrell. Give me some of your fancy
words to show me I'm wrong. Convince me what I felt was
off base, some misfiring in my brain, some delusion brought
about from losing blood. Tell me Somebody was with me in
my time of need."

"I can't, son," Ferrell says. "I wish I could."

At dinner that night, he and Rilla do tag team parent-
ing. It's a scene reminiscent of most that have come before:
Levon as captive audience, grilled by his interrogators while
he tries to eat.

"There's still the question of paternity," Rilla says, reaching to quell Levon's fidgety fingers on the table.

"There's no question in that department. I know what I did and when and how often."

Rilla rubs her face with both hands. Ferrell knows she's about to try another route. "Honey, what's your plan after proving you're the father?"

"W-e-l-l," Levon says, getting mileage out of the word, "I plan to do fatherly stuff. You know, teach him to play ball, show him things, tell him what he needs to know."

"That's a detailed plan," Ferrell says.

Rilla frowns at Ferrell. "Those are good actions," she says to her son. "Worthy and important."

"Don't do your freakin' counselor act."

"I'm simply suggesting the child will value time spent with his natural father."

"What I never had."

Rilla looks hurt at that one, the boy having learned his targets well. "You know that wasn't my doing, Levon. Your father left us and never looked back."

"Well, I'm looking back. What's the harm in that? You should be proud of me for wanting to be around."

"No one's talking harm here," Ferrell says. "Or pride. We're talking obligations."

"We're talking money. I want to see him, but I'm not interested in that tidy monthly sum."

And here they've come, full circle at last. Ferrell examines the tabletop with acute interest. He considers banging his forehead on the wood, but first he'd need to move his plate and bowl, negating the effect. Reasoning with Levon never fails to put him in the foulest of moods, makes him feel someone's torn holes in his precious cloak of logic. He ends up schoolteacherly again, days he hasn't minded leaving behind.

"Well, that puts us at an impasse, honey. The Coles aren't about to give you visitation without blood tests and established paternity. After that you'll be officially assuming child support."

"That's lawyer shit for bribery," Levon says, pounding both fists on either side of his plate, the table rattling nicely. "So I have to pay to see him? Like he's a rent-a-kid or something?"

"Someone's got to pay," Ferrell says. He's talking, of course, about raising Levon, a dangerous game to play. He has sided with Harrison simply because the man's reliving Ferrell's arduous stepfather days.

Levon leaps to his feet, the chair clattering to the floor. He stands over them, breathing hard. "I want to fucking see my son and you two find fault. If I stayed away from him, you'd bitch even more."

It's Levon's earned closing line, his ace in the hole, and Ferrell will let him have it, knowing the bitter truth it contains.

On the bookcase in the den sits a perfect coyote skull, the double rows of teeth still wanting to howl. Last month, during a routine stroll, Ferrell found the skull amid the jumbled puzzle of the skeleton, near the linked vertebra. He brought the skull home cradled in his palms, amazed at the intricate hingework of the jaw, how the upper and lower teeth were completely intact. He put the skull on the bookcase to guard the chair where he reads. When he tromps past during the day, the skull rocks slightly on its curved jawbone, nodding to Ferrell about things he hasn't asked.

Tonight Ferrell stands eye level with the skull to choose the night's reading. Ahead lies a beloved book and the halo of his reading lamp, the orderly lines of print smoothing out the creases of his mind. He stares into the eyeholes of the beast, wondering what those eyes have seen, pondering what thoughts have crackled through the skull like summer lightning. Ferrell chooses Stegner for his evening companion, then pours himself a shot glass and settles in. As a sunset drinker, he's never sure if he's toasting the night to come, or pleased to have put another day behind him.

The lowing of cattle drifts through the window screen. Ferrell listens to the altercation and closes his book. When he steps outside, the full moon blazes down like lantern light. The beasts protest and complain, bellowing as if the world were about to end. Ferrell's just eased into the rocker when Rilla steps onto the porch in her robe.

"What's the ruckus?" she asks, her voice raspy with sleep.

"Calving, I suppose. There's probably heifers on the ground and the whole herd's stirred up."

"The renegade coyote?"

"That's the thought I'm trying not to have."

"Do you think Cole's up?" Rilla says.

Before Ferrell can open his mouth, the rumble of a shotgun rolls over the porch—two angry shots, seconds of calm cricket chatter, then two more shots in rapid order. As the blasts fade, the cows holler and moan. Ferrell imagines a demented Cole out in the moonlight, hunting his own cattle.

"Think he got anything?" Rilla says.

"Cole couldn't hit a barn if he stood directly in front of it. He's scaring his animals more than anything, maybe even working up an old-fashioned stampede."

Rilla falls silent, waiting, most probably, for the sporadic beat of shotgun blasts, the music of strange rites performed beneath the watchful moon. Ferrell reaches out and takes her hand. He knows Harrison is hunting down Levon's ghost this evening, not the shadows of the coyote he imagines he sees.

In the starry hours, Ferrell wakes as if choking blackness has settled over the bed. He lies beside the snoring Rilla, envious, as always, of her talent to sleep through strife and discord. His mind on overtime, he'd stayed awake long after the shots had stopped and the crickets reigned supreme. Now sleep has fled after barely saying hello.

Ferrell gets up and tugs on his overalls. On the porch, he laces his boots and heads to the barn. He needs to occupy his hands, to distract his mind from its teeming thoughts. When he flips on the bright fluorescents, his 1947 John Deere appears as if by magic, centered on the barn floor like a museum piece. Since buying the tractor at an estate sale in Oreana last month, Ferrell works on the engine as his own brand of therapy. He opens the window to the brisk night and gathers his tools.

In the heavy quiet, Ferrell changes the fouled plugs.

While the oil drains into the pan he tries to loosen the filter, but the threads won't budge. He steps back and studies his nemesis. He grabs the grimy filter with both hands, summoning whatever vitality he can muster at two in the morning. His arms shudder and quake, his heart a noisy riot in his ears. He's about to quit when he loses his grip, the knuckles of his right hand raking against the frame.

"Well, fuck me," he yells, impressed with such eloquence managed under dire conditions.

The door creaks open in true horror flick fashion. Ferrell turns to face not a living ghoul, nor the undead startled awake, but Melody Cole, standing in the doorway in a long nightgown and faded jean jacket.

"A provocative invitation." The young woman gazes at Ferrell, her eyes crammed with words he wishes he could read.

"I truly doubt that." A stab of pain flickers in his right hand, swells speedily into a deep smarting hurt. Ferrell looks down to find his knuckles torn and bleeding.

"You're hurt."

"I'll live."

Melody crosses the spacious barn, angelic in her nightgown and pale bare feet, her blonde hair aglow in the light flooding down. Though he knows it's his tired eyes, Ferrell has the distinct impression her feet aren't touching the floor. Melody takes his right hand into hers, inspects the wound as if she has the power to heal.

"I saw the light," she says. "I was out walking."

"In your bare feet?"

"I like to feel the sand between my toes."

"So do the coyotes."

"Oh, I often see eyes flash in the moonlight, catch sil-houettes here and there. I always *feel* their presence around me."

"Aren't you afraid?"

"When Levon and I would meet in the scrub, we'd hear them circling constantly around our blanket. Once, when we were caught in the throes of passion, the pack began to howl, like they could feel what we felt. I'd never heard such banshee shrieking before. I knew from that moment on the coyotes would never hurt me, nor I them."

"That's why you trusted them in the ravine last winter."

"Of course."

"Your husband doesn't share those sentiments."

"Harrison doesn't hate the coyotes. He just hates Levon. He'd hurt him bad if he got the chance, I'm afraid. I've never seen him so beside himself. He looks like a monster."

"Levon has always had the knack of bringing out the worst in people. He's helped me discover emotions I didn't think I possessed."

"Me, too, but not the ones you mean."

"Which then?"

"Excitement. Elation. Ecstasy. The amazing rush of mix-ing fear and guilt with pleasure."

"I bet making love in front of coyotes accomplished those pretty well."

Melody reaches down and deftly tears the hem from her nightgown. She takes Ferrell's hand and wraps the strip of cloth over his bleeding knuckles, sparks shooting up his arm. She ties off the impromptu bandage and releases his hand.

"My husband is a decent man, Ferrell, but he's a dull decent man. I needed something more than raising trees and cows. It's a real familiar story."

"And such stories never end well."

"Oh, Levon will lose interest in us soon. Your son can't stay in one place for too long."

"That boy is no blood relation of mine," Ferrell says.

"Yet you raised him."

"Fed and clothed, but did not, alas, impart instruction."

"You know he speaks of you quite fondly. Maybe he's learned more from Ferrell Swan than you think. He's not done anything terrible yet."

Ferrell nods at her hopeful words, but his heart doesn't believe. "You'd best be getting back, Melody. Harrison will think you and the boy are keeping the coyotes company again. He's already been out once with his gun."

Melody offers Ferrell a smile that breaks his heart. She steps in close, her physical proximity stealing breath from his lungs. She rises on her tiptoes, or perhaps levitates, and kisses him tenderly on the lips, her mouth a private gift. When she breaks their brief connection, Melody rests her head on his chest, hugging him with an intensity that pleases. He puts his arms around her, daughter he has never had, embrace he has never given.

The next morning, Ferrell wakes hours after sunrise, groggy from the heat pouring through the open windows. He sits up in bed, dejected to have missed the morning cool. He wonders where Rilla has gone, if she and Levon are once again matching wills. He finds them chatting at the kitchen table, a Norman Rockwell vision of ease and contentment.

"Kick-ass gunfire last night," Levon says as Ferrell heads for the coffee pot. "Like a war zone or something."

"Just Cole guarding his herd, as is his right."

"Holy Jesus, Ferrell, enough with the rights and regulations. Sometimes a man needs to do whatever the hell he thinks is best, others be damned."

"That's your code, son, not mine."

"If you say so," Levon says, his voice raising the specter of buried lambs, of secrets shared.

Rilla pushes the creamer toward Ferrell when he sits down. "Cole called this morning."

"Did he get any coyotes?"

"No, but two calves are no more. He said it wasn't a pretty sight."

"How's he taking it?"

"He's not. He says he wants you hunting up on the ridge by noon, or he'll get the BLM people involved. He plans to visit the Boise headquarters this afternoon with one of the dead calves as proof."

"Wow, this is like *Shane* or something," Levon says. "Which one of you is the big bad landowner? Who's the outlaw trying to hang up his guns?"

"Neither of us," Ferrell says, taking his coffee to the porch.

When the lunch table is set, Rilla finds that Levon has disappeared to parts unknown. She searches the cabin and barn, even the outbuildings, but her son is not around. Ferrell decides Levon can only be down the road, visiting Melody and his son while Cole is miles away. A risk taker to the end, flirting forever with disaster.

By late afternoon the heavens cloud, a strange occurrence in this land of relentless sun, Ferrell's cabin and barn cast in gray. He sips coffee on the porch, unwilling to take to the hills with gun in hand. He's doing his best to divert his mind from the conflict at hand, avoiding Cole's threat as if it were never made. He feels old angers take root, remembers how he detests being told what to do. Here he is surrounded by acres of his own damn land, his property lines far from the cabin, and he's got neighbor trouble. There's no way he will march into the ravine today, intent on blasting that clever coyote, protector of his twilight years.

When he hears the gunshots, one after another after another, his mind goes in all directions at once: Levon crumpled outside the neighboring Victorian, Cole slumped over the steering wheel of his truck, Melody sprawled in her living room, the child wild-eyed as his mother's blood pools. The shots ring off the hills, confusing Ferrell. He can't place their origin, believing they somehow come from everywhere. The concussive recoils make him jump, hot coffee sloshing over his hand until he sets the mug down. With each gunshot, he ages beyond his natural years.

The screen door slams and Rilla rushes to his side, her face betraying her thoughts: Levon has finally acted out the climactic scene he's been rehearsing his whole life, an act both monstrous and irrevocable, their lives forever changed. Ferrell puts his arms around her.

"Oh, God," Rilla says when the shots end at last. She

seems even more worried now that the gunfire has ceased. "Go see about my son, Ferrell."

Ferrell hurries to the tack room, but the gun case stands open, the double-barrel nowhere to be found. He sprints outside to the truck and fishes for his keys. He's about to open the door when something catches his eye, movement, he thinks, on the ridge above him. A man is hurrying sideways along the drop-off, heading toward the trail that winds down to the cabin. He moves in a loose-limbed slouch, the dark length of the shotgun in his trailing hand, and Ferrell knows what Levon has done.

In his mind, Ferrell sees the big coyote on his side in the sand, utterly dead and gone. He studies the poor beast as surely as if he's down in the ravine himself—the splendid coat barely stirring in the breeze, the fur silky as he runs his fingers along the muscled flanks, the tender belly. Ferrell can even see the months to come: he and Rilla visiting the coyote while sun and wind, blowing grit and brief rain, take their toll, matted fur giving way to clean white skull, to bleached foreleg and hip bone, revealing the small curved cage that held the captive heart. *Dust of planets and stars*, he'll say in improvised prayer, *now dust once more*. When the skull is bare, just bone and strong sharp teeth, Ferrell will lift the head from the skeleton and carry it home. He'll set the skull on his bookcase beside the other one, faithful companions, huntress and hunter, reunited at last.

Levon reaches the trailhead and stops, for all appearances surveying the homestead below. He seems to spot Ferrell beside the truck but doesn't show a sign, the gun, in the crook of his arm, aimed vaguely in Ferrell's direction. With clumsy effort, Levon slings the double-barrel off the ridge, the shot-gun cartwheeling, stock to barrel, down the steep embank-ment, sand churning high, then sliding a dozen feet to wedge against a tumbleweed. Ferrell watches his stepson watch him, the boy in precise silhouette, dwarfed by the space between Ferrell and the ridge. Levon raises his empty arms to the side, brings them even with his shoulders, and stands absolutely still, a dark figure against the bleak sky.

Solstice

By the end of May the sun has pulled closer, harsh and ever bright, the days blistering by noon. The heat bears down on the steel roof of the cabin, floods the ceaseless sage and rocky hills, the distant Owyhees baked hard in the sun. Ferrell and Rilla hike this metallic world as if inside a kiln, their skin deep brown, their bodies lean and agile. Beneath the scorching sun, Rilla wears fewer and fewer clothes, then she wears nothing at all, heading out in hiking boots and tanning oil. Soon Ferrell does the same, grows used to being au naturel in the wilds of Idaho.

Amid this bare-skin walking, this hiding nothing from the world, Rilla decides baring their souls comes next. "If our bodies are naked," she says, cupping her breasts to prove her point, "then our thoughts should be too."

On the ridge, the pair sit on boulders the size of SUVs. Their boots dangle three hundred feet above the desert floor. From this solemn lookout point, Ferrell thinks the planet looks too damn hostile to support life. He imagines them

lone survivors of something too terrible to utter, the apocalypse already come and gone.

"We will talk until no word's left unspoken," Rilla says,
detailing her grand plan. "We will leave no question about
our past without answer, no motivation unexplained."

Ferrell feels daunted by the task ahead. He has forever
known the past belongs in his rearview, shrinking quickly
from sight. He doesn't want to look over his shoulder, now
or ever, doesn't want to view a land where nothing can be
changed.

"That sends chills, Rilla. Gets me scared and trembling."

"A dark storm on the way to our personal safe harbor.
Not easy, but worth the sweat and blood."

"Blood?"

"Only a symbolic bloodletting, Ferrell. Nothing that
will really hurt."

"Easy for you to say."

In the days that follow, Rilla rises with the sun, bangs
kitchen cupboards and drawers shut, rousting Ferrell from
sleep's brief reprieve. She throws open the curtains as if the fat
orange sun cannot be denied. Yanked from his dreams, Ferrell
believes himself a deep-sea diver shooting to the surface, his
return to the world too abrupt for his blood to handle.

"Can't we sleep in?" he asks on the third day of glaring
sun and stark confession. "Maybe take a day off from all this
sharing?"

"Too much to talk about."

"But we don't *work* anymore. We have nothing but time."

"Oh, hell, Ferrell, there aren't enough hours in the day for you to explain yourself to me."

On the porch, Ferrell downs his coffee while Rilla fills their canteen. The night chill lingers over the sage, and he breathes air sweet enough to taste. Left to his own desires, he would stay put and relish the morning.

"Let's go, champ," Rilla says. "This ain't Starbucks, last time I checked."

Ferrell slings coffee dregs into the yard and balances his cup on the rail. Rilla's treading dangerous ground taking his java time. He can feel his mood turn blustery, can feel black roiling clouds bear down. Next comes that fluttery, airy sensation he recognizes as the urge to be alone.

Rilla hustles to the top of the ridge with Ferrell in tow. They take their places on her favorite boulder. "Today," she says, pulling off her shirt, "we explore your reasons for leaving me." She slips out of her canvas walking shorts.

"You were there."

Rilla's eyes narrow to slits. He can feel hostility radiate off her skin. For months the slick switchbacks of their divorce have been avoided, but today she wants to speed headlong into danger.

"Ferrell?"

"I'm thinking."

"Don't think, just let the truth gush forth."

Ferrell tugs his shirt over his head, then wriggles from his faded cutoffs. "What if I don't *know* the truth?"

"Everyone knows *their* truth."

"What if I have more than one?"

"Then tell me all of them."

"What if my leaving came from unknown urges and baffling impulses, from half-formed ideas that never reached fruition?"

"What if you're an asshole?"

Rocks smack together behind Ferrell. His skin goes flushed then clammy, and he springs to his feet, whirling to face their doom in one form or another—cougar or coyote or other wild creature. He discovers Din Winters instead. A handful of people in fifty square miles and here one stands.

"Howdy, partner," Ferrell says, acutely aware of his manly parts hanging in the breeze.

"Sorry to disturb your sunbathing."

Rilla keeps her back to their nearest neighbor. "Out for a stroll?" she asks.

"I was tracking some coyotes," Din says, his eyes locked on what parts of Rilla he can see. "I thought I saw them run up here, toward the ravine."

"Are you sure it wasn't my bare butt again in those high-powered lenses of yours?" Rilla asks.

Ferrell watches Din turn red and not from the sun. Whenever the guy meets Rilla, profound loneliness strikes him like a horrible affliction. Anymore, Ferrell considers him a lost cause.

"Well, I did have the binocs out this morning."

Rilla slips back into her T-shirt. "And you could not resist the closer view?"

"No lie, I do get a little crazy out here." Din toes the sand with his torn tennis shoe. "You know, you two look like

Navajo warriors right now, waiting on their spirit helpers."

"Our what?" Rilla asks.

"Your spiritual guides. Visions that appear after days of fasting to offer secrets about the future."

"Lordy, we could use them," Ferrell says. "We really need some answers."

"What were you two talking about anyway?"

This dear man, Ferrell realizes in a rush, might rescue him from today's foray into unforgiving truth. "Why, we were talking about when one spouse leaves another. The possible reasons and so on and so forth."

"That's something I sure know about."

"Then have a seat, neighbor."

"Do I have to get naked?"

Rilla yanks on her shorts and stands to face them. "For today's session, Ferrell Swan, you ask poor Din what it's like to be left. You have *him* tell you how it feels."

Before either of the men can speak, Rilla storms down the trail, her boots lifting wispy clouds of dust.

Summer takes over Ferrell's land: chilly dawns before morning heat, afternoons above one hundred, the sun a heroic burden he must carry all the way to dusk. After mornings of frank revelations, he and Rilla seek the porch shade because they must, attempt fitful siestas that provide little sleep. With the sun high and holding steady, Ferrell believes night will never come, imagines a world of perpetual noon, every living thing burned away.

One afternoon they hike south into the rising mercury,

along the maze of ditch laterals feeding water to his pastures. At the head gate they climb the steep ditch bank, their boots slipping in the loose shale, and emerge on the dirt road that hugs the wide irrigation canal.

"It's like some weird oasis," Rilla says. "I never expect to find it here, like my mind can't imagine such a place in the middle of so much rock and sand."

Stretching from the Snake, the green waters of the canal drift lazily in the sun. Hardy cottonwoods rim the south bank, and cattails thrive in the leafy shade below. Rilla strips down and dives in. Near the opposite bank, she splashes to the surface and waves.

"Hurry up, slowpoke. We're not getting any younger, you know."

Ferrell undresses and folds his clothes along the water's edge. He eases down the bank on tender feet and wades to his thighs. Heavy cold grips his legs, rattles his brain like a good hard punch. He dives headfirst to get the shock over with.

"Oh, Mommy," he says when he comes up for air.

Rilla swims almost fifty yards against the current, then floats toward him on her back, exposing her glory to God's watchful eyes. Ferrell himself gets a pretty fair look as she sails past.

"Our daily baptism," she calls to him.

Downstream Rilla dives back under. She moves slippery and cool in the jade water, her feet kicking up spray. She reminds him of a playful otter, happy for water and sun. He wishes for once to feel what she feels.

Ferrell senses a presence overhead, then a squadron of

shadows flits across the water: the silhouettes of ancient
pterodactyls, he thinks, broad wingspans and angular heads,
legs stretched behind. Ferrell looks up at a flock of great blue
herons, sixty or seventy in haphazard formation, their huge
wings held steady. The flock glides over the canal, banks
awkwardly to the east, then swings around to where Ferrell
and Rilla tread water. Ferrell points to the cattails along the
bank, and he and Rilla slip among the thick green leaves.
The herons call to each other in odd chortles as they near
the water. Ferrell glances at Rilla, her eyes wide and staring.
When he looks back, flapping wings blot out the sky. Dozens
upon dozens of herons light on the canal banks, tall on their
black stick legs. The elegant birds keep landing until he and
Rilla float among the rookery, hidden in their secret spot.
The air fills with raucous laughter, with the exotic cries of
some alien race.

Ferrell stares through the itchy leaves, the sunlight hued
in green, watching the herons stroll the bank on thin stilts.
One large bird stops directly beside their hiding place, so
close Ferrell can smell its damp feathers. If he wanted, Ferrell
could reach out through the leaves and touch the slaty-blue
wing, stroke those feathers glistening with oil.

And that is exactly what Rilla does, her hand easing
through the leaves, fingers stretched across the bright inches
to the slick feathers. When the great blue screams its warning, the air explodes around Ferrell's head, so many wings
pounding the air he can feel wind on his face. The water
churns as the birds ascend into the refuge of the sky. The herons stream out due north, regrouping in flight. He watches

the flock until it blurs into the horizon. He turns to Rilla, her hand still reaching through the leaves, her fingers trembling. She brings her hand to her face, presses those shaky fingers to her lips.

"It was like touching a part of me," Rilla says, her voice strange to Ferrell's ears. "That heron was old, Ferrell, her days of being needed far behind her. There was freedom in that, and total fucking heartbreak."

Rilla dives through the cattails, popping up yards downstream. She rolls onto her back, her breasts skyward, her nipples taut. She makes no effort to hold herself against the gentle current, and floats steadily away from Ferrell, growing smaller in degrees.

During the new moon, nights turn extra dark, as though the barren satellite has wandered off to be alone. Soon a thin crescent shows above the ridge, then the moon transitions to quarter and half, gaining heft by the night. Ferrell marks each day of confession by the phases of the moon, amazed almost a month of introspection and tears has gotten them nowhere that he can see.

After supper one night, Ferrell steps outside to soak up the blessed cool. Above his ridge, the round moon throws yellow spirals into the black. Rilla steps from the house to join him in the yard.

"We're going nocturnal tonight, Ferrell. We *must* hike out beneath this magisterial sky."

As the moon climbs, spooky shadows stretch from the chaparral. The whole of the desert seems a weirdly lit stage.

He imagines a curious play will soon commence, perhaps a creepy Noh drama, complete with high-pitched flutes. Nothing would surprise him.

"Let's move out, soldier," Rilla says, and off she goes.

When he catches up with her, Ferrell marvels at the incandescent light pouring down, his world tinted platinum, a negative photograph of the landscape he loves. He could be walking through a glowing dream, trapped between wakefulness and the place where nightmares reside. In the distance come the faint shrieks of phantoms: a coyote pack miles away. Ferrell and Rilla stop and wait. Nearby a single coyote barks once, clear and distinct, then barks twice more. Next the entire resident pack begins a chaotic chorus. Tonight Ferrell hears mayhem not mischief in their bickering squalls. The pack sounds tense and uptight, about to run across the brilliant desert with trouble on their minds—social deviants, netherworld ninjas, ready to wreak havoc on the sleeping world.

"I tell you," Rilla says, "I hear them now and it just gets me sad."

"They do sound riled up."

"I don't mean that."

"What then?"

"When I hear them lately, I can only think they are so utterly doomed. To call out the way they do is to summon their own deaths. Any day you know that damn government plane will be overhead, and then we'll hear the shots. So much beauty, wiped out just for being alive."

"I can't argue that."

Rilla shakes her head. "This whole summer's turned mystical on me, Ferrell. All our long talks and insights gained. It's too much to process."

"That's what we're doing? Gaining insights?"

"What would you call it?"

"Tearing each other down. Saying things that can't ever be unsaid."

"But leaving things a secret has been the real problem, Ferrell. We were married almost twenty years and didn't know our private selves."

"Maybe privacy isn't such a bad thing. Maybe our mysterious natures are meant to be just that."

"Maybe that's a copout. Maybe you are just a private man who wants to stay that way."

"Goddamn it, Rilla, don't you ever think you might not like what you'll find if all of me is revealed? What if we aren't supposed to know our deepest secrets?"

From somewhere above their exposed heads, a horned owl screeches. Ferrell ducks at the idea of those sharp talons cruising the dark. He finds something unsettling about birds with seven-foot wingspans that fly silent as specters. He scans the inky sky and its roof of white stars, feeling himself a target on the open plain. Directly overhead a flying shadow soars before the moon. Ferrell has the distinct impression the bird stalks his paltry soul. The owl screeches louder than before, then pivots and wheels south, flying straight toward the irrigation canal.

"Wow, Ferrell, I thought we were goners."

"Maybe we are."

Up ahead, Ferrell spots a ghost hovering in the silver
light. He recognizes Din Winters in his white EMT jumpsuit from days past.

"Are you stalking us?" Rilla calls.

"I don't sleep so well these days. It gets pretty hot below
the ground."

"How about a swim?"

"In the desert?"

"Follow me," Rilla says and turns south, Din's personal
tour guide of the desert wasteland.

Ferrell glances at Din and shrugs. Together they fall in
step behind her, hurrying to keep pace. High in the vaulted
sky, the moon dims the lights of their celestial neighborhood.
Din huffs and puffs beside him, out of shape or nervous as
hell, Ferrell can't figure.

"Where are we headed?" Din asks.

"You'll see."

At the canal embankment, Rilla scrambles to the top. She
stands looking down at them, slightly sinister in the eerie
moonlight, then she is gone. Ferrell climbs the loose shale
with Din struggling behind. On the canal road they stand
side by side, catching their breath. The moon throws a glit-
tering white ribbon on the water, while higher up, branches
loom in a black tangle. Ferrell can't find Rilla, but he does
see her clothes, piled on the bank. Then she swims into the
spotlight beaming down. She waves her arms at them, wet
skin reflecting the moonglow.

"You boys going to watch or swim?" she calls out.

Ferrell pulls out of his clothes, a common task over the

course of this strange summer. Din stands stock-still, peering at where Rilla splashes about. Between her full tan and the dark water, Rilla's hard to distinguish, but when she swims across the tunnel of moonlight there isn't much left to imagine.

"You ever skinny-dip before?" Ferrell asks.

"When I was six or seven. This feels a bit different."

"Most things are."

When Ferrell slips into the canal, he believes his heart might freeze. The cold grabs his body and squeezes hard. After several false attempts, he catches his breath. On the bank, Din stands pale in his naked skin. He seems as white as when he wore his jumpsuit. He puts a foot in the water and yelps.

"Cowboy up," Rilla shouts.

"But I drove ambulances. I've never even been on a horse."

"Just jump in," Rilla says and the poor man does.

Din resurfaces and whoops at the sky. Ferrell can hear the man's teeth chattering from yards away. His neighbor swims over and holds steady in the current.

"Where's Rilla?" Din asks.

Ferrell scans the shimmering surface, flat and empty. He shouts her name, but she doesn't answer. She was floating beside Ferrell when Din cannonballed off the bank, and now nothing.

"Ri-lla," he yells, long and full. The word is swallowed whole by the night. Honest panic hits his chest, and Ferrell knows he trembles from more than the cold. Beside him Din shouts Rilla's name over and over. Ferrell's about to float down the canal, searching beneath the black current, when he hears something from the direction of the bank.

Rilla stands slick and dripping on the road. Her supple body shines beneath the moon. "Looking for me?"

"You scared us," Ferrell says.

Din swims toward the road, staring as if his favorite movie goddess has undressed on the screen. Ferrell thinks he can see the man's eyes glow in the night.

"Sometimes it's good to be scared," Rilla says. "Sometimes that's the best thing you can be."

In the morning, Ferrell wakes heartsick as hell, too little sleep and too many thoughts over the drawn-out night. Downstairs Rilla can't be found, each room as if he lives alone. On the porch emptiness prevails, not a sign of her in all those open miles. He slumps in the rocker and stares into the whiteness of the sky.

By afternoon, the heat crosses the century mark and continues to rise. Ferrell dreads how the temperature won't peak till dusk, growing hotter as the sun slips down. He finds those last blazing hours hardest to take, when the heat becomes something tangible, a dense heaviness on the air. In the kitchen the radio reports 110. Ferrell laces up his hiking boots, squares his cowboy hat on his head, and pushes out the door. He crosses the dusty corral and climbs the fence, the horse watching from the shade of the barn. Her eyes tell Ferrell he's a damn fool to be out in such heat.

"No secret there," he says aloud.

With the sun low and fierce, Ferrell heads out alone into the sage. He hikes at a sure pace, his legs feeling strong. It almost seems he moves through water, the ancient seabed he walks over full once more. A trio of turkey vultures attempt clumsy circles in the sky, bald heads watching his progress from the cabin.

"Not yet, you bastards," he yells, but they don't seem to care.

Near his northern property line, Ferrell stops to wipe his salt-stung eyes. His tumbleweed heart threatens to break free on the hot wind. Hiking solo, he finds the silence too great. The terrible calm has amplified his thoughts, has cranked his inner monologue up way too loud. He tries to quiet his head to match the mute country. He wonders if he's confused silence with contentment over the years, emptiness with peace.

Ferrell circles to the ridge and looks down. *I'm a speck*, he thinks, *a proverbial grain of sand*. He turns his head at a sound he can't name. From out of the ravine, Rilla comes walking like some daytime apparition.

"Where were you?" he says when she gets close.

"At Din's."

"I thought being underground gave you the creeps."

"He's a kindred soul, Ferrell. He understands the hurt I felt."

"Have you been there all day?"

"Mostly."

"Why?"

"I wanted someone to talk to."

"But we've been talking for weeks."

"To no end, Ferrell. You're the first to admit that."

"But why Winters?"

"He understands what I went through when you left."

"I know what you went through. You tell me every day."

"You were the one who did the hurting. I understand now you can never know."

Ferrell doesn't disagree.

Sometime past midnight, Ferrell wakes to find Rilla not in bed. He stumbles to the front door, his head foggy with sleep, and steps into the yard. Above his cabin, the stars have fled the sky. Delicate drops drizzle from the clouds like a sacrament on his head. Ferrell waits for his eyes to adjust, wondering where Rilla could be. With something like relief he finds her car beside his truck, the fine rain inaudible against the roof and hood.

Ferrell imagines Rilla's walked straight into some dreadful harm—a chance encounter with escaped convicts or a famished cougar miles from its territory. Right when he decides to retrieve the shotgun, Rilla emerges naked from the mist, looking more spirit than flesh and blood.

"Are you friend or foe?" he calls.

"Neither," she says. "Both."

"Where have you been?"

"I walked to Din's."

"Naked?"

"I had clothes on the way over."

"Where are they now?"

"Beside his bed."

Ferrell doesn't trust his tongue. His frayed wiring shorts out everywhere—legs weak, arms heavy, lungs unable to pull air. He feels betrayed and gut shot. His head slumps to-

ward his chest, as though his neck cannot support the burden
of his thoughts.

"I didn't fuck him."

Ferrell drops to his knees in the sand.

"He undressed me. He took off my boots, then my shirt
and bra, my shorts and underwear. We didn't say a word the
whole time. I felt like a melancholy queen, attended to by a
dutiful servant."

Rilla steps closer, her mouth down to his ear. "When he
caressed my face, it hit me. I wanted neither one of you."

During summer solstice, the moon rises orange as the
sun. Ferrell sits on the porch alone, privy to a spectacle he
does not wish to see. Since last night's news he has kept himself apart, unable and unwilling to speak.

Rilla comes out on the porch to sit beside him. "I'm leaving, Ferrell. I don't belong here anyway. This is your place,
your solitude. I was a fool to think you wanted someone
around."

"You're the one who can't be happy."

"I'm just noise to you, an interruption to your days of
tranquillity and repose."

Ferrell stares at the rising moon. "You should have left
well enough alone."

"And settle for chronic loneliness? For living with a
stranger?"

"We haven't gotten that bad, not like before."

"I'll leave before we do true harm."

An hour later, Rilla has both suitcases packed. She showers with the bathroom door locked, emerging fully clothed, something Ferrell hasn't seen in weeks. She wears a black dress like she's in mourning, hair pinned in her formal counselor style. She looks more defeated than angry, as if living with Ferrell is a battle never to be won.

Ferrell watches Rilla gather forgotten things about the house. He nurses a tumbler of fine single malt and keeps a wide berth. Dozens of significant sentences tickertape across his brain, but none make it out his mouth. A piercing coldness fills his skull, thin mountain air passing through his thoughts. He feels oddly detached from the theater of her departure, strangely removed from the scene playing out. He knows he should protest, should shout and scream and raise holy hell. Or maybe he should calmly talk her out of leaving, offer apologies, concessions, innumerable compromises. He could even renegotiate the terms of their daily lives. For Christsakes, he should be called to some kind of action, but gravity holds him fast.

It's not that Ferrell doubts she'll go. Acutely he understands he will sleep night after night without her, will wake alone in his bed. Rilla won't be there from morning coffee to final nightcap, which he knows can be some tough, protracted hours. But then he imagines taking extra time at wake-up coffee, pictures downing more than one sunset scotch. He can meander through the day at his own finicky pace, subject to every whim and flight of fancy. He feels all that solitude as pent-up desire, as something he's craved. He knows he'll pay the heavy toll of loneliness, will miss her many hours of the day. He'll feel the knife-edge of regret and nurse its lingering scars, but right now he doesn't give a rat's ass, believes he could drive with ease through the red gates of hell.

At dawn Rilla stands beside her car, keys in hand. Ferrell teeters before his ex on shaky legs, ample whiskey in his veins.

"Did you have to drink all night, Ferrell? Has the party already begun?"

"I drink to forget. Or remember. One of those."

"You drink for all reasons. Most times you drink to drink."

"Cheers."

Rilla studies Ferrell so long he feels nearly sober. If she looked any sadder, Ferrell worries he might go ahead and break down.

"It's not for good, Ferrell, at least not for me. I just need a break from this parched land. It's making me nuts in the head."

"I'll be here."

"I know." Rilla checks the keys in her hand. "Then this is good-bye?" she asks.

"If you're leaving it is," Ferrell says. "If you're staying, then it's good morning."

"Good-bye, Ferrell."

She turns and swings her car door open. "Our spirit helpers never showed, did they? The fuckers left us alone to fend for ourselves."

"Just like always."

"I'll call in a few months. When what we say matters once again."

"What if Levon comes to visit?"

"He won't. That young man knows when to stay away."

Rilla reaches out to touch his face. Her cool fingertips brush his temple and cheek, his mouth and the stubble on his chin. "You wouldn't want to make love one last time, would you, Ferrell?"

"Make love?"

"In the car. Like when we were young."

Ferrell steps within Rilla's gravitational pull. He rests his palms on her shoulders, then pulls her to him.

With Rilla gone, Ferrell has choices to make. He could stagger to bed and watch the room spin. He could jump in his truck to feel his own wheels turning, to believe movement is a sort of accomplishment. Instead he tightens his laces and swaggers into the rising sun.

At the trail to the ridge, Ferrell stops to regroup. His night of drinking has left him miles beyond tired, but his feet seem ready to climb. He starts up the steep hillside because he has no other choice. At their confession place, Ferrell drops to his knees. When he stretches across the flat boulder, the sky revolves as if the earth were dead center of the universe.

"I left because I fucking wanted to," he shouts to the sky and its inhabitants. "I left because I damn well could."

Ferrell senses someone near and whirls to his feet, fists clenched. Out of the morning haze, a strange creature approaches with deliberate steps. He recognizes Rilla's brown naked body—glistening with sweat, the hard muscles moving beneath her skin—but not the sun-bleached horse skull where her head should be.

"I am your spirit helper," the creature says in Rilla's voice. "I am here to guide you through the days to come."

Ferrell stands blinking in the heat. "You, my dear, are the mistress of the horse god. You are a vision concocted of whiskey and no sleep."

"And that makes me less real?"

Ferrell frowns. He's been wanting his own spirit helper, has finally welcomed her into the world, and she turns out to be none other than his former wife.

"What do you want?" he says.

"I want what you want."

"I don't know what I want."

"Then I want to know what it's like not to know."

The creature brings its bony snout near his face. The eye sockets show nothing, but the blunt teeth along the jaw blaze in perfect rows. Ferrell's thighs quiver until he almost falls. Rilla's lean arm reaches out, her palm resting on the side of his face. Cold fingers splay along his forehead and temple. Somehow he understands this peculiar contact allows her to invade his troubled mind, to bypass flesh and bone. Ferrell closes his eyes and tries to focus. Today she can behold any thought he has ever had.

When he wakes he is lying naked on the boulder, the noon-white sun at the top of the sky, a blind eye staring down. Someone or something touches his arm, and he turns to find Din Winters hunkered beside him.

"I thought you were dead."

"I might have been."

"Where's Rilla?"

"Probably Rock Springs, or nearabouts. She wanted to make Wyoming before she stopped to rest."

"She left you?"

"I like to think of it as her getting even with me."

"Is she coming back?"

Ferrell struggles to sit upright. His head feels about to roll off his shoulders. He looks at Din and those mournful eyes. "Kind of like she left you too."

"You're wrong to treat her the way you do, Ferrell."

"And what way is that?"

"Like you don't need her."

"Maybe I don't."

"Like hell."

Ferrell studies the desert floor fanning out below. "What did it really feel like when your wife left?"

"Like I'd been castrated with a dull pocket knife. I didn't care if I lived or died. I even thought to speed the process along. Get things over and done."

"You'd have killed yourself over her?"

"I'd have killed myself to end the hurt. I never felt such a pain as that. There was nothing I could have done to make it lessen, let alone make it go away."

Ferrell climbs swiftly to his feet. His head becomes a confusion of lost images, of murky figures and dark vague shapes, coalescing into a time and place he once knew, but has ceased to recall. He staggers to the edge of the drop-off, palm heels pressed to his eyes, hoping to stem the memory rushing behind his closed lids.

His old house, the gravel drive, midnight. His mother in her red nightgown, beside the family car, her balled hands smacking the windshield in dull thuds. From behind the wheel his father looks perplexed, as though he doesn't know the woman pounding his green Ford LTD. He backs the car away, then steers down the steep lane, bright white cones skirting the trees.

His mother watches the taillights reach the bottom of the hill. Ferrell almost expects her to raise a hand and wave. He steps from the house and walks toward his mother, careful not to startle her. He will lead her back into the house, tuck her safe in bed. He will sit by her side in the hours to come.

When he touches her sleeve, she screams. She sprints down the long driveway, bare feet slapping the loose stones, and is overcome by the dark. Ferrell stands listening, then breaks into a run. Despite his tennis shoes, he cannot catch up to her.

At the bottom of the hill, he stops to listen. His pulse thumps in his ears like something out of control. He hears her first as a quiet whimper somewhere up ahead. He finds her in the shallow ditch as if tossed there, something broken and discarded, something unwanted.

"Mom," Ferrell says, stepping into the ditch. He sits on the bank and reaches for his mother, drawing her to him as one would a hurt child. Once in his arms she grabs him so tight he can barely breathe.

"It's okay," he says, knowing it isn't, knowing it won't ever be. "We'll be all right."

The cry arising from his mother starts as a low growl, then erupts from her mouth, not a wail or scream but something altogether different, something primal, a sustained howl that scares him more than he's ever been. When the air leaves her lungs, his mother gasps. He pulls her against him as if to smother her. In that moment of mother and child, of death and rebirth, the two of them cease to be who they had been.

"She sounded like a coyote," Ferrell says out loud. "Like a starving coyote caught in a trap."

Din furrows his brow. "Who?"

"My mother," Ferrell says, shaking his head. "It was like she forgot who or even what she was."

"I don't know what you are talking about."

"Yes, you do." Ferrell reaches down and pulls him to his feet. "Did you eat yet?"

Din shakes his head. He looks perplexed, his woeful eyes wondering what the afternoon will bring.

"Let's go make some lunch." Ferrell puts his arm around the man's shoulders. "You can tell me what Rilla truly felt."

Swan in Retreat

Despite years in the Owyhee rangelands, Ferrell hates the wind as never before. He imagines the howling gusts as soundtrack to his lackluster life, accompaniment to those nightly dreams of Ohio and his youth. In his waking hours the wind pervades his thoughts, as if to scour his mind clean of memory and regret.

Today Ferrell is moving the last of his sheep, a thankless chore. When he bought the animals his thinking seemed right: combine hot, rainless land with the durability of sheep. But the beasts turned out to be more stupid than the colleagues from his teaching days, and between coyotes and the scorching sun, he loses more lambs each year than he takes to the sale yards, where hundred-pound lambs bring thirty dollars, more highway robbery than business transaction, if someone were to ask him.

Ferrell circles the barn with his face turned from the blowing grit. At his side pasture, he opens the gate and sends the dog wide. His border collie flanks the sheep in a fluid arc, lambs and ewes turning as one. Hattie reverses direction, wheeling back in another sweeping turn, then aims the flock toward the holding pen. When the sheep have scurried through the gate, Ferrell closes it.

The man had called yesterday from Kuna asking if Ferrell had sheep to sell. Ferrell couldn't make out much on the bad connection, but he heard the word *Sarajevo,* and the rest he could figure. Some of the ranchers near Melba sell lambs to the local Bosnians, getting twice what the sale yards can offer. The Bosnians, rumor has it, arrive en masse—husbands and wives, kids and grandparents, distant relatives—and butcher the lambs right on the property, skinning and gutting with patient inefficiency, leaving hours later in their minivans or station wagons, content and happy, the blood on the ground the only sign of their efforts.

"Are you going to do this?" Rilla says, coming up behind him in her English riding getup. She's headed to the public lands, her basic plan to miss the day's events. On this latest visit to the cabin, Rilla prefers to ride Chroma straight across the BLM, no longer content to circle the corrals.

"I guess."

Last night, Rilla argued bitterly about the Bosnians: how she couldn't fathom a retired history teacher taking up sheep killing, why the hell he moved to the Wild West in the first place. Ferrell listened and shrugged. In recent years, Rilla has divided her time between the cabin and their former house in Dover, staying with Ferrell until she can't stand him another hour, then winging for Ohio to recuperate and forget his difficult ways. The arrangement has become something they never could have imagined for themselves.

"I can't believe you want holy sacrifices on your land, Ferrell," she says, taking up where she'd left off at bedtime.

The flock mills about the holding pen, bleating reassurances. The beasts have already calmed down, the ordeal of the dog fading from memory. In the bright sun they look almost wise, though Ferrell knows there isn't much wattage in the dark caverns of their skulls. Beside him, the dog sits wild-eyed and trembling, her work ethic too strong to suit Ferrell. He knows the dog could herd all day and still not be satisfied. It makes him tired thinking about it.

Ferrell glances east to a caravan negotiating the lane, dust plumes blown sideways. Rilla huffs and walks off. He watches her leg-up into the saddle, adjust her riding crop to her left hand, straighten her black helmet. Without visible signal she moves the horse into a walk. As the cars and vans park beside the cabin, Rilla canters down the drive, then moves Chroma into a run, each hoof raising small explosions of dust.

When the caravan has parked, Ferrell waits, but nothing happens. He stands buffeted by the wind, perhaps a dozen pairs of eyes trained in his direction, then doors open and slam until he's surrounded. An older man dressed in white steps forward, the designated spokesperson, Ferrell assumes.

"We come for sheep," he says, the voice from the phone. "I am Javad."

Ferrell points to the holding pen, deciding directness and simplicity is the way to go. "Take your pick," he says.

The visitors crowd the fence, as if in reverence. Ferrell guesses four generations stand before him, a single bloodline reaching from the toothless man leaning on the gate to the babies bundled in their young mothers' arms.

"How many do you want?" Ferrell asks when the leader has looked the sheep over.

"All."

"You want to buy every one of them?"

"Yes, all." The man studies Ferrell as if he were slow-witted. "We take seven today and then come back. We take all by two weeks' end."

"That's twenty head," Ferrell says. "What will you do with them?"

"We cook and eat, in the park. We have many family and blankets on the ground. We eat and have drink as we have always done. In Bosnia, we do this. So here, of course, we do this."

Without discussion, three of the younger men enter the pen and wade into the flock. Javad speaks to them in their mother tongue, points and gestures. One of the moorit bucks is singled out and cornered. The men wrestle the lamb out the gate and onto the driveway.

"Here?" Javad asks.

Ferrell notices for the first time the substantial knives the women carry. Javad slides his finger across his throat in a way that doesn't warm Ferrell's heart. He pictures Rilla riding down the blood-soaked drive.

"Behind the barn," he says.

On bad days Ferrell wonders where his life has gone—an age-old inquiry, he understands, but knowing his thoughts are timeless doesn't help his mood. His flesh and bones may be sixty-plus, but his eyes still see with the same crying ache as ever, as if acute yearning were the natural order of things, as if his smoldering heart were about to catch flame. At dusk he gushes at the setting sun like a Hallmark poet, like a lovestruck boy swooning for the first time.

This morning the melancholy clings to Ferrell like a second skin. Nothing but blue overhead, the sun a great gold star, yet Ferrell walks beneath a dark gloom. He ponders the source of his unease, not sure why he feels so rattled. Is it yesterday's knives and those horrible last gasps? The black blood on the ground? He pushes these questions from his mind, puzzles to save for his evening shots, the only time he tries to figure out his life.

Ferrell spends the morning avoiding chores around his homestead. After eight years in Idaho, these last five with Rilla often at his side, the novelty of physical work has worn off, and Ferrell knows why he wasn't a farmer to begin with: busting your ass gets old, however noble the calling.

In the forenoon, Rilla saddles up without speaking a word. Ferrell is pumping water into the trough beside the barn, but he might be invisible for all Rilla notices him. She hasn't spoken since the Bosnians' visit, returning from her ride with the sole purpose of avoiding him. She stayed on the porch while he cooked dinner, her anger bringing an early dusk. After going to bed, he heard her in the kitchen, the clinking of flatware the loudest sounds in the night.

Now Rilla canters from the cabin, riding with a purpose he wishes he shared. She looks for all the world like she isn't coming back. Ferrell watches until she and the horse fade into the wavering horizon, a final scene from a Western he once saw.

With Rilla physically gone, she gallops back into his head.

He thinks of every time one of them has stormed off mad, the decades of tempest and turmoil they've shared. Against better sense, Ferrell still wakes believing this will be the day they get their lives on track.

Growing up, Ferrell often heard his dad promise to *be a better person.* "Tomorrow is a day of monumental change," he would announce at dinner. "A new me from now to god-damn eternity. I'm turning over a new leaf. Just watch me shine."

But to Ferrell, his father only got worse. Maynard cultivated aloneness like it was the key to salvation, his mood storms coming with greater frequency and duration. On the bus to school, Ferrell could feel his father's curse harbored in his own blood, encrypted in his cells: those inexplicable angers and festering grievances, against loved and unloved alike, that lack of passion and joy. He'd watch the fields slide past, the corn as tall as the man he was becoming, and wonder if willpower alone could thwart the dictator seeking to rule his heart.

In the late afternoon Rilla rides through the gate, dust-covered and sweaty, an English princess abandoned on the American frontier. In her eyes is that look she gets when she rides long and hard—as if she's had a few words with God and has some inside news.

Rilla reins Chroma to a halt beside Ferrell and dismounts. "That was almost worth it," she says.

"How far did you go?" Ferrell says, surprised she has spoken. If he can keep the conversation in gear, they'll be rolling to another temporary reconciliation.

"Far enough."

"Did you see any coyotes?"

"No."

"Mustangs?"

Rilla rolls her eyes. "I know prompting when it comes my way."

"We can change, Rilla. Do better."

Ferrell toes the powdery dust with his boot. He hadn't planned on blurting things out, especially tired lines from daytime soaps, but the words had leapt before his lips could block the way.

Rilla stops in the drive, legs braced. She looks surprised at his invitation to enter the fray.

"Oh, hell, Ferrell, it's been hit or miss for years. You want to be alone more than you want someone around. You want to make love when the urge strikes—and god bless you for that—but beyond sweaty sheets you don't need or want much else."

"At least we're not codependent."

"If I wanted absolute freedom, I'd have stayed in Ohio. Alone, I wouldn't have to put up with your moody disposition. I'd have the perks of going solo, and none of this extra work."

"But you like it here."

"Ferrell, it's like living on the face of the moon. For awhile you're Neil Armstrong, getting inspired over distance and space, that view of your planet far away. But then, in short order, you miss home."

Rilla touches him lightly on the sleeve. "I miss seeing things grow," she says. "I miss the smell of rain."

"What about your riding, all those acres of desert to roam?"

"Riding the open range has been seriously overrated. Usually, I get out there and feel all shrunk down, like the planet's too big or I'm too small. Maybe both."

"When are you leaving?"

"Dammit," Rilla says, stepping close. "Don't always accept my leaving like that. Beg me to stay this time, or beg to come with me. For Christsakes, beg for something, anything."

"Okay, stay."

Rilla takes his face in her sweaty hands. Her eyes show neither anger nor pain, only something he'd call calm weariness. "Let's get the hell out of Dodge," she says. "Move back home with me."

"I'll think about it."

"You and your damn head, Ferrell. I wish you'd run on pure want for once."

"I can try."

"You don't fucking *try* to want something, Ferrell." Rilla starts toward the cabin, then turns to face him. "We weren't raised here, you know. These stark rhythms aren't in our blood. Our brains aren't used to daily dust and wind."

Friday at noon, the caravan returns. Ferrell steps onto the porch as the Bosnians pour from their vehicles, an invasion of his secret desert stronghold. As before, dressed all in white, Javad alone approaches him. Ferrell remembers that as Javad drew the knife across on their first visit, his youngest son had let go of the lamb. The animal's head and chest had heaved from the ground, splattering Javad in his pristine clothes. Red drops had arced gracefully onto Ferrell's boots. He'd gone inside to wipe them clean.

"Mr. Swan," Javad says. "Today is my daughter's date of birth. We will need your best ram for this, and two others, if possible."

"You know what I have," Ferrell says.

Javad signals to another of his sons, a gangly boy in his teens. The whole mob turns together and moves toward the barn. Javad steps forward and climbs the porch steps, a place he's not yet been. He takes out a small leather purse and counts the money into Ferrell's palm.

"How many children do you have?" Ferrell asks.

"Ten in all, from the ages of eight to twenty-one."

"That's a lot of mouths to feed."

"As well as many strong hands."

"My stepson wouldn't lift a finger when he was home. He ran off at seventeen. We see him mostly to handle the trouble he finds. I don't even know where he's living."

"I had such a son. My Sali would not expend himself for anyone. He also refused to share our roof, once he came of age."

"Where is he now?"

"We buried him before we left Sarajevo. He did not last on his own two years with his reckless ways." The man studies Ferrell with rapt attention, his eyes seeing him, it seems, as mythic fellow traveler and not a man selling sheep. They've moved from a transaction older than Moses, from something other than the exchange of Roman coins.

"I'm sorry," Ferrell says.

"When it came to Sali, everyone was sorry. Even the police who shot my son were very much sorry. They knew him well and do not want to pull their triggers." Javad glances at the empty driveway. His extended family has disappeared behind the barn. "We still wake expecting Sali to come home. We open our eyes and think we hear him shouting and stumbling about."

"Our Levon always seems confined in his own skin."

"Confined?"

"Held captive, like a prisoner."

"Ah," Javad says. "Yes, a prisoner. I, too, feel like a prisoner without having a proper place to rest my head."

"But you're in a new country," Ferrell says. "A new home."

"New country, yes, not home." Javad motions to the distant mountains sprawled before them. "This is where we live, but Bosnia is where our mothers birthed us."

"Will you go back?" Ferrell says, not sure why he wants to know, only that he does.

"God has not told me, but I hope he allows my bones to sleep beside those of my son." As if about to fall, Javad reaches for the rail in front of him. He holds on tight with both hands, his eyes raised to the sky. Ferrell believes himself witness to another siege in a prolonged war. With everything we have to endure, Ferrell thinks, it's a wonder we get out of bed.

Someone shouts for Javad, and he nods once to Ferrell—all the communication, it seems, he can offer. He starts down the steps, raising his hand over his shoulder in silent farewell.

Ferrell watches him go, the man's shoulders slumped in the posture of defeat.

In the days that follow, Rilla books a flight, rescues her suitcases from the anarchy of her closet. Despite feeble attempts at affection, Ferrell fails to win her back. He decides it's best to respond to the call *before* she loses faith in him, not in the smoking ruins after.

At noon on Sunday, the Bosnians arrive for the rest of the flock. Rilla stays inside the house, refusing to leave the bedroom. Ferrell keeps a low profile as the Bosnians go about their tasks, which will take the rest of the afternoon. After Javad pays him in all twenties, Ferrell sits on the porch with his evening whiskey. He needs a soothing cocktail hour, despite the high altitude of the sun. He's had his fill of sheep death, wants no more of the heavy scent of their blood, of those smooth shiny organs revealed to the air. He pours whiskey and stands the bottle beside the rocker. His tumbler looks molten in the sun. Rilla, he decides, will never understand the miracle of Lagavulin.

Javad climbs the steps when everything is done. "If you have more lambs, please use the telephone."

"No more sheep," Ferrell says, shaking his head. "Just that horse there is all I'll be caring for."

"And your wife."

"She hasn't been my wife for years."

"And still she stays."

"Comes and goes, more like."

"Your ways are different from ours."

"Same problems, though," Ferrell says, letting the whiskey decide which words he'll use.

"Your way offers no solution to your troubles."

"Are you some kind of priest?"

"In my country, I was the operator of a truck. What is your occupation?"

"I *was* a teacher," Ferrell says. "History."

"You are very special, then," Javad says, reaching out to shake his hand. "You understand all that has come before. You know more than the common man."

"Not even close," Ferrell says.

As the Bosnians drive off for the final time, Ferrell raises his glass to their dust. The screen door slaps and Rilla stands at the porch rail, her back to him.

"It's done?" she says.

Ferrell's not sure if she means the sheep or them. "There's no one here but us."

"That's never been enough, has it?"

"Sometimes it has." Ferrell can feel the bravery of the whiskey. True courage or not, he'll take what he can get. "You must have nothing but regret, Rilla. I mean all this time spent on a man who always lets you down?"

"We're too old for self-pity." Rilla reaches down for the bottle, refills his glass. She takes the glass from his hand like an offering. "This stuff any better than last time?"

"Besides you, it's the one thing that gets better with age."

Rilla ignores his lame remark, sips whiskey instead. "Jesus Henry Christ," she says, wiping her eyes on her sleeve. She gives him a look of cool intensity he'd like to escape.

"What gets better, Ferrell Swan, is our ability to spend time apart."

"That's saying something."

The sun hides behind the barricade of the mountains. Rilla hands Ferrell the glass, and he drinks his share of the communion they've begun. "We'll make love when it gets dark," she says. "Right here, on the porch."

"I thought we didn't plan?"

Rilla takes the glass, drinks, and doesn't sputter. She delivers it back to his hand. "We'll do things in your honor tonight. Drinking and fucking."

Ferrell looks at his glass. He can't rally enough enthusiasm to protest her remark.

"Okay," she says, "that was low and mean. Undignified, too."

"Probably true, though."

"Oh hell, most things are true about most of us most of the time."

"Where's that from?"

"I just made it up." Rilla takes her turn at the glass, eyes shut. "I'll leave the horse, decide what to do with her later."

"She'll be here when you come back."

"I'm not sure I'll be back for a while."

"Then I'll ride her to Ohio on the Swan express."

A spell of quiet falls over them, and Ferrell knows they've depleted their pitiful stockpile of words. He watches a redtail turn on the late afternoon thermals, circling high above the barn. As the hawk passes directly over the cabin, Ferrell admires the undersides of those terrific wings, the intricate design fired in the afterglow.

"I'm looking forward to missing you," Rilla says after more time has passed. "To feeling those good feelings once again. Isn't that something, Ferrell, to look forward to missing someone?"

"I guess I look better from a distance."

Rilla drinks as if taking the bitterest of medicine. "Out here, it's like we are the last people on the planet sometimes."

"Or the first."

"No, it's definitely more end-of-the-world." Rilla sets the glass on the porch boards. "No more talk," she says, rising from her chair. She settles into his lap and runs her hands over his bald head. She brings her lips to his own in a long kiss of good-bye.

"I'm dying, Ferrell," she says when the kiss is done.

"What?"

"You are, too."

"You mean bit by bit?"

"I mean no matter how you cut it, we are running on fumes. Our time's nearly expired, the ride's about over. Lord, I can feel the cold breath of mortality breathing down my neck as we speak."

"Then don't speak."

They drive out at midnight beneath those billion stars, the pale mist of the Milky Way dividing the sky. As they drive, dying stars spew fiery trails, sear imprints upon Ferrell's eyes. Rilla stays turned from him, facing the black desert as if she expects her savior to appear. They cross the Snake and stop for gas past the bridge. As the tank fills, Ferrell searches for the water slithering into the distance. Rilla comes back from the restroom and climbs into the cab, a stranger he is taking to the airport in Boise, a hitchhiker picked up along the deserted highway. Ferrell marvels how dawdling their progress has been toward peaceful coexistence, yet how fast they reverse direction—become separate at warp speed, unknown to each other and themselves.

Ferrell pulls onto his dusty lane around midmorning. He parks in the drive and shuts the motor off, staring out the bug-spattered windshield at his barn of faded red, at the side pastures now empty. From the corral, Rilla's horse watches him intently. Chroma knows Ferrell's the new keeper of the hay.

As he expected, the house isn't the same inside: just walls and a ceiling, a few rooms. His hours ahead loom uncharted and full of rocky shoals. He feels inclined to take to bed and skip the daylight altogether. Back outside Ferrell stands at the fence, his arms folded on the top rail. He stares at the mountains heaved straight from the desert floor. He notices the air is absolutely calm, the still leaves as if painted on the trees. He wonders why it's always this way: too little, too late, the day perfect and Rilla half a continent gone. With this pretty day unfolding, Ferrell does the only thing he can. He gets the scotch whiskey from the kitchen, clinks two ice cubes into a glass, and takes to the porch to await the desperate fall of the sun.

Ferrell's enjoying the second half of the bottle when he spots the car—Rilla somehow returned. But he knows it can't be, not with her airborne at six hundred miles per hour. The car parks beside his pickup and sits idling, its dark tinted windows full of menace. Has violence found him at last, he wonders, sought him out across the wide expanse? When the door opens, the old Bosnian steps out like a messenger from afar. He's dressed in white, as always, yet no entourage follows him from the other doors. Javad strolls alone to the steps of the porch.

"I come for lambs," he says in some weird desert déjà vu.

"You bought them all," Ferrell says. "Their mamas too. I told you there'd be no more."

"People change ideas. You may have birthed more lambs."

"Without any ewes?

"One can hope for anything."

"One can hope too much."

Ferrell hears the scotch call his name, but he doesn't want to drink under the scrutiny of another man. Javad glances at the glass in Ferrell's hand, then at Ferrell's feet, where the bottle sits waiting.

"You are celebrating?"

"Opposite, more like."

The Bosnian stands patiently in the sun, a pilgrim come a long way for truth and willing to wait.

"Oh, hell," Ferrell says. "My ex went home again." He reaches for the scotch and pours himself three fingers, plus a few extra for good measure. "Can't live with 'em . . ."

"With whom?"

"Wives," Ferrell says and raises his glass. "I've had three myself. Lord bless them, every one."

Javad folds his arms across his chest. "You have two glasses?" he says.

"What?"

"A second glass?"

"You are a fan of the demon rum?"

"Is that not Lagavulin?"

"Oh, Lordy," Ferrell says.

By dusk Ferrell has a new best friend, the two men bonding, he knows, in ways only two bottles of the finest scotch
can achieve. Beside him Javad rocks in Rilla's rocker, sipping
from a shot glass Levon stole in Jackpot. From the porch
the scrubland extends to where the sky swoops down, and
Ferrell has the distinct impression they sit inside a stupen-
dous theater. He imagines they're awaiting the start of the
world's greatest show, though what that show will be he
won't guess.

Sunlight fans into columns, spotlighting the corral where
Chroma prances for her evening hay. Ferrell pours their shot
glasses to the brim. In the past hours they've discussed sheep
raising, truck driving, their boyhoods, and the weather in
Sarajevo. They're men speaking with time between their
sentences, men thinking and drinking more than anything
else. To Ferrell's dismay he notes the sun will soon set, and
darkness will wash the cabin from its foundation.

"Won't your wife be worried?" Ferrell asks. "Sun's going down."

"Worried, yes. Angry too."

"Will you be in trouble?"

"Oh, very much trouble." Javad holds his glass up, then drains it like a gunslinger. "Sari will yell and break some things, perhaps slap my cheeks. She is a very vibrant woman."

"Then what?"

"Some things are private, even between men."

Ferrell reaches out and pats Javad on the back. "So how long under the yoke?"

"If you mean wedded bliss, thirty years and still not parted." Javad winks with elegant flair. "You think I should have instruction for you? Wisdom of pearls?"

"Well?"

"Sari and I have no more harmony than the governments of foreign nations."

"You must get along?"

"In God's name, no. Fights, grievances, indiscretions never forgotten or forgiven. Sari harbors angers at words I spoke when we were young and without common sense. Yet we stay. We battle, we rest ourselves. We threaten and shout loudly, we lovemake with great vigor. Always we wake with our wedding bands still on our fingers."

"Hallelujah," Ferrell says.

"All big joke, men and women seeing eye to eye. My idea is God is more mischievous. He makes women so nobody gets bored. God has much humor in his heart. He has laugh lines around his eyes."

Ferrell feels expansive tenderness toward this new friend at this side. "Amen."

"Do you know how to ride that horse?" Javad says.

"Some."

"When I was a boy I was often on a horse's back. My father had much land, and many horses. Now I don't own the small space beneath my family's feet, nor the roof over their heads."

Ferrell stands and leans against the rail. He surveys the darkening horizon, the earth curving down to circle back behind them. He understands what they are destined to do.

"Follow me," he says.

In the corral, Javad slips on the bridle and saddle with ease. An evening wind picks up, blowing dust and grit. The coolness jolts the horse like a shock, her head swinging up and down, her hooves sidestepping as if she cannot contain her elation. Javad puts his foot in the stirrup and swings gracefully onto the saddle. He reaches down an open hand.

"Grab," he says. "We'll ride together."

Ferrell extends his arm and is pulled right up. He scrambles to sit behind the cantle, arms encircling Javad's plump middle. The man smells of cheap cologne and exotic spices.

At the gate, Javad unlatches the hook while mounted on Chroma's back. The horse is beside herself with the call of the desert dusk, and Javad can barely hold her from breaking into a gallop. When they reach the place where the BLM runs far and deep, Javad reins up short, those ten thousand acres as if they've never been crossed.

And then they are free, with nothing but the ground beneath them and the first stars above. In this open territory, Javad lets the horse have her will, and she trots, then canters, then gallops flat out, leaving Ferrell hanging on, wild with delight. He clings tight as Javad steers toward the flaring sunset. Chroma runs like no sun will ever rise again, her legs seeking all the speed she can find.

Ferrell leans close as gravity pulls. He hears Javad's breath billow from his lungs, the man struggling to keep them both onboard. Against his will, Ferrell thinks of his lonely father, years dead in the terrible ground, that black curse surviving in his son. He pictures Rilla unlocking the door to her vacant home, imagines Levon out in L.A. or Vegas, Jackpot perhaps, hunting trouble down. Javad's own son, finding too much as the bullets fly. Ferrell's no sheriff in pursuit, he understands, but the one pursued, an outlaw of his own design. He imagines himself and Javad as desperadoes without hearth or kin. Butch and Sundance, on the run. His heart rides high, and he yells because he must, yells into a world both damned and saved.

Swan's Home

For my soul is full of troubles,
and my life draweth nigh unto the grave.
Psalms 88:3

The call comes at high noon, with the sun bright on the rocks and sage, not in the dark midnight hours like Ferrell has always expected. On her cell phone from Ohio, Rilla asks if he's sitting down.

"You bet," Ferrell says, standing at the porch rail. He looks across the sun-blasted country, knowing the news is about Levon. Such trouble from preschool to high school, and not a whole lot's changed.

"What'd he do this time?" he says when she doesn't volunteer the words.

"He crashed his car."

"Bad?"

The quiet on the line sets Ferrell's knees trembling. He

hopes for anything but Levon being dead, anything else but that. He tries to steer his thoughts from the tragic, but that never helps when it comes to a child, whatever the age.

"Real bad." Rilla goes silent again, allowing Ferrell to hear every mile between him and the charming brick house where Rilla huddles alone.

"I'll get a flight," Ferrell says, already planning the two-hour drive to the airport. "I'll try to be there tomorrow."

"Try very hard," Rilla says and hangs up.

Ferrell pockets his cell phone in disgust, high-tech messenger of bad news. He studies the colossal smoke columns above Oregon, a half million acres, the radio reports, burning out of control. It has been the worst fire season in a century, months of no rain and hundred degree days, the air itself ready to burst into flames. Over the summer, Ferrell has seen wildfire from each direction of his isolated home, nights lit in garish orange and red, the horizon aglow as if the fires of hell have broken through. In daylight hours, the smoke pouring from behind the Owyhees seems a sign of distant war, the bombing of far-off cities.

Last night, Ferrell recalls, the full moon had risen so deeply crimson it scared him, a horrible sunset, he imagined, run backward in the smoky haze. Watching the smoldering moon, Ferrell heard his dead mother quoting scripture, something about the moon running the color of blood, a signal terrible events were about to begin.

The plane ride east might as well be a rocket trip to the stars, following as it does Ferrell's Wild West years. After his oil lamps and solitude, his propane fridge and woodstove, lifting off into the clouds seems a sort of miracle.

Once out of Boise, Ferrell can see burning in the remote forests near Cambridge, another locale in flame. He refuses the complimentary beverage, anticipating the unsteady trek down the wobbly plane. Of late, he seems to drink less and use the bathroom more, wasting away a day at a time. He understands now why his great-grandfather lived on gin in his twilight years.

As the plane steadily climbs, Ferrell thinks of young Harry, four years old now and growing each hour. Last night, Ferrell had to walk down the road with the news about Levon. Melody stood in the Coles' spacious living room, Harry riding her hip, and seemed crippled with fear, her face so white Ferrell worried she would faint. He reached out and gently took the child, and Cole helped his wife over to the couch, where they sat in their mutual shock, trying hard to process the crash and its implication for their lives.

Looking out his small glass portal, Ferrell pulls himself back from the slippery slope of his thoughts, knows the absolute futility of pondering one's knotty life.

Rilla stands outside security, looking worse for wear. She smiles bravely at seeing him, holds him tight when he comes close. For the last year, Rilla has wanted Ferrell to come home, to give up his desert exile and move back to the place of his birth. You need people, Ferrell, she has said. You need family. No, he's told her. I do not.

"Levon?" Ferrell says when she releases him.

"Still critical, but they may upgrade today."

"You know Levon won't give up the ghost. He's too afraid he'd miss something."

Rilla's lips tighten into a thin line, as if he's criticized Levon in his hour of need. "Let's get your bags."

On the ride south from Akron, Ferrell learns the specifics of the crash, of the damage velocity times weight imposes upon a healthy young man. Levon was coming home late from the bars in Dover, racing the winding back roads, when he plowed into a tree. A common fate, Ferrell knows, often repeated in their rural hinterland.

Moths to a flame, he thinks.

Rilla relates this information staring at the complicated freeway traffic heading to Columbus. Ferrell studies the lush countryside sliding past, awed by miles of rich green corn and wooded hills. After living among the tumbleweeds, his heart tightens at what he's been missing. Compared to this flowing teat before him, he lives on arid Mars.

Hours later, off the rushing freeway, Rilla steers them through their old stomping grounds. The shady streets of New Philadelphia look mostly the same—trim lawns fronting immaculate houses, impressive brickwork. At the domed county courthouse, the lone cannon still guards the front steps. They pass Tuscora Park with its Ferris wheel and sparkling swimming pool, its green pond with an armada of white ducks. Ferrell had expected more change—all that not-going-home-again business—but the town doesn't seem that different. What is different is the traffic, as if most of Cleveland has driven south for the day, the main thoroughfares snarled and congested in a way that makes Ferrell feel trapped.

As he worried she would do, Rilla drives him straight to Union Hospital. Scaffolding covers the building like a cage, a brand-new wing under construction, the room where Ferrell was born blocked from view. Rilla wheels them into the shade of a parking garage Ferrell doesn't remember.

"Be ready, Ferrell," she says. "He's done it good, this time."

While she guides him across the lobby and into a crowded elevator, Ferrell feels a growing dread. He has never been fond of hospitals, reminders of mortality as they are. He's always been a weakling when it comes to dying. As a young man, he'd been thrown violently off track when J.F.K. went down, when Marilyn wasn't alive in her bed come morning. Martin Luther King, lost on that quiet spring balcony. Saint Bobby on the floor, haloed in blood. Janis and Jimi, that whole legion of dead musicians, O.D.'d or plane crashed, it mattered not. Superhuman Bruce Lee, dying without a whimper in his sleep. *Challenger*, a fireball in the sky.

Princess Diana, Lord almighty.

On the third floor, Rilla leads Ferrell through the double doors of the ICU. She heads to a petite nurse behind a futuristic desk, command central to five glass rooms. In each chamber, a fellow human lies amidst props from *Star Trek*—electronic gadgets too strange for Ferrell to imagine their purpose. He spots Levon in the last of the rooms. Rilla urges Ferrell in first, her hand to the small of his back. He stands beside the metal rails of the bed, looking down upon the boy he had once rocked to sleep. Levon's face is unrecognizable, bruised and swollen until his features have disappeared. The dozen black stitches along his hairline seem too neat and tidy in the bloated face.

"Christ," Ferrell says.

"Take his hand. Let him know you're here."

Ferrell grips Levon's cool dry palm. The boy has always sought freedom from his own hide, and here he is at last, brought to the brink of actual release.

"Does he ever wake?"

Rilla shakes her head. "It's not a coma exactly, more like sleep they tell me." She circles to the opposite side of the bed, reaches down and takes Levon's other hand. "Swan's home, sweetheart," she says. "He's come back to see you."

If this were television, Ferrell knows, the hand would squeeze him tight, let him know recovery hangs around the bend. Nothing happens but the beeping machines and Levon lying still.

The next morning, Ferrell wakes into his past life. He lies on his back and studies a ceiling he'd studied for seventeen years. When he lifts his head, a stage setting surrounds him: her scratched armoire, his ancient dresser, the frayed love-seat they'd bought at a yard sale in Baltic. After she moved back into the house, Rilla must have put everything where it had originally stood. Ferrell sits up in bed, an actor in his own dismal life story. It's another day at Dover High, Rilla already dressed for work, their mutual coffee brewed. In this other time, Levon would be asleep in his room down the hall, all-night heavy metal blaring forth, not across town in the ICU.

Downstairs, Ferrell does find Rilla and fresh coffee, but she wears a frayed terry cloth robe, her long red hair tinged with gray.

"Welcome home," she says, handing Ferrell a steaming cup.

"Good to be."

"I was thinking how strange it is to have you in this house. You know, for years I've only seen Ferrell Swan with those Idaho distances behind him, spectacular mountains and boundless chaparral. It's like you don't seem you without the panoramic backdrop."

"Well, good morning right back at you."

"Oh, Ferrell, I'm not being mean. I'm just in an odd frame of mind, saying my thoughts out loud. I'm not trying to start anything."

"Cheers," Ferrell says and sips his coffee.

As if abruptly forgetting him, Rilla sits down at the kitchen table. She looks bewildered and forlorn. Why such a good woman has needed this many hard lessons, Ferrell has never understood. It seems she long ago got the message: life will fuck with you until you're dead. He joins her at his old place setting before he knows what he's done.

"Have you called the hospital?" he says, real pain in his heart.

"He's improved some. They said he'll probably make it out of the ICU by the weekend."

"That's good."

"He scared me bad this time, Ferrell."

"You and me both."

"For real?" Rilla reaches out and takes his hand. "I mean you and he have never been best buddies."

"But deep down I want the boy to pull it together. I always hope something will click in his brain, that he'll figure out a way to find some peace."

"Some people don't get it out of their system until they reach their thirties or forties."

"You're saying Levon might have years of hell-raising left?"

"We can only hope."

In the coming days, he and Rilla hold vigil outside the ICU. They take turns driving home for showers and short furious bouts of sleep, eating something only because they must. Levon doesn't wake, and so they keep their eyes open for him, guarding their son from an unforgiving world. Ferrell's mind grows hazy from lack of sleep, the hectic halls of the hospital viewed as if inside a dream. On the evening of the third day, Ferrell parks in Rilla's drive, once his driveway, too, and stares at the house. The pale red light fanning out behind the roof seems not the sunset, but the glow of burning close at hand, destruction on an epic scale. He believes the fires of the West have hunted him down, traversed the Great Plains in search of his scrawny ass.

Ferrell is an intruder inside the house. At the kitchen table he drinks coffee besieged by ghosts of their former selves: Rilla on the couch with case studies from work, Levon destroying his room, Ferrell himself at this spot, grading papers with his trusty red pen. In his head he is everywhere at once, at all points in time, each moment so vivid he wants to cry. Through the doorway, he spots their wedding portrait hanging in the hall, their faces airbrushed to make them blissful, clueless about the struggles ahead. Ferrell lifts his cup to his younger self, wishes him the best of luck.

Five days after slamming into a tree, Levon wakes up. Ferrell and Rilla are in the room, standing at their places on either side of the bed. Levon looks at Ferrell as if *he* were the one returned from the shadowy netherworld.

"What the hell?" Levon says. "Ferrell's in O-HI-fuck-ing-O?"

"I thought cheating death would make you more personable, son."

Rilla interrupts their standard father-son repertoire. "You scared us, honey."

"Was it bad?"

"It was touch and go." Rilla brushes Levon's bruised cheek with her fingertips. "You're going to need some time to recover."

"So I'm back from the dead?"

"In a manner of speaking."

Levon turns to Ferrell and winks. "What do you know, Ferrell. A new goddamn start."

"Your forte, son."

"What do you remember?" Rilla says. "Do you remember what happened?"

"I remember "Born to Run" on the radio. You cannot *ever* drive slow to that song."

"The police estimate you were doing seventy when you hit."

Levon looks at his mother. "And what *did* I hit?"

"A tree, honey. You hit a tree."

"This fucking state always did have too many trees. I should be out there with you, Ferrell. Your dustbowl only has a couple puny cottonwoods."

"And you'd probably run into one of those."

"That's for sure, Ferrell. That's for damn sure."

With Levon intent on recovering, Ferrell has extra time on his hands. Rilla carts him across Tuscarawas County like a zealous tour guide, compelled to prove the splendor of their land. She takes Ferrell to Der Dutchman, an Amish restaurant perched on a scenic hill, where they eat lunch with hundreds of bus tour folk from parts unknown. Afterward, Rilla wheels past the photogenic Amish farms, dodging those creeping black buggies as if on her own private obstacle course.

Late one afternoon, without revealing their destination, Rilla drives toward the hilltop plots of Ridge Crest. When she turns up the steep drive, he protests loudly. If hospitals make him squirm, then cemeteries do something worse, have been places to avoid his whole life. Rilla parks at the highest point in the county and sits holding the wheel. Far below, the town is one of those realistic train tableaux Levon used to build: scale-model streets lined with little trees, the thin silvery Tuscarawas and the diminutive factories along its banks, the two-lane bridge next to the old trestle.

"I'll stay here," Ferrell says.

Rilla gets out and waits at the front bumper. She leans against the hood until Ferrell climbs from the car.

"You know I get the willies," he says.

"I know."

Rilla starts down the hill, working her way between the scores of flat bronze markers. Ferrell hesitates, then follows her across the grass. Rilla weaves slowly among the markers, searching left and right. At last she kneels before a grave. When Ferrell catches up, he reads the fancy-lettered names of his mother and father. Below their names is Ferrell's own, already forged into the bronze:

FERRELL SWAN

1941–

BELOVED SON

After the old man's death, Ferrell's mother asked if *Ferrell Swan* could be scripted onto the new family marker. She wanted all their names added at the same time, said she wanted to join them now as they would be joined later. Though a small matter at the time, Ferrell doesn't care for seeing his name among the dead. A man, he decides, should not view his grave while standing on his feet.

"I thought it would be good to visit your people, Ferrell. Pay your respects."

Ferrell doesn't take his eyes from the marker. Two yards below their names his parents rest side by side, united in death as they never were in life. "I'll be here plenty when the time comes," Ferrell says. "We'll visit then."

"You take self-absorption to new heights. I swear you're the most inconsiderate man ever to draw air."

Due west, the descending sun turns vaporous over the

town, such a picturesque little village. Ferrell wonders if sadness reigns inside *all* those pretty homes.

"Is this really the place to argue, Rilla?"

"Better than most." Rilla waves her arms to include the entire hillside. "You won't say anything these souls haven't heard, and they sure as hell can keep a secret."

"I wouldn't be so sure. You don't know but all of purgatory isn't whispering our secrets as we sleep."

"Look, Ferrell. I thought you'd experience some family history here, maybe feel part of a bigger something. We're looking for connection, a sense of belonging to a place."

"Who says you *belong* to the damn place you're from?"

"Well, no one *belongs* in the middle of nowhere."

"Some do."

"Ferrell, you've had years in the desert. Isn't that enough?"

"But I still *want* to live out west."

"Oh, Ferrell, you've always done what you wanted. You've never figured out there are other people involved. Every action you take will somehow affect the ones in your sphere of influence. Someone pays a price for everything you do, Ferrell. Nothing's without consequence. Not a goddamn thing."

"Well, I guess I shouldn't breathe then."

"Think about your father. Or mine. Levon's own deadbeat dad. Each man doing whatever the hell he wanted, others be damned. Where did it get them, Ferrell?"

"It got them the life they chose."

"But what did they leave behind? Shouldn't something be left behind, other than wrecked hearts and fucked-up lives?"

"I'm sure those boys made someone smile."

"When my dad died, the words for the eulogy came few and far between. And *your* dad had no one at his funeral but your mother, his brother, and us. Doesn't that tell you something?"

"That no one will come to my funeral?"

Rilla sits on the nicely mown grass, as if the effort of her words has taken her strength. "Almost everybody's here, Ferrell," she says and draws her knees to her chest. "We live in a world of strangers."

Ferrell eases down onto the grass. He slips an arm over Rilla's shoulders and pulls her close. He wants to say she's absolutely right, that we are only ever among strangers, either with family or friends, lovers or spouses. Hell, on any given minute of any given day, we're strangers to ourselves.

Days add up to weeks, and Ferrell's still home. He and Rilla make daily pilgrimages to the hospital, where Levon continues to mend, but afterward find themselves without plan or obligation. As they slalom through the twisting back roads, Ferrell notices the leaves have gone to red and orange and yellow, the earth tilting into a new season. He hasn't seen this much autumnal glory in years, and feels more than inspired.

On a brisk Monday morning, Ferrell volunteers to do the weekly shopping. He steers Rilla's car down streets of nostalgic fall trees. When he passes Dover High, the curb is lined with yellow buses, kids streaming into the school's double doors. Another school year has gotten under way. Out of habit, he pulls into the faculty lot and parks.

At the flagpole in the quad, Ferrell stops short. Before him sprawls the brick citadel where he served for three decades. In his blood he feels the old stirrings, recalls that quivery excitement of a new semester. He could be thirty years old right now, leather satchel in hand, gearing up the day's lesson in his head—bloody Gettysburg, the Louisiana Purchase, the grueling Oregon Trail. If he were thirty the year would be 1971: Rilla not yet back in his life, Levon not born, divorced bachelor living. With commanding authority the tardy bell rings in the building, the year '71 or '05 Ferrell's not exactly sure. When he flexes his right hand, the satchel isn't there.

Faced with deserted hallways, Ferrell hesitates for the second time since stepping from the car. He doesn't know why he's here, let alone which direction to take. Across the lobby, glass showcases preserve time. Portraits of Dover High teachers since 1920 hang above a forest of polished trophies. His young self peers out with too much confidence, and Ferrell does an about-face on this trip down memory lane. His hand reaches the door as footfalls approach.

It's Tom Decker, his buddy from grad school, matchmaker of Ferrell and Rilla. Decker and he started at Dover the same year, but while Ferrell avoided administrative duties, Decker sought them out. For years he's served as principal of the school. "Ferrell Fitzgerald Swan, back from the promised land."

Ferrell extends his hand, but Decker embraces him instead, pounds hard on his back. "My god, Ferrell, you're a damn string bean. Can't you trap enough food out there in the wilderness?"

"Looks like you haven't had that problem."

Decker rubs his round paunch. "Enough manly repartee, Ferrell. Come to the office and we'll catch up."

Ferrell and Decker stroll the quiet halls, passing classroom after classroom, old friends—Neil Marks, Jim Nixon, Gertrude Hertz—standing before new kids. In one classroom he spies Randall Myers, his archrival, a teacher spellbinding in his mediocrity.

"Your best buddy," Decker whispers as they pass.

"How's he doing?"

"I'm still amazed the man can find his pecker."

When Ferrell enters Decker's outer office, Gladys Smythe, veteran secretary and confidante, hugs him in a cloud of lavender. It's more physical contact than he anticipated when he left for the store.

"You old dog," she says. "Never even a Christmas card."

"But always in my heart, Gladys."

"You were never a good liar," she says and hugs him a second time.

Decker leads Ferrell into his private office and closes the door. He opens the bottom drawer of his desk and pulls out a fifth of Jim Beam. "Are you still a fan?"

"Not for breakfast."

"For old time's sake then?"

Ferrell gives the nod. He thinks he wouldn't mind taking the edge off this reunion excitement. Decker sloshes bourbon into coffee cups and screws the cap onto the bottle. Ferrell's cup says *1984 Teacher of the Year* in bright red letters.

"So how long, Ferrell?"

"A bunch."

"And never home?"

"First time."

"I heard about Levon. Is he doing all right?"

"He's improving by the day. It would take more than a tree to do that boy in."

"I'll never forget the afternoon Levon jumped out the window of the second floor science lab."

"He broke his left arm and his right leg."

"I don't recall why he jumped."

Ferrell sips his bourbon. "He thought he could skip class that way. Avoid the hall monitors."

"How's Rilla handling all this?"

"Tough as always, but the strain wears. I worry about her."

The two men raise their cups, their decade of not seeing each other a widening canyon. Too much remains to be told, and so they don't even try.

"Ferrell, do you ever think of coming back? Maybe teach another year?"

"To be honest, Tom, I never do."

"But haven't you missed the kids?"

"The kids, yes, some of my colleagues, no."

"You never did suffer fools well."

"I'm one myself is why."

Decker pours another slosh into his cup. He wags the bottle at Ferrell, who shakes his head. "No, Mr. Swan, you were never a fool."

"I don't think Rilla would agree."

"Nor Donna about yours truly. Thirty-eight years, and

the woman up and walks out. It'll be three years alone for me this Christmas."

"She left you?"

"Christmas Eve, eight P.M. Used the kitchen door while we were unwrapping presents in the living room. Lots of *where's grandma?* and tears and shit. It was really quite dramatic."

"I'm sorry, Tom."

"Me too."

Ferrell experiences a need to bolt. He's never been good at shouldering his own sorrow, let alone the sorrow of others. "I won't keep you, Captain. You got a ship to run."

Decker stands with Ferrell and shakes his hand. "I mean that, Ferrell, about coming back. We can always use you. For godsakes, someone has to offset the damage Myers inflicts on the youth of tomorrow."

"Has the school changed?"

"Two gun scares in two years, a knife fight in the boys' locker room, lots of blood but they both lived. The worst was five years ago: two sophomore girls picked up some lowlife in Dover while returning videos. The punk forced them to drive out of town, killed the one and the other jumped off the Sugarcreek trestle and pretended to drown. It crushed us here, Ferrell. Good girls both, so much promise. No one can figure why they decided to give the fucker a ride. The whole school could hardly bear to go on. My toughest year by far."

"Did they catch the guy?"

"He's rotting up at Mansfield right now. Life without parole, and that's too good for the bastard. I wish him a horrible death nightly in my prayers."

Decker grips Ferrell's shoulder with a big strong hand. "Maybe you're right for living the way you do. Maybe the world *is* too far gone."

It's Ferrell's turn to hug, and he does it well, holds Decker close as his eyes ache and burn.

Another week, and Ferrell and Rilla settle into a rough approximation of their married years. Together they shop for essentials, eat their meals, wash evening dishes. Twice a day Rilla drives Ferrell to the hospital, where they pull up chairs beside the bed, visiting with Levon as they've never done before. Always a talker, Levon seems to relish the captive audience. He regales his listeners with tales of the days since he left home, a litany of self-inflicted mishap. In each saga Levon is the star player, centerstage in this drama of job firings and bungled schemes. For every relationship after Melody Cole, what begins in a fury of hormones and thrill ends in shouts and broken things, the woman unwilling to go the distance with Levon's twitchy ways.

Twilight on Saturday, as the boy winds up his latest story, Ferrell claps his hands. "Then what?"

"She piled my stuff in the yard and burned it," Levon says, looking like a court jester in a lime-green smock. "And my wallet was in the pocket of my jeans."

Rilla gathers her cloth handbag. "I'm craving some of that cafeteria espresso. You boys want some?"

Ferrell and Levon shake their heads, and she hustles out the door, leaving them alone. Without Rilla, the room has changed into something quite different, and Ferrell decides to make that cafeteria run. Before he can stand, Levon reaches out and takes his hand. The boy looks on the verge of something terribly emotional.

"I know I disappointed you at every turn," he says solemnly.

Ferrell tries to free his hand, but Levon's grip is surprisingly strong. "Hell, you weren't that bad."

"Let's not hide behind our false rituals, Ferrell. Let's speak from our inner selves for once and be done."

"You sound like Melody. Like your mama too."

"And why not? Why not confess our deepest truths in this stark hospital light?"

"All right, you first."

"I'm sorry for failing you as a son."

"Good, we've gotten that out of the way."

"Dammit, Ferrell, that's not what we are after here. We're after honest communication and freely spoken minds."

"What have you been reading?"

"It's what I've been *thinking*. Most nights, after you leave, I sit with the TV off and think for hours. Even before I got hurt, I'd been doing some 'soul searching,' as Mom so fondly calls it."

"And what do you want from me?"

"I want us to *talk* for a few minutes, stepfather to stepson, and say the things that need to be said. If I'd died squashed against that tree, none of these words would have ever gotten aired. Remember how Mom always begged us to talk?"

Ferrell gives another half-hearted tug to loosen his hand, but Levon holds tight. "Okay, son," he says, resigned. "Let's talk."

"Do you think if I'd been more like you, a straight shooter

and such, you would have treated me differently?"

"What do you think?" Ferrell says, the reliable opt-out from his classroom days.

"I think you'd have ridden my ass either way. I think I could never have pleased you. I think you'd have found fault with Christ himself."

Ferrell suffers the nagging futility of too many words spoken. "Is this getting us somewhere, Levon? I mean really."

"I just want to say I know I fucked up in legendary fashion, and I know you tried your best and only wanted what you thought was right for me. That said, I want to say I'm sorry and I forgive you. And I want you to do the same."

"You want me to apologize?"

"A full-fledged apology for any and all wrongs, plus unconditional forgiveness of any and all things I've said or done. A clean slate from this point forward."

"That sounds a mite idealistic, son."

"What's the alternative? Sophisticated grudges and festering resentment?"

In the time it's taken for Levon to speak his mind, the sun's angled low, and now the room is awash in crimson light. Ferrell decides there's nothing to lose and thus reaches out, taking Levon's other hand. To his surprise, Ferrell feels at peace with this young man whose history he shares. He doesn't think for a minute the feeling will last, but he'll always have this one time, this tenuous truce.

"I hereby forgive your trespasses, dear Levon," Ferrell says in his most assured voice. "Accept my unconditional and repentant apology?"

"Fuck, yeah," Levon says. He pulls Ferrell down into a hug, holds him fast until the sunlight has slipped below the window sill.

When the phone rings in the brilliant autumn morning, every hope seems possible. Rilla rises from the breakfast table, laughing at the memory of the sunny noon she hiked naked on the ridge, Din Winters spying from below. Ferrell watches Rilla lift the receiver from the kitchen wall, then looks out the picture window, today a framed painting of Sunday repose: prim brick homes, lawns like golf course greens, fat newspapers on concrete porches.

Rilla hangs up the phone, and is stricken somehow, as if blood has drained from her face. Her expression turns impassive, though a funny smile worries the corners of her mouth. In the few steps she needs to reach the table, one world passes away and a new one begins, and Ferrell knows he will remember this minute for his remaining years, knows this is how it feels to have terrible wrath swarm down.

According to the hospital's finest, the cause of death was pulmonary embolism, a fancy way to say what Ferrell learns was a simple blood clot, lingering undetected in Levon's thigh until he rose near dawn to walk the halls. He collapsed while chatting up the night nurse, a young and pretty woman, Ferrell recalls, with auburn hair. Despite immediate attention, Levon died within five minutes.

In the numbing days that follow, Ferrell guides Rilla through the necessary arrangements. He chauffeurs her from

appointments at Lingler's Crematorium to the church where
the services will be held. Their home fills with Rilla's aunts
and uncles and cousins on her mother's side, plus friends from
the counseling center in Akron. Neighbors bring an assort-
ment of casseroles and cakes, pies of every description. It is
a ritual of solace, and Ferrell moves through the crowded
rooms glad for the faces around him.

The night before the funeral the doorbell rings. Ferrell's
alone in the living room, and he rises like a weary doorman
to admit the latest kind neighbor with a covered dish. He
opens the door on Harrison and Melody Cole. Levon's son
slumps in Melody's arms, staring at Ferrell as if he doesn't
know him. Neither Cole nor Melody seems able to utter a
word, so Harry announces their arrival with a tired whimper. Before Ferrell can find a greeting for this precarious situation, Rilla pushes him aside.

"Help Harrison with their bags, Ferrell." Rilla reaches
for the boy, and leads Melody inside, the men, as always,
left to flounder with their inadequacies. Ferrell follows Cole
to the rented car, and together they truck luggage into the
house.

"These bags new?" Ferrell says.

"I haven't gone anywhere for so long, I had to buy."

"How was the flight?"

"I'd forgot how weird it feels to be six miles up in a noisy
tin can."

Ferrell leads Cole upstairs to the spare bed, Levon's old
room, the ironies coming too fast to acknowledge. With the
luggage stowed in the closet, he and Cole stand with their
hands in their pockets, nothing between them but the ring-

ing air. Cole seems a different man with his big frame stuffed into a suit and tie.

"I don't know, Ferrell, how I feel."

"Nobody does, I imagine. There's never only grief and sadness in times like these, but a dozen or three other feelings thrown in."

"Melody said she was coming, whether I came or not. I didn't know what else to do."

"I think you did right, Cole."

"Remember those crazed mustangs?"

"Is that the way you feel?"

"You bet." Cole looks over the small bedroom, his eyes wild as a stampeding animal's. "The boy's room?"

"None other."

"You know, if we were home, you'd have a drink in my hand by now."

"I can remedy that."

The morning sky dawns bright and mocking blue, a feed-store calendar of midwestern splendor. It makes Ferrell's regret that much harder to endure. Surrounding him is everything Levon will miss: the sunshine on his head, that trace of woodsmoke in the breeze, the lulling drone of nearby lawn mowers.

Outside Rilla's church, Ferrell paces the sidewalk in his tight dress shoes. He found them in the bedroom when he put on his suit, the first time he's dressed up since retiring. The formal clothes remind him of the lengthening distance from the rugged Owyhees, from jeans and hiking boots and open space.

A somber dark exodus converges on the white clapboard building, Levon's charisma, his easy charm, having touched more folks than Ferrell would have guessed. Given his solitary ways, Ferrell wonders if anyone will mourn him when it's his turn to go. Across the lawn, Rilla waves from the doorway of the church. She's sad and lovely in her plain black dress, red hair pinned beneath a black hat. She meets him on the cobblestone path.

"So many people, Ferrell. Levon would be surprised."

"He left his mark."

Ferrell sits at Rilla's side in the front pew, clasping her hand. He does his best to listen to the young pastor, a stuffy, boring man Levon would have despised, read from his typed notes. The eulogy is a carefully edited and cleaned-up account of Levon's short life, his various transgressions turned into achievement, his sins redeemed. From the sterile phrases and stock images, none of Levon's frantic exuberance comes forth, none of his nervous fervor, that feeling the boy was about to break into a run. Soon Ferrell ceases to listen to someone Levon never met speak of him as friend.

Instead he sorts through thousands of days, the good and the bad now strangely neither. He settles his thoughts on the time Levon played electric guitar, Ferrell's birthday gift when the boy turned sixteen. With Levon loony from the doldrums of summer, Ferrell put a used Stratocaster in his fidgety hands. In what seemed like only days, the hodge-podge of noise and sour notes coming from Levon's room coalesced into coherent sound, classic riffs Ferrell knew by heart: Skynyrd and Zeppelin, The Who and Hendrix, some godly Clapton.

One swampy afternoon, Levon hacksawed the neck off an empty Rolling Rock bottle, plugged in his amp, and from the doorway to his room rang the slide guitar intro to "Free Bird," Ferrell's personal anthem to his thirties, an era when he liked sour mash whiskey more than a little. Ferrell was reading in the den when the lonesome notes turned memory alive, and he closed his book and listened with approval, as if Levon had finally acquired the ability to speak after years of being mute. Over that stifling summer, Ferrell dug out his old Martin acoustic from the garage, a relic from his own teenage days, and damned if the boy and he didn't jam in the muggy hours after supper. For once it seemed the two of them *could* magically communicate. The ceasefire didn't last long, and come September battles raged, but for those dog days of summer Ferrell had found a kindred soul.

The house is crammed with people and tables of food, a solemn party under way on a weekday afternoon. The crowd spills onto the patio and into the backyard, the entire cast from Levon's life holding paper plates and plastic cups. Once Rilla has her food, friends from the counseling center escort her away. Sharp backward glances tell Ferrell what he needs to know about their view of him. At fund-raisers over the years, Rilla's fellow counselors had tolerated his presence, but the unspoken sentiment seemed obvious: she could do better than Ferrell Swan. If her friends were frosty before the divorce, the years since have turned them outright hostile, their cherished friend quitting her job to languish in the dust and sun of the West, returning home dejected, a nomad, a vagabond, her orderly life torn asunder.

Ferrell opens the fridge to choose his poison. He pulls out a cold Coors, Levon's favorite, and pops the tab in his honor. He plots his escape route to the kitchen door, and is about to venture into the throng, when Cole drapes a burly arm over his shoulders.

"I'll lead," he says, and uses his bulk to clear a path to the yard. Cole stops at the spot where Ferrell's favorite oaks had stood before the power company cut them down.

"Thanks," Ferrell says. "I don't do well at things like this."

"I wouldn't have guessed. You're so damn sociable back home."

"Fancy words." Ferrell sips beer and watches the crowd, his next couple hours looking to be slow and arduous.

"He had a lot of friends," Cole says.

"More than you or I."

Cole takes a generous swig of beer. "Ferrell . . ."

"Careful now."

"I just want to say I didn't want him dead. Despite everything, I'm not happy this happened."

"Oh, lord, I know."

"I keep thinking how Harry's daddy is gone. I guess I always thought the boy would know his real father when he grew up. It's strange, but I feel sorry for Harry the most."

"How's Melody taking all this?"

"I couldn't tell you."

"She hasn't said anything?"

"She's talked, but secrets stay in her head." Cole stares at Ferrell, though his eyes appear to see someone else. "After Levon visited Melody and the baby, I knew that's how it would be. A part of her locked away and private. I know she still loves him, and I know she can't stand next to me and not compare. And that's one matchup I'll always lose."

Ferrell feigns interest in the cloudless sky. Never in the mood for frank confessions, he finds this occasion even less desirable.

"Now that he's gone I'm doomed, you know. He's done turned martyr."

Ferrell doesn't know whether to be angry or sad. Everyone's been talking about themselves instead of Levon, about how his death affects *them,* more selfishness than mourning, it seems. Levon's drunken header into a tree has left Cole with a lousy hand of cards, his bluff called. Right when the conversation can't turn more awkward, help arrives in the person of Tom Decker, taking the afternoon off. As the principal joins them, Cole mumbles something about beer and heads to the house.

"Did I interrupt?"

"Saved me, more like."

"There's sure a ton of unchecked emotions swirling about. It seems Levon left an impression on *everyone* he ever met."

"Hear, hear," Ferrell says and raises his beer.

"I'd bet the hearts he broke in school never healed." Decker cuffs Ferrell on the shoulder, a gesture he remembers from their teaching days, times when Decker knew him too well. "How you holding up?"

"I can't complain. I'm not the one dead."

"Fair enough."

"Dammit, Tom, I'm worn thin right now. Don't mind me."

"No harm done. You could shout and scream and it'd be okay."

"That's what makes you a great principal. You always have empathy for others. That's something I can't muster."

"Have you given my offer any thought? Rilla will need you more than ever."

"Right now, I couldn't imagine teaching."

"It's not the time, I know. But keep the idea in the back of your mind. I was damn disappointed when you had the nerve to quit on us. It'd be a shame for you to be two thousand miles away when you could do so much good in your hometown."

"You make teaching sound like the priesthood."

"Maybe it's ours. You know you've changed some lives over the years. You know there's kids you've influenced."

"God help them."

"I'll call you in the next while. How long will you be in town?"

"I wish I knew."

Decker rests a reassuring hand on Ferrell's shoulder. "You've got some things to sort out, Ferrell. I don't mean to push. But promise me you'll make Dover High one of your possibilities?"

Ferrell nods, unable to trust the spoken word. The man's so persuasive Ferrell may make promises he can't keep. Decker gives his shoulder a squeeze, then turns in his black suit and walks away.

Hours of condolences and polite mingling, everyone a story to tell. Small respectful groups converge on Ferrell and then disband, never the same faces twice. Now and again, through the thinning crowd, he spots Rilla in the embrace of family and friends. She looks wearied and drawn, as if wasting away over the course of these awful hours.

When the crowd shifts, Ferrell finds himself alone. He escapes out the gate and hurries into the coming dusk. The unfurling sidewalk feels like something he needs, and he walks along the placid houses at a sure clip, heels echoing on the concrete, tie flapping over his shoulder. He heads down Oak Grove and turns right, onto the shaded tunnel of Maple Street. His pace slows as he gradually unwinds. Most of the homes have curtains drawn wide, and in these exposed rooms lights snap on against the gloom: *here we are, good neighbor, nothing to hide.* Flatscreen televisions flash pictures from across the spinning globe. The sight fills Ferrell with a sense of order and purpose. He knows these families have taken their blows, have been driven to their knees, yet here they remain, staving off the dark in their bright cheery homes. *Tribes,* he thinks, *huddled around their fires.*

A stationary figure watches his approach from under the trees. Ferrell contemplates crossing the street, but keeps to his course instead. Up close, he recognizes Melody's yellow hair, the boy straddling her hip. She's been elusive during the reception, tending to Harry in the upstairs rooms, and Ferrell is surprised to have her materialize from the dusk.

"I knew you were you," she says when he stops before her. "Either Mr. Ferrell Swan, or a genuine walking scarecrow."

"Tired of the crowds?"

"I'm just plain tired. The long flight, Harry not sleeping

well, the oddness of seeing Levon's home under these circumstances."

"Should we walk?"

"If you take Harry. He's too big to carry around like I
do."

Melody steps near, a hint of jasmine wafting up. She hands
Levon's son to him, and in the simple act Ferrell becomes the
grandfather he should be. Harry rests easily against Ferrell's
chest, eyelids fluttering. With Melody at his side Ferrell starts
for the house, a family on an evening stroll.

"I saw Harrison and you from the upstairs window," she
says.

"He was talking about Levon."

"We've had our moments, even before Levon."

"Everybody does. It's never like the movies."

Melody loops an arm behind Ferrell's waist. "I could
never have imagined this for myself. Married to a man decades older, a child from someone younger than me who's
already left this world. It's like I've gotten totally confused
along the way. Like I can't even figure out who I am."

"Join the club, sweetheart." Ferrell shifts the sleeping
Harry carefully in his arms. "How will it be when you get
back?"

"I don't think I'm going. I feel closer to Levon here. It's
strange, but thinking of him growing up here makes me feel
he's still around."

"What will Cole do?"

"Grow his trees and raise his cattle. He needs those things
more than he needs me. He needs sky and unobstructed views,
hour upon hour of being left the hell alone. Like you."

"But he about lost it when you left him."

"He only thought he would. We all have dues to pay." Melody's touch is soothing as they walk. "What about you? You've been gone awhile."

"Well, I'm thinking of staying as well. They've offered me my old job back. Rilla will need some time and attention."

Melody brings them to a stop. "You know, Ferrell, the fires came three weeks ago. Took our house and barn and all the trees. Killed dozens of cattle. The fire scorched Din's land and most of yours, a huge chunk of BLM. Fifty thousand acres in our part of Owyhee County."

"Why didn't Cole tell me?"

"He thought you had enough to deal with."

"What about Chroma?"

"Cole let her out of our barn as the fire got near. He spotted her days later with the mustang herd. He says she'll be with foal by the time he catches her."

"Is the cabin all right?"

"The fire came within a few hundred feet. Burned your barn and corrals and fences. We're living out of a tent. You wouldn't recognize the place, Ferrell. It's not the same."

"What about Din?"

"He fared the best of all of us. We hid with him in his bunker when the fire roared through. He kept us safe."

"I'll be damned," Ferrell says. "The guy was right all along."

"Din offered to help build us an underground home. Cole took him up on the idea. The two are best buddies right now. Before we left, they'd already started excavating with

Cole's new backhoe. I'd never seen Din happier. Or Cole, for that matter."

As they walk on, Ferrell tries to digest the news. His mind fills with miles of blackened earth. He pictures Din alone on the land, waiting for Cole to return. Ferrell recalls working beside Cole on the dead trees, that single purpose they shared. He's glad for Din to have companionship in the days to come.

The streetlights buzz and blink to life as the sky fades. Near the house, Melody sighs and shakes her head.

"Levon didn't mean any harm, Ferrell."

"Never on purpose, no. But harm done nonetheless."

"I won't tell you my Levon stories."

"I understand."

"He's with us now, you know?"

"In my arms?"

"In your very arms."

At the house, Ferrell hesitates on the sidewalk. Harry lifts his head without opening his eyes and settles back down. Melody watches them with her mysterious thoughts.

"Mind if I take him around the block?" Ferrell says. "Just one more spin before we head inside?"

Melody rises on tiptoes and kisses his cheek. "You and I aren't a whole lot different, Ferrell."

"How so?"

"We're both dreamers, I think. We'd rather live in the world our head creates, not the world we see."

"You bet."

"You're such a damn chatterbox, Ferrell."

"I love the spoken word, I guess."

"I'll be with Rilla for a while," Melody says and ambles down the front walk.

Ferrell waits until she closes the door, then continues past the house. Harry seems to note his mother's absence and rubs his eyes like a storybook lad.

"Where's my mom?"

"In the house back there. We're getting some fresh air, then we'll go join her. That sound okay?"

"There's fresh air in the backyard, you know?"

"That's true, but out here it's fresher."

Ahead shadows pool under the large oaks, despite the glowing streetlights. Ferrell's relieved this day of formal grief is soon to pass. Harry rides like a little prince, his arms across Ferrell's shoulders.

"Are there tigers around here?" he asks.

"Tigers?"

"In the jungle. You live in the jungle, don't you?"

"Ohio has trees, son, but it's not the jungle."

"What is it then?"

"Mostly farms and fields. Like *Charlotte's Web*. You ever read that book?"

"We have the video. I don't like the spider dying. That's stupid."

Out of the mouths . . . , Ferrell thinks.

As they walk around the block, the tug of Rilla's house increases, everyone waiting on their return. He isn't sure what he expected from circling his onetime neighborhood with Levon's heir, perhaps a stirring of memories from when Levon was four. Ferrell prays hard to shed twenty-one years in the next steps, to find himself with a young excited Levon, those unblemished days of playing father, hope and promise on fire in his chest. But despite this desire to bend space and time, he stays a divorced old man with a dead stepson, bearing a fatherless child back to his mama.

"Are we almost home, Grandpa?"

"Almost, Harry," Ferrell says. "Almost."

Near midnight, Ferrell wakes with gripping sadness full upon him. Rilla said true grief would arrive after the funeral, and right on cue Ferrell lies beneath its cruel weight, as if something dank covers his skin. The deep chill seeps into his eyes and ears, floods his heart until it aches. He has always lived on the fragile edge of his moods, able to turn dark and woeful at a wrong word spoken, but with real tragedy at hand, he knows those flights of despair were practice runs.

In the living room, cable news blares from the television. It takes Ferrell a minute to understand the shape on the floor is Rilla, cocooned in a sleeping bag from their family camping days, her tangled hair spilling from the faded green. The loud TV sends a torrent of tragedy over her sleeping ears, a lullaby of murder and terrorist bombings, freak accidents that have wrenched more souls from the world. Ferrell stands hypnotized by the violence issuing forth. Something about this heartsick hour, with Levon's absence palpable on the air, has transformed the day's news into the Book of Revelation, read aloud by an attractive woman with flawless hair.

Ferrell makes coffee and carries two cups back to the living room. He stops in front of the fireplace, where Levon's urn sits on the mantle. In the disparate thoughts roaming Ferrell's head, Levon seems a trapped genie with wishes to grant. But then synapses fire in a different direction, and Levon is simply ashes in a blue urn.

"Everyone's dying everywhere," Rilla says from the floor. "I counted seventy-five killed since I started watching. And those are the ones that make the news. Imagine how many died today. I bet last breaths are being drawn right now."

"Coffee?" Ferrell asks.

Rilla offers Ferrell a look that scares him. She has awakened into a life forever altered, with new rules she has yet to discover. Rilla emerges from the sleeping bag still in her black dress, and she walks straight to the dining room table, where she pours single malt into a shot glass. She downs the scotch and returns to her camping spot with bottle and glass.

"Is there anything I can do?"

"You can bring my son back."

Ferrell closes his eyes, his thoughts worthless and stupid. He knows Rilla knows each possible condolence he could offer. For most of her adult life, she'd comforted scores of the grieving, kids who'd lost mothers and fathers, sisters and brothers, best friends known from kindergarten. Ferrell was always amazed at her talent for soothing such raw wounds, how she used words to talk someone out of their pain. Now, he understands, her special prowess has left her defenseless against her own sorrow.

"If I could, Rilla, I surely would."

"You would not."

His hands tremble badly, and Ferrell sets the cups on the end table. He mainlines a dangerous dose of remorse and self-pity. He looks to the front door, and his overriding impulse is to flee.

"You never liked him, did you?"

"Rilla, please."

"I mean you rode his ass all those years. The damn kid couldn't do a damn thing to please you."

"I did my best."

"Your best wasn't fucking good enough. Your best wasn't even close. Finding fault with his every move, never a good word. That boy grew up believing he wasn't worth shit. That's what you were, Ferrell, a constant reminder of his shortcomings, his many and varied flaws."

"I thought I was keeping him in line."

Rilla pours another shot, her eyes daring him to utter a word. "He's dead, Ferrell, and what good did he hear from you? Bitch and moan, criticize and find fault. Did you ever let the kid feel good about himself?"

Ferrell considers revealing their heart-to-heart, that last prophetic meeting between father and son. But to open his mouth would be to contradict her, a rebuttal to the blazing vision she sees.

"You take a person's delight," she says. "You steal their fucking bliss. You know that, Ferrell? You steal a person's goddamn bliss."

Tears scald his eyes. Invisible hands clench his throat. He stands dumb and blind, resigned to his fate.

"I'm just setting the record straight," Rilla says and drinks from the bottle.

Ferrell can't seem to get enough air. He feels feverish and weak, ready to collapse under this blackness raining down. He wonders if despair can kill him outright, if his heart might finally seize.

Oh, God, he thinks, *take me now and be done.*

When he opens his eyes, Rilla looms before him, an angel of judgment come to sweep him from the earth. Her eyes show suffering, then the fires of hate brightly burn. She turns her back to him, shoulders slumped, head hung low. He notices how rumpled her mourning dress has become, the black cloth creased and wrinkled. Heaving sobs wrack her small frame, and he reaches out to comfort her, the one thing he knows how to do.

As Ferrell's hand touches her shoulder, Rilla whirls. Her arms become a confusing blur. His head twists on his neck, and fine sparks shower the room, then the thudding blow registers home. Rilla hits him with her fists, slams his temple and chin, the bridge of his nose. Her punches sink into his belly, his ribs, the bone plate of his chest, and he watches her through bursting fireworks of silvery red. These are not wild flailing blows, he realizes in a detached way, but punches calm and calculated, Rilla intent on putting him down. He opens his arms to accept her gift.

In the night, Ferrell sleeps among the wretched and the damned. He hovers on the ragged border between rest and dream, his wounds smarting whenever he moves. In fleeting fragments of a shifting world, he lies in the steamy torture rooms of Hades, beaten by beings he cannot see or hear. Then he's in the hot sand of the ridge, pinned beneath a creature sinister and grotesque: a naked woman with a horse skull for a head. This beast grips the cannon bone of a horse, and strikes Ferrell in the head with the blunt white shaft, his nose spurting red. She clubs his eyes until he's blind, his mouth until he cannot speak. Where his teeth have broken free, his blood runs bitter as spoiled wine. Next Ferrell sits alone on his cabin porch, watching wildfire pour off the ridge, the tumbleweeds thousands of miniature suns. Orange flames rise into the night, a sharp crackling roar. Soon fire engulfs the corrals and barn, then the porch boards smolder and reach flashpoint, flames blanketing him in a horrid heat. He raises his hands to protect his face, but his skull melts beneath his fingers like wax.

Ferrell wakes to fierce light filling the room. He considers the water stains on the ceiling as if secrets will be revealed there. His head hurts a billion ways past Sunday, his ribs bruised and aching.

He finds Rilla sitting cross-legged before the television. A deluge of CNN misery washes over her, and Ferrell gets a quick hit of indignation at these constantly talking heads. He walks in front of the screen, blocking Rilla's view, but she doesn't lift her eyes to him. He reaches back and shuts off the television.

Rilla stares straight ahead like a statue of defeat. Ferrell doesn't move and he doesn't speak, and she finally looks up. She seems to study his damaged face with honest wonder.

"You look terrible," she says.

"You don't look so hot yourself."

"I haven't slept in days."

"Maybe the doctor can do something."

"Can he bring my son back?"

"Look, Rilla . . ."

"Christ, Ferrell, I'm sorry."

When he steps toward her, Rilla raises both hands from

her lap. Her fingers have swollen twice their size, the knuckles not visible beneath the smooth taut skin.

"You're hurt," Ferrell says.

"I want to be."

"But you might have broken bones."

"It's my punishment. For hurting you. For failing Levon."

"You didn't fail Levon."

"I couldn't keep him alive. My role was to protect him."

"But you weren't there. You couldn't have been."

"Always driving so fast. Always so reckless. Damn him, Ferrell, why couldn't he slow the fuck down?"

"To slow down wasn't an option, honey. You more than anyone knew that boy had only one gear."

"Knowing didn't help. All my training, and I couldn't do a thing to save him. I can't even do a thing to save myself."

"At least you understand what's happening to you."

"It's like a disease," Rilla says and shakes her head. "It's inside me when I sleep, when I'm awake. It feels like it's in my damn blood."

"They say it gets better."

"It doesn't. It'll change and become something else, but it'll never relent."

"How can I help?"

"I want to see where it happened. Can you take me there?"

The anguish in Rilla's eyes gives him no choice. "If you think it's for the best."

"There is no best anymore."

Rilla rides shotgun and Ferrell drives, the car leaving their little town and edging quickly into the pastoral. Ferrell

notes the leaves on the wooded hillsides have mostly fall-
en, and in the fields hollow cornstalks quiver in the breeze.
Much of the cropland has been plowed, dark earth prepared
for the long wait to spring. Ferrell feels secretly comforted at
how life has been going on despite their grief, but he keeps
such observations to himself.

At Broad Run Dairy, Rilla points out a gravel road and
Ferrell swings the car east. Stones ping off the undercarriage,
and he slows to a crawl, delaying their arrival as long as he
can. He doesn't want to see this spot, Rilla or no, doesn't
want to view what stopped Levon's rowdy ride.

"We should be close, Ferrell. The police said a mile past
the dairy, before the abandoned coal tipple."

Ferrell brakes even more, peering over the hood for signs.
Ahead a lone birch towers beside a straight stretch of road.
Ferrell parks as far to the side as he can, without getting stuck
in the shallow ditch. First off, he sees Levon had to veer wide
right to leave the road. Indeed, the boy managed not only to
lose control on a straightaway but to hit the only tree in the
whole hundred-acre pasture. The irony would not be lost on
Levon.

Ferrell opens his door and climbs out. He counts off the
number of paces to where tire tracks cross the ditch. Torn
sod leads from the busted fence to the broad trunk, its white
pulpy wood exposed. He feels the crash could have been yesterday, such an aura it still casts. Rilla walks into the pasture alone, her funeral dress dark against the sallow grass,
and Ferrell hangs back, leaving Rilla to her private thoughts.
She stands before the tree for minutes too painful to witness. Ferrell returns to the car and sits on the hood, but each

time he looks up he wonders how Levon rammed a tree that far from the road. Another black crying jag swoops down, and Ferrell presses thumb and forefinger to the bridge of his nose, as if stemming the tears will stem the sadness. Try as he might, he can't imagine Levon never again wreaking glorious havoc upon the land.

"Are you all right?" Rilla stands in front of him, a gap in time somehow.

"Are you?"

"It takes the mystery out of it, that's for sure. It's just a tree, and Levon ran into it at seventy miles an hour." Rilla reaches out and touches his knee. "You want to go over?"

"I'm hard put as it is."

"You always were a softie, Ferrell, beneath your cranky gruff act." Rilla sits beside him on the hood. He recognizes the most common pose of their early days together: side by side on the hood of a car, single lane stretching from the front bumper.

"You loved him, Ferrell. I know you did."

"I know that too."

"I'm sorry for what I said. What I did."

"You just can't hold your liquor, Rilla."

"Humor aside, beating your ex-husband is not legal in most states."

"It is in Idaho."

"Let's go, Ferrell. I'll drive."

Rilla accelerates past the tree and keeps going, Levon's original route that fateful night. The coal tipple drifts by ghostly on their right, its wooden tower hidden in the trees. On Willy Slater's Lane, Rilla bears left where the road forks.

Ferrell's been gone long enough this maze of back roads eludes him.

"I'm lost," he says.

"I'm not."

The car enters woods so dense and dark it seems night has abruptly fallen. Ferrell stares into the tangled limbs of the trees, primordial and uninviting, even to him and his love of wild places. The car tops a brief rise, then swings down into a low hollow. Rilla slows and leans forward in her seat, searching for something in the murky light.

"There," she says and turns onto a dirt path Ferrell would have never seen: rough car ruts passing through poison ivy and nettles. Tucked in the heavy shadows, a battered single-wide hunkers parallel to the road.

"What the hell?" Ferrell says.

"Levon's home," she says. "He lived here for almost a year. His longest residence ever, not counting our house."

"This place would make a hermit proud."

"Maybe he took after his stepdad more than we knew."

When Ferrell gets out, thick branches press down until he wants to duck. Without sunlight the air is damp and cool, and he wishes he'd worn his coat. The mobile home is an eyesore at best, probably a Fleetwood from the seventies. Most of the metal siding has peeled in sharp curls, revealing yellow insulation.

"He won it in a poker game," Rilla says before Ferrell can ask.

"High stakes."

The trees crowd in close around the trailer. It's calm as his Idaho home, some birdcall above, a light rustling of leaves.

He visualizes Levon living in this spot, an utter lack of stimulus to a young man who'd always injected agitation straight into his veins. Almost too much to believe, this Levon he never knew.

Keys clink softly as Rilla searches for the right one. She fits the key and shoulders the door, a mother simply checking on her boy. Ferrell tries to rein in his galloping heart, then follows her inside. The interior is another surprise in a morning of surprises. Though beyond its better days, Levon kept the place clean—no dirty dishes in the small sink, no dirty socks or rumpled boxers in sight, the carpet vacuumed. Even the cabinets in the kitchenette have been painted.

"Cozy," Ferrell says and means it.

In the back of the trailer, the bed looks meticulously made. Ferrell has to smile—year after childhood year of insisting Levon straighten the covers, to start the day with a little order, not stagger from his room like an orphan boy. Above the bed hangs a blown-up snapshot of Ferrell and Rilla on the cabin porch, neat whiskeys raised to the setting sun. Rilla has her mouth open in laughter, some joke of Levon's before he snapped the photo. Ferrell picks a small gilded frame from the nightstand: Melody and the child, faces turned from the camera. He walks back down the narrow hall, passing the bathroom with its cramped shower and commode and sink. Rilla sits on the ratty couch, a sheaf of notebook paper in her hand, Levon's loopy script scrawled across the lines.

"What's that?"

"His journal, I guess."

"He was different these last months."

"He had this plan to call Melody and have her come.

Raise Harry as his own. He wrote how he wanted to do for his son what you did for him."

"Levon wrote that?"

"Cross my heart."

Beyond the thin walls, Ferrell hears not a sound. "Sure is peaceful, Rilla."

"He said he liked it that way. He said the noise in his head grew hushed out here." Rilla sets the papers aside and rises to her feet, as if remembering something she needs to do. "I'm going to check the bedroom, too."

Ferrell watches Rilla pass down the hall. Her bowed head, her measured steps, remind him, spookily, of a penitent approaching an altar. He walks to the front window to pass the time. Outside, the sun is unable to penetrate the trees. In this sheltered place, he pictures Levon strolling the woods in thoughtful meditation, hidden from the temptations of town. Ferrell understands how this unwanted strip mine became shelter for Levon, reprieve from the clamorous places where trouble always found him, where neon bar signs called his name in such hoarse, urgent whispers, where women could not stop needing what he had, his virility opiate to their famished needs.

Ferrell stares hard into the woods, searching between the dark trunks rising everywhere, and he sees the boy himself, Levon in the flesh, as much in the physical world as the black trees. Levon walks with his head down, a posture never witnessed when the boy was alive. Ferrell blinks at this crazy trick of his old tired eyes, leans closer to the filmy glass, but Levon's still there, tramping slowly by the trailer. He won't look at Ferrell, ruler of his domain for years, king of law and

order. If Levon would give him some sign, Ferrell knows
absolution has come his way, but the boy keeps his unbroken
pace, moving deeper into the shadows.

Down the hall Rilla calls his name, and Ferrell glances
from the window, dazed at his return to the living. It takes
a moment to gather his wits. Rilla calls to him once more,
and something in her voice raises gooseflesh on the back of
his neck. His feet move of their own accord and Rilla calls
yet again, his name murmur and shout. He looks down at
the black leather shoes she was wearing, then, inches far-
ther, finds the crumpled dark pile of her mourning dress. Her
pure white undergarments mark the threshold to the room,
but Ferrell doesn't raise his eyes to the bed. His fingers find
the buttons on his shirt, and he slips free from the cloth. He
bends and pulls off his boots, one echoing thud after another,
while ghostly Levon wanders the woods outside.

In the morning, Ferrell wakes to monochrome clouds
encroaching from the west. The weather so matches his
mood Ferrell feels an odd calm, his inner frequencies tuned
perfectly to the physical world. An exhausted heap, Rilla
sleeps her first bona fide sleep in days. Ferrell sees how this
will never stop, how Levon will always be dead, and Rilla
will wake again to the knowledge of his death, her own private curse.

Downstairs, Ferrell showers and dresses in jeans and a
flannel shirt. He pours hot coffee into one of Rilla's fancy
travel mugs, silver and tall with some kind of confounding
lid. On the phone last night, his uncle asked if Ferrell wanted
to ride along to Mineral City. Walt said he thought it would

be good for Ferrell to visit the old Swan place, to remember his roots.

A car horn beeps from the driveway, and Ferrell hurries out the door, waving at his uncle to cease the racket. Walt waves back with unbridled enthusiasm, beeps his horn three more times. Not yet in the car, Ferrell regrets agreeing to the trip.

"Haven't had your coffee?" Walt asks when Ferrell slides in with his big mug. "I've had mine."

"Good morning," Ferrell says.

Walt backs the Oldsmobile down the drive, swings onto the street, points them at the red climbing sun. When Walt mashes the gas pedal, Ferrell's pinned against his seat, thankful for the heavy-duty coffee lid. His whole life, Walt has wound his springs too tight. He talks fast and often, hurries about as if deadlines threaten. Rumor has it Walt used to pleasure Aunt Ethel and be back in his trousers in three minutes flat.

"You remember the way?" Walt asks, his belly snug against the steering wheel.

"Mostly."

Walt delivers the directions in their entirety, including alternate routes and their distinct disadvantages. He follows these details with an extended account of the construction of the Swan house, including a historical overview of the region. To Ferrell's continued amazement, his uncle finds inventive ways to pack sentences with more words than seems possible. Ferrell imagines a glassy glaze covers his eyes, pictures his skull imploding. His uncle launches into story after story, and Ferrell can't tell where one stops and the next begins. He rarely discerns the point of the tales, or why one prompts another, even what decade Walt's recounting. Never blessed with much patience, Ferrell's reserves run dangerously low.

To his relief, Walt retrieves a ham sandwich from the dash. He spends precious minutes eating and driving. Ferrell begins to recognize the farms along the road, their particular arrangements of house and barn and silo, as familiar as if *he* were raised here and not his father. He sits straighter in the seat, more excited than he anticipated to return to the land of his people.

"You know where we're at, Ferrell?"

"I most certainly do."

Under such bleak skies, the house resembles its grainy black-and-white counterpart in Ferrell's photo album. The north side of the two-story looks to be in good shape, that part of the roof intact, but the entire south end has fallen to the ground.

"She's nearly finished," Ferrell says.

"Gravity's been pulling at her, that's no lie. The bedrooms caved under the snow five years back, and the rest is soon to follow."

When Walt shuts the engine down, Ferrell scrambles out first, leaving the big man to struggle free of his car. He wants a minute to stand alone before his father's house, such place of origin. His namesake grandfather, Ferrell Martin Swan, émigré from the Alps of Switzerland, bought the house in 1912, and raised three sons and two daughters under its sheltering roof.

His uncle lumbers up beside Ferrell, huffing quietly.

Silver beads shimmer on Walt's brow. Ferrell feels a biting surge of empathy: the man's not long for this world.

"It's strange, your daddy dead all these years," Walt says.

"He never was around when he was alive," Ferrell says.

"But still we knew where he was. All those postcards."

"He never came home the last two decades."

Walt pulls a white linen handkerchief from his pocket. "Little Maynard never seemed to *have* a home, even as a kid. He was a loner, that's no mystery."

"What was he like as a boy?"

"Son, your daddy was the same, child or man."

"And how was that?"

"Peculiar."

Tightly woven vines hide the cobblestone walk. Walt steps heavily onto the slab of the porch and knocks on the bare clapboards. The door rests in the raggedy weeds.

"I love to do that," Walt says. "Let the family know company is calling."

"Can we go in?" Ferrell says.

"Not unless you want to visit the cellar. The floors can't be trusted, at least not with my extra pounds."

Ferrell trails his uncle along the front of the house, not a pane of glass in the window frames. "Damn kids," Walt says. "Why the young feel compelled to destroy everything not guarded or tied down is beyond me." Walt circles the south end of the building and stops in the backyard, beside some smaller collapsed structure.

"Would you look at that?" Walt says. "She finally came down."

"What?"

"The summer kitchen. Mother cooked out here in hot weather to keep the main house cooler. You know, when your daddy got old enough, maybe fourteen or fifteen, he asked to live in this place."

"What did Grandpappy do?"

"He told Maynard to drag his mattress from the house. He told him he never was family to begin with, always off on his own, never offering to help. Come haying you couldn't find his sorry ass if your life depended on it. Pappy told him he was a born solitaire. Said if he wanted to be a goddamn refugee, then have at it. Poor Maynard was pretty much on his own after that. He lived out here till he was seventeen, then got that Shenango job and moved to Dover. He never spoke to us much after the wedding, and when he left your mama and you we heard even less."

Ferrell stands before the heap of wood and shingles. He tries to imagine his father as a teenager, living in the summer kitchen while the family shared the house. He thinks of his father building that extra room in their basement, an outcast once more, self-imposed.

"Do you ever wonder why my dad was so different?"

"Sure, wondered, but no conclusions. My guess is some are born without a need for others, without the natural wiring for affection most people have. Me, I go crazy without someone to talk to. My thoughts stay in my head too long they get funny and odd, like they ferment or some such thing." Walt pulls jangling keys from the pocket of his trousers.

"You know, Ferrell, you've got a fair amount of the antisocial in you, latent though it may be. I hear you live in the middle of not much, miles from nowhere."

"I do like my privacy."

"Your privacy don't have much to say, Ferrell. It don't give no hugs, nor offer a gentle touch. You live alone too long you forget who you are, where you come from. Having folks around gives you something to measure yourself against. They hold up a mirror and show you who you are. Think of those Kern boys. Crazy as loons, those two. Lived in that school bus with the stovepipe sticking through. Came to town on grocery runs once in a blue moon. You ask me, those two were alone way too much."

"People go crazy, together or apart. You just choose your demons."

"Oh, clam it, Mr. Educated. You were wrong to leave. No matter what fancy thing you choose to say. A man should stay where he was born. Your brain gets tuned to the land you come from, to these trees and hills, these pastures and fields, this very air. When you are raised in a single place, you get hardwired for it, programmed into the seasons, summer thunder and winter snow, all the rest. I bet you've been out of sync since you left. I bet you wander that wilderness like a lost man seeking water. This damn patch of ground is where you were born, and this is where you should end your days. You were *made* of these elements and these alone, and your bones should be returned to this exact ground, dust from whence it came and so forth." Walt stands breathing heavily, as if he's labored at something taxing. "I've spoken my mind because I don't have many days left. You can regard it as the rantings of a crazy old fool."

But Ferrell intends no such thing. He stands humbled

before this man, alter ego to his nomadic brother, someone who stayed put and saw more of what there was to see. Ferrell turns from Walt's gaze to look at the house. Above the ruined farm, Ferrell believes he can see the captive truth set free.

With night nearly upon the graves, Ferrell parks and sets the brake. He eases the car door shut, not wanting to disturb the dead. He plots a course down the darkening hillside, careful to stay between the brass markers. Ever since he was a little boy, stepping upon someone's grave has been a mortal sin. God would surely smite him for such disdain.

As light fails, Ferrell navigates the familiar names. Whole families have lived and died around him, as though Dover High were the focal point of the town. Here are classmates from his own school days, longtime friends, occasional enemies. Here are neighbors and fellow teachers, erstwhile drinking buddies. Here are those from parent-teacher conferences: store owners and cops, bankers and farmers, truck drivers and dentists, factory workers. Here are dozens of his past students, much younger men and women who should not be in the ground before him. Why these particular souls lie dead and not others seems as arbitrary as Ferrell can imagine. Somehow he has survived a burst appendix, a lost hiking trail in a freezing whiteout, a couple good car wrecks that shook him to his toes. But more than these, he has outlasted heart wounds beyond measure—three grueling divorces, a child raised and irretrievably lost, days on end of petty colleagues and sullen students, uppity store clerks and gas station jockeys with their egos on their sleeves, telemarketers who learned nothing from their mamas. How, in God's holy name, has *he* managed to keep from the comfort of his grave?

Ahead Ferrell spies his name, barely visible in the twilight. He stops before the family marker, then sits on the grass beside the graves. As he traces the raised letters of his mother's name, he feels emptiness in the space she used to fill, the world forever smaller, more diminished, with her passing. But when Ferrell touches his father's name, his fingers halt over the letters, a blind man encountering some bizarre and frightening Braille. He wants to break the connection but can't move.

Ferrell rocks back in the damp grass. He yanks his hand free of the name—a rejected son then and now. Sitting beside his father's grave, he knows forgiveness should come: flashes of insight, cleansing wisdom, all good things. But these feelings don't come. Maybe it's *his* private curse, or some fundamental flaw in his character, some deficiency in his makeup, that prevents his heart from opening. Perhaps he makes two of a kind with the old man, cut from the same cloth, a selfish man begetting a selfish son.

Ferrell slumps against his bent knees. He has come a long way to sit here, traveled far with little rest. His muscles recall only effort, as if he's been tethered into a harness, breast strap across his chest, and forced to pull an incessant load. And how can this be? He spent his work life in pressed chinos and dress shirts, strolling air-conditioned classrooms, his voice low and soothing. Yet beside these graves, Ferrell Swan feels a weariness he's never known. He might not ever stand up and leave this place.

This sanctuary of buried bones puts Ferrell near final defeat. He has returned from too many battles fought and lost. With the resignation of the vanquished, he decides to move back to Ohio, this night his personal Appomattox, his formal surrender. He will finish his days among the keepsakes of his youth: cicadas in summer, autumn woods, chimney smoke on winter mornings, the fireflies of spring like tiny pulsars on the dusk. Perhaps his uncle is right: his mind *was* formed from these elements. Maybe he needs the place of his birth like the living need air. He will live at the house with Rilla, if she'll have him, teach some at the school, return to civilization once more. *I will fight no more forever,* he thinks, *and God have mercy upon my soul.*

Early next morning, Ferrell descends the steps to greet his new home. Rilla is hustling about the kitchen, an unknown holiday fast approaching.

"There's sleepyhead," she says.

"Greetings," Ferrell says, trying hard to gauge the situation into which he's stumbled. "Salutations."

At his place setting, Rilla sits him down to a banquet of her own design. She has scones on the table from their English past, and rahmschnitzel to honor his Swiss bloodlines. She keeps ferrying things from the stove: blueberry waffles and wild honey, hash potatoes browned to crisp loveliness, cheese omelets stuffed with onion and bell pepper. The table crowds and still she makes the trip from stove to table, countertop to table, adding warm tortilla shells and fresh salsa, a platter of huevos rancheros topped with sliced black olives and sour cream. She brings hot bran muffins from the oven, and Italian sausage bubbling in its juices, brings flapjack stacks with pure maple syrup from the trees of Vermont. In the last square foot of real estate on the table she parks a plate of homemade donuts, the sugar glaze lit by the window sun. An international breakfast of epic proportions, and despite his hunger, Ferrell can only stare at the feast she has made.

"Guess you thought I'd have an appetite."

"I wanted to celebrate the homecoming of the famed mountain man, before his return to the wilderness."

"I'm wanting to stay, if that's all right. Decker's offered my old job, and this house feels pretty good."

Rilla stares as if reading his deficient thoughts. "Don't flower it up so much, honey."

His radar picks up something ahead. He keeps his mouth closed, for the time being.

"Lookit, Mr. Romantic, you've covered job and home. Do I fit in there somewhere?"

"Oh, hell, Rilla, you know better."

"Do I, if you never say?"

Another conversation headed straight to sea. Rilla seems to recognize his panic, and lays her hands on top of his.

"Don't get scared. I'm not looking for a fight. I'm just amused."

"At me?"

"At us."

"Why are we so funny?"

"Because I was about to tell you I want to go west. I want to live at the cabin, walk your desert trails, commune with the coyotes."

"But what if I belong *here?*"

"You don't know where you belong. Neither do I. Maybe nobody knows."

"That's awfully mystical for six in the morning."

"The thing is, Ferrell, we don't have to decide. We can pick up and leave when we want. Be wanderers like days of old."

"But what happened to our Ohio roots?"

"My son's dead. I can't be around the place he died right now, with ten dozen reminders of him everywhere I look. I want to be down in that ravine and see nothing at all. I need my forty days. You've already had yours."

Rilla gives him a heroic smile. She studies the table so long Ferrell feels ignored. She breaks a cinnamon scone in two, her movements full of intent, of meaning beyond the simple act. She holds half the scone to his lips, the scent of sweetened flour in his nose.

"Eat, Ferrell," she says. "Eat until you are full, until you feel as if you will never be hungry again."

"And after that?"

"We'll sleep until we are replenished, then we'll rise into our new lives, reborn into the people we've always wanted to be."

Across the room, the oven pours out wondrous heat, and sunlight floods the tabletop in the new day about to begin. Ferrell opens his lips, takes the bread as offering into his mouth. Rilla bites from the other half, and together they eat.

Days later, Ferrell rises in the dark for the trip to the Akron airport. He loads their packed suitcases into the car, calls to confirm their departure time, his mind tied to the weary routines of travel and not the consequences of the act: leaving one place for another.

Rilla guides the car through town without speaking. On I-77 she brings them to speed, merging with the long-haul truckers blasting down the north–south corridor. In the pre-dawn, the brightly colored running lights turn the trucks into spacecraft from other worlds, visitors to their pitiful planet. He wonders what aliens would think of this place, packed with creatures like him, singular in their devotion to their greedy hearts.

Without Ferrell noticing, light has begun to come up. From the height of an overpass, he discovers dense fog haunting the bottomland, scattered farmhouses and barns, tall silos, like shadows of their real selves. Ferrell imagines they hover above some dreamworld, he and Rilla its indifferent gods.

The flight west retraces the dusty route of covered wagons and washboard oxen, that fabled Oregon Trail five miles below Ferrell's feet. He tries to wrap his mind around the physical fact of Rilla, asleep in the next seat, but can't seem to fathom the *how* of his new traveling companion, his amiga. From the requested window seat, Ferrell keeps watch on their steady progress across the sprawling continent—the tabletop plains with those lonely intersecting roads, then the heaving snowy spires of the Rockies, reaching to scrape the underside of the plane.

At last the terrain below turns lunar and forbidding, fold after fold of the featureless hills near Boise, such oddly contoured land. Soon the subdivisions hove into view, then the Outlet Mall and Micron Technology and the neat square blocks and bare trees of the city. The runway rises up fast and jars Rilla awake, and she turns and kisses his cheek, their second life begun.

While Rilla waits at the luggage carousel, Ferrell buys the truck out of long-term parking, a debt from a previous life. A different man left two months ago, and someone else has returned to take his place. With the bags roped down in the bed, Ferrell and Rilla climb into this other man's truck. Ferrell follows the blue exit signs through acres of parking lot, wheels out the tollbooth and onto the freeway, merging with the traffic of a Boise afternoon. The truck rattles in revolt at the speed, and Rilla leans against his shoulder, young lovers headed into the western sun.

"This feels weird," Rilla says. "We're like new people, driving to our new home."

"Next stop the promised land," Ferrell says. "Manna raining down."

When Ferrell reaches the bridge over the Snake, night has fallen. He drives through a blackness total and complete, the high desert invisible all around, though beyond his headlights he knows the road touches tomorrow. He's as tired as ever, but doesn't feel the need for sleep, only an urgent wish to stop and be still. Above a road that keeps spooling out, stars pack the sky.

Parked at the cabin, Ferrell sits with the highway rushing his closed lids. Rilla stirs at the absence of movement, and she sits up in her seat, staring into the dark.

"Are we here?"

"We are."

"When does the moon come up?"

"Should be soon."

"Will it be full?"

"Only a quarter."

"Good enough."

While Ferrell hauls their bags inside, Rilla waits on the porch in her coat. He traipses from truck to cabin, cabin to truck, Rilla's creaky rocker keeping cadence to his work. After the luggage is stowed, Ferrell carries an oil lamp from room to room, checking on his possessions. Beyond the log walls, the acrid scent of soot and ash permeates the air, but his cabin's unharmed and for that he gives silent thanks.

Ferrell brings the lamp to the porch, casting fluttery light on Rilla and the rocking chairs. In her arms she cradles Levon's blue funeral urn, which she must have packed in her carry-on when Ferrell wasn't looking. He understands in an instant what she intends, and he blows out the flame, darkness enveloping them. A radiance shows above the ridge, then comes the sharpened edge of an exotic scimitar. The quarter moon clears the ridge, scary and rising fast.

"Are you ready?" he asks.

"I am."

Ferrell lets Rilla lead this sacred pilgrimage he knows too well. Around their feet foul ash floats up, and he wonders how Rilla can find her way in this unfamiliar landscape. He's convinced they've entered the charred ruins of hell. Rilla stops and takes her bearings, checks the stars like a captain at sea. Ferrell squints into the night, surprised to discern the white boulders of the wash.

"I'm amazed you found the place."

"I had help."

Tucked beneath the embankment, the entrances to the dens seem hidden portals to other worlds. He knows the dens are vacant this time of year, occupied only in late winter when the alpha female has her pups. Rilla sits at the opening of the largest den. Ferrell recalls their previous visit to these dens with another funeral urn, the damp fog and snow of a Thanksgiving morning. They took a private sacrament that day, such bitterness on his tongue.

Ferrell walks over to Rilla and lowers himself down. He knows the endless motion of the day has finally ceased, that he has arrived someplace where he can rest, where some measure of stillness can be found. He pulls his coat closed against the chill.

"He never met my father," Rilla whispers. "Do you think he would have liked him?"

"They had the same blood in their veins."

"That's never enough."

"But Levon would have understood your father. They fought the same hard battles."

"That's right, Ferrell. They *will* get along."

Rilla's hands do something in the shadows, then she reaches out to Ferrell. He opens his palm to receive the glass top of the urn, cool on his skin. He cradles the lid in his lap.

"He'll like it here, I think," she says. "He'll have plenty of room in which to roam."

"And a traveling companion," Ferrell says.

"And a traveling companion."

When Rilla moves quietly once more, Ferrell holds out his hand. He feels the ash as something fine and weightless on his palm, with substance and yet not there at all. He wishes beyond reason for Levon to be among the living, then feels he still *is* among them, not ghost or spirit, not memory encoded in the creases of his brain, but somehow in the air around them, perhaps pure energy as some believe.

"He will be part of us," Rilla says, hopeful wish and absolute truth.

Ferrell raises his hand as he did years before, touches tongue to bitter ash, eyes shut so tightly they ache. He sees behind his lids the windswept ridge, the ravine with its mustang skull glowing like the moon. He feels the heated rush of forgiveness, not from *without* but *within*, forgiveness of himself for his myriad failings, for hardships imposed upon those under his watch. At his side Rilla tosses her handful of ash before them, and Ferrell does the same, then she upends the urn and ash whispers down. Ferrell imagines the coyotes sniffing this strange scent, this peculiar ash hinting of man. When the coyotes pace this sacred spot, traces will cling to their swift paws, carry Levon with them as they run beneath the steadfast eyes of heaven.

When Ferrell wakes shivering in the dark, years may have passed. He lies next to Rilla in their cold bed of sand, the sagebrush around them like guardians of their sleep. His mouth tastes of sooty ash, and his bleary mind recalls Rilla slipping into his arms after emptying the urn. They stretched out under the electric stars, the moon pale as weathered bone, and slept fast and deep.

Now the stars have dimmed, and he finds the moon on the other side of the sky. To the east the horizon has brightened—another day, he thinks, neither sought nor desired. If Rilla was the guide through their surreal night, then Ferrell will lead them into this impending day, and he nudges her awake. He must witness dawn from atop the ridge, a desert ritual of his own.

"The sun," Ferrell says. "We've got to hurry."

Ferrell hikes surefooted through the chaparral, and Rilla follows without protest, trusting him as he trusted her. He reaches the trail to the ridge and starts to climb, drawn as if a rope pulls him up. His boots guide him past loose rock and twisted roots, the aching in his legs a forgotten pleasure. He can hear Rilla breathing hard close behind, but he doesn't slow until he reaches the top.

On the ridge he and Rilla hunch over, winded but laughing. They've beaten the sun, and Ferrell is pleased at this small victory, happy to have raced the day and won. He stands with Rilla at the drop-off's edge: the two of them and nothing else but the comfort of immeasurable distance. He'd forgotten how tremendous the vista from his ridgetop, how much joy the sight hundreds of miles can bring, so inhospitable a place he feels more alive.

Rilla grazes her fingertips across his cheek, reminding him of the sustenance she provides. He puts his arm across her shoulders, such a fit over the years, their puzzle of two, and they remain embraced as the sun breaks the horizon. In that moment they are Nez Perce elders, Mayan priests,

monks in the temples of Kyoto. They are the leaders of their
Cro-Magnon tribe, or Adam and Eve, overseeing another
dawn. Somewhere in Ferrell's mind voices whisper of war
and rampant carnage, but he refuses to hear.

"Damn, Ferrell," Rilla says.

"Damn straight," he says.

In the rising light, Ferrell studies the impressive reach of
August's fire. What he hoped was night shadow is miles of
scorched desert, the pitch-black skeletons of sagebrush and
tumbleweed, the indigo bunchgrass. Rilla walks south and
looks down upon their homestead, and Ferrell joins her to
discover how close the cabin came. Below he sees the sweeping turn the fire made, his northward corrals and fences
blackened, his burned barn like a razed ship. A dozen paces
to the west the log cabin sits untouched, as though the callused hand of God intervened.

Toward Cole's spread, the tall stone chimney is all that
remains of his Victorian, rising like a monument from the
heap of black timbers. Ferrell makes out the white dome of a
tent, pitched beside the collapsed barn.

And then, unexpected but utterly perfect, a lone coyote
calls from the ravine. It's one sustained cry, not a yip or bark
but the mournful howl of a coyote seeing who's around. *I'm
here*, it asks, *anyone else?* The call lasts ten seconds at best,
then cuts short, ringing in Ferrell's head like a struck bell.
No answer arrives from the rocky spine of the ridge, and the
coyote doesn't call again. Ferrell and Rilla look at each other
and raise their voices to the sun.

The answer comes not from beast but man, and Ferrell
turns to see Harrison Cole and Din Winters stroll out of the

ravine. They wave but do not speak, and when they cover the distance each simply shakes Ferrell's hand. The two men hug Rilla in turn, their lonely tribe rejoined. From a hawk's-eye view, soaring the thermals high above the ridge, four tiny figures huddle in a burned-out world.

Mitch Wieland is the author of a novel, *Willy Slater's Lane* (SMU, 1996); his short fiction has been published in such venues as *Southern Review, Kenyon Review, TriQuarterly, Yale Review, Shenandoah,* and *Sewanee Review.* He teaches in the M.F.A. program at Boise State University, where he is founding editor of *The Idaho Review.* He is the recipient of a Christopher Isherwood Fellowship and two literature fellowships from the Idaho Commission on the Arts. He is presently working on a novel set in Tokyo, Japan, where he taught English for four years before earning his M.F.A. from the University of Alabama.